# Divine Legacy Series, Book 1:

# Divine Legacy

## By

## C.J. Peterson

*The Next Generation Is Taking Over*

Texas Sisters Press, LLC.

Published by Texas Sisters Press, LLC, Lufkin, TX, U.S.A.

The characters and events in this book are fictitious. Any similarity to real persons, living or dead, is coincidental and not intended by the author.

Texas Sisters Press, LLC

2020

Second Edition

This book is dedicated to my loving husband and dear family who love and support me. You mean more to me than you will ever know. Thank you! I love you!

A portion of the proceeds of this series will go to Airborne Angel Cadets of Texas – a non-profit group of hardworking volunteers who send care packages to our soldiers overseas. You can find them at: http://www.airborneangelcadets.com

To learn more about C.J. Peterson, find her online at:
http://cjpetersonwrites.com/
"While the stories are fiction, the journey is real!"

# Summary

*The Holy Flame Trilogy* and the **Grace Restored Series** come together in the exciting and much anticipated next generation series: ***Divine Legacy Series***.

As the children of Nico and Kit Sullivan: Joshua and Rachel Sullivan, along with Mark and Casey English's children: Jon, Jesse, and Angel English, make up the original members of the new A.N.G.E.L.s Unit. Their job is to gather their remaining teammates. While this should be a simple task, the adventure is anything but effortless. In the process of acquiring the two members listed in the United States, they run across a situation that isn't on their agenda. Amber Jones was in need of miraculous intervention, and God answered her call with the next generation of A.N.G.E.L.s. The A.N.G.E.L.s find some unique help along the way, and learn valuable lessons that will change how they function and see the world from that point forward. Read along as the next generation picks up the torch, claiming their ***Divine Legacy***.

**Joel 1:3**

Tell it to your children, and let your children tell it to their children, and their children to the next generation.

**Hebrews 13:2**

Do not forget to show hospitality to strangers, for some who have done this have entertained angels without realizing it!

# Contents

# Chapter 1
# Many Are Called, But Few Are Chosen

"Whose bright idea was this?" Rachel snapped, while she and Jesse dove behind a rock just in time to escape getting shot. As a barrage of gunfire ricocheted off the rocks around the pair, debris rained down. Praying for the safety of the rest of their team members Rachel knew were getting away, she brushed off the debris, took a deep breath, and looked around the rock to find her target before firing her weapon in the direction of their pursuers, praying those attacking would focus on them and not those escaping. Emptying her magazine, she then ducked back behind the rock to change it out. "I only have three more magazines. Do you know if they're clear yet?"

"I saw them heading for the helicopter," Jesse assured her. "Pretty sure they're clear by now, but I haven't seen the chopper take off yet."

"Should we make a break for it?"

"I don't know if we can get clear enough to make it out without putting the others in danger," Jesse said, and then emptied his weapon. "I've only got two magazines left."

"Well," Rachel said on a sigh with her thick Australian accent. With her face coated in dirt from the rock and dust-filled terrain surrounding them, she said, "If this is it, I want t' let ya know it was an honor t' serve the Kingdom with you."

Jesse shook his head. "Don't think like that." Seeing a cave a short distance away, he grabbed her hand and pulled her with him. Dodging the flying debris the gunfire created as it ricocheted off the rocks, he was thankful each shot missed its mark. When his eyes adjusted to the dim light inside the cave, his heart filled with hope at the tunnels that jetted in every direction. "Looks like the Lord's not done with us yet. Ever play hide-n-go-seek?"

Ignoring the hope in Jesse's voice, Rachel resigned herself to the idea that this was the end. "If it wasn't Josh, I'm glad it's you here with me."

Cupping her face with his hands, he kissed her. "I love you, Rachel. Focus for me."

"Was that just to distract me?"

"Did it work?"

"Yeah. But if you do it again, I'll have t' kill you."

Jesse chuckled as he continued to pull Rachel down one of the dimly lit, chilly tunnels. Unable to form a plan in his mind, he prayed for God's leading.

"We're gonna die, an' you're laughin' at me?"

"It's because your hair is a disaster. I even saw dirt on your teeth."

"We're being shot at an' you're concerned with my looks?"

Stopping in the tunnel, he spun toward her. "You may have given up, but I'm not done yet."

"I haven't given up."

"Then snap out of it! We *are* getting out of here!"

"Are ya sure?"

"If not, we're going to give it our best shot. The others got away. Now it's our turn."

* * *

Six Months Earlier

As a group, the Mexican and American A.N.G.E.L.s had a meeting to discuss the future of their teams. With the children old enough to take over, they had to decide whether to part ways after working together for more than twenty years down in Mexico, or stay together.

After graduating from a local college, Angelina, Mark and Casey's youngest child, was set to begin her Master's Degree in Anthropology at the University of Nevada in Reno in about two weeks.

Mark and Casey also had a set of twin boys, who were older than Angelina. The older of the twenty-four-year old twins, Jonathon (Jon), finished his degree for Physical Therapy the previous year. Meanwhile, the younger twin, Jesse, finished his schooling for Graphic Arts. Both of the boys had been doing internships to gain experience in their selected fields down in Mexico while they waited for Angelina to finish.

Once Angelina graduated, the question came up regarding the status of the teams. The group decided since the children were older, the Mexican unit was at a viable size to handle Mexico's issues, and this would free the American A.N.G.E.L.s to return to America and rebuild their unit.

After the American A.N.G.E.L.s did some research, they decided since Angelina would be going to college there, that the family would relocate to Reno, Nevada to make their start and rebuild their lives. They researched and took a couple trips up to Reno area until they found their perfect home for them. Once papers were signed and money down, the moving date was set for two weeks out.

The two weeks went faster than they anticipated and with the move being the next morning, things around the house were a bit chaotic.

There were two other American A.N.G.E.L. members who lived with the English family, Major Derek Cruise and Colonel Ethan O'Donnell. Packing their rooms upstairs kept them occupied, while Jon and Jesse were out gathering more boxes around town. Mark and Casey were packing the kitchen when twenty-three-year-old Angelina walked in and leaned against the wall.

"Have you finished packing your room?" Casey asked, shoving wrapped plates into a box.

"Yeah," Angelina said, trying to decide how to ask the next question.

Mark could never get over how strongly Angelina resembled Casey at her age. With her long chestnut brown hair and thin build, her green eyes even sparkled like Casey's when she smiled. Angelina, who they now called Angel, also had many of the same habits and mannerisms as her mother. He knew by the way she tucked a portion of her hair behind her ear and nibbled on her nails, that she was hiding something or wanted to talk. He crossed his arms, leaning on the counter. "What is it?"

"Well, I was finished packing my room, so I started on the storage area off the master bedroom…" Glancing toward the bedroom, she nervously looked back at her parents.

"Oh, good!" Casey smiled, clearly happy progress was being made. "We'll get the packing done in no time with initiative like that."

Mark's heart skipped a beat at the mention of the storage area. "Um," he cleared his throat, "you, uh, started packing the storage area?" He asked, rubbing the back of his neck.

"Yeah."

Casey narrowed her eyes while she studied Angel's body language. "Did you find something?"

"Yeah. Just a minute."

"Oh, boy." Mark sighed, looking up toward the ceiling, praying she didn't find what he thought she found.

Angel went into the storage area and picked up a locked metal box that was approximately three feet in length, two feet wide, and two feet tall. When she brought it into the kitchen and sat it on the ground between them, Casey gasped, covering her mouth in shock, and Mark groaned.

Angel rested her hands on her hips. "What's in the box? I could have picked the lock and just looked in it myself.

However, around here if there's a lock on something, I've learned it's on there for a reason."

"So, you *didn't* open it?" Mark asked. Now sixty-two, he spent the last thirty years protecting its contents. Unable to find a safe place to bury the box outside of the home, the men decided to hide it in their storage area, buried deep within the boxes and crates. The only entrance to that area was through the master bedroom. The room itself was made of cinderblock, so they knew no one could access it from the outside. Keeping the box close to them would be safer. While Mark knew time was past to open it, he knew once opened, it would bring the other side running.

"No. You look really nervous. Would opening it be that scary?"

Mark hesitated before he admitted, "It would."

Glancing down at the dark-green, aluminum A.M.A.L. military box in question, Angel looked her dad in the eyes as she crossed her arms, not backing down. "What's in the box?" she demanded.

"That's a long story. Tell ya what. When we're moved and landed in Nevada, I'll open it with –"

Mark was cut off by the now sixty-five-year-old Colonel, who was coming down for a bottle of water, "That's not what I think it is, is it?"

"You know it's past time to open it," Mark pointed out.

Derek, who was two years younger than the Colonel, came down the stairs into the kitchen. Without a word, he went over to the refrigerator and pulled out a soda. Stopping with the door mid-way opened, he looked up, heart racing as tingles flooded his body. "Why is the hair on the back of my neck standing on end?"

Knowing Derek's gift was sensing the other side, Mark ran to the front door while the Colonel ran out the side door to see if they could find them. "Out here!" Mark yelled.

As everyone joined them, Casey ordered Angel to stay with the box. Disturbed that the visit occurred as soon as the box surfaced, Angel was instantly on guard. Also noting the reactions of her parents and the Colonel in regards to the box, she moved so her back was to a wall, allowing her to keep a lookout in the other three directions. Sliding the box on the floor beside her in order to protect it, she prayed for protection for all of the A.N.G.E.L.s she knew were in the area.

The Colonel and Casey were the only two who immediately returned. "When are the boys due back?" Casey asked, practically throwing the plates into the box as quickly as she could. At this point she didn't care if something broke.

"Any minute. What's going on?" Angel asked.

"That box holds vital information the other side is just itching to get a hold of," the Colonel explained, as he helped Casey in the kitchen by tossing cookware into a box. "They know the time is long overdue, so it needs to surface. They also know who had it last."

"Meaning?" Angel pressed, crossing her arms.

"Keep a lookout," Casey ordered, moving to pack the glasses.

"Yes, ma'am," Angel said, backing down at the tone in Casey's voice. Shifting to a position that would allow her to see the two main doors, she asked, "What do you mean by it's long overdue to open it, Colonel?"

Colonel sighed. "Look, I know you'll know soon enough, but now is not the time. We have to get out of here as quickly as possible. They've found out where we are and what we have."

"Who?"

"*Them,*" he snapped.

"Do you want me to call Jon and Jesse home?"

"Please…and thank you," Casey said, focused on getting the kitchen packed.

Angel called her brothers and explained what happened. When she finished, she placed calls to a couple of the Mexican A.N.G.E.L. members. Part of them already knew what was going on, and had met Mark and Derek on the race to intercept the visitor. Because of that, others were already on the way over to help pack the remainder of the house. They would also be escorting them to the border for their move. Once in America, though, they were on their own.

*   *   *

Planning on taking off in the middle of the night, the collective group of A.N.G.E.L.s sat around the house after the truck was loaded. The only items still in the home were sleeping bags to sit on and *the box*, which sat in the middle of the group.

"Do we dare open it?" Cristina asked around midnight. She was Juan and Claudia's daughter. Juan was head of the Mexican A.N.G.E.L.s.

"It *is* past time," Juan reminded them.

"We have ample people here to look out as well," Derek added. "If we stay on guard, we should be able to protect it."

Casey shuddered as she remembered the torture Jackie Monroe put her through to gain access to the box. At that time, Casey had no idea what she was talking about. Now, the very box that cost so many lives was not only sitting in front of them, but also about to be opened.

"How often does it get opened?" Angel asked.

"Once every hundred years. The only exception was when we transferred it to a more secure box once Jack got his hands on it. At that time it was in a metal trunk, before that it was a wooden box. However, the AMAL boxes are airtight, allowing for better protection. We found out about these boxes through a military friend of mine who used these in Vietnam.

By the time we got to where the box was last sighted, it was missing and the person guarding it until we could get there was dead. My friend suggested we put it in an AMAL box once we found it again in order to better protect it. With it being in a pretty much indestructible box, it would be easier to hide it in obscure places.

Well, it took us a bit to figure out where the box went after the other side stole it. Once Jack recovered it, we put it in the safest box we could think of – the one you see in front of you. While I realize the storage room doesn't seem safe, it was never alone. Once landed in Nevada, finding a better hiding place will be top priority. Now, if we ever get our hands on the *other* box, we'll do the same."

"There's another one?" Antonia, Raul and Ana Maria's daughter, asked, stunned. "Why don't we have that one too?"

"Because *they* do. That's why they want *this* one," the Colonel said, gesturing toward the box. "This is the other half."

"The other half of *what*?" asked Jesse, the blond-haired, green-eyed, muscular young man, who took a seat beside his identical twin brother, Jon.

The Colonel sighed, shaking his head. "I guess there's no other way around it. We have to open it for you to understand. Now keep in mind, what's in here has cost many their lives. While we do know in general what's in the other one, we need to get our hands on it just as much as the other side needs to get their hands on this one. Angel, pass around pens and paper. You *cannot* take a picture of this. There *cannot* be any possible electronic access to the information in here."

"Just open the blasted thing already," Mark snapped.

"You know the importance of this."

"Yes, sir, but you're wasting time. The longer you draw it out, the worse it'll be. They'll sense it as soon as it's opened. They already know it's surfaced."

"I know." The Colonel slowly let out a breath of air. "That's why I don't want to open it. Jesse, do you sense anyone from the other side?"

"They're around, but they're distant," Jesse confirmed. Having the same gift as Derek of sensing the other side, over the years Derek helped Jesse fine-tune it to an even higher level than Derek's gift.

"Keep sensing," the Colonel warned before he unlocked the locks on the box. With every latch he released, anxiety built among the group. When he took off the lid a bright light filled the room. The first thing he pulled out was a towel, folded and stored in a vacuum-sealed bag. "This is the towel Jesus used the night He washed the feet of His apostles at the last supper." Delicately placing it beside him, he then pulled out a velvet bag. When he removed the scroll the bag contained, collective gasps filled the room.

"That looks like a copper scroll," Angel squealed in excitement. "Like the Dead Sea Scrolls."

"Exactly," the Colonel said. "This particular one is of the book of Revelation."

"Fascinating! Has it ever been studied?"

"No need," the Colonel said with a twinkle in his eyes. "It was handed directly from person to person, starting with the apostles themselves. It was stolen a couple of times throughout the years, until an archangel came to me and told me where it was and what was in it. These are the genuine articles."

"You're serious?"

"Yes. These were placed in here to let the person know who opened it that what else is in here is genuine as well. While these are valuable, what's contained in the remaining pots is priceless." Gesturing toward the three ancient airtight pots resting in foam packaging. Pulling the pot marked with Roman numerals "MM" on it, he left the other two. One was marked "MMM" and the other was "MMMM."

"Ready?" he asked Angel, who had already handed out pens and paper to everyone who would write.

When she nodded, to her horror, he went to break it. "STOP!" she shouted.

"How else am I going to get into it?"

"Oh for Pete's sake!" She huffed. Getting on the floor with him, she took the pot from him. "You can get in without breaking the entire thing. Please don't tell me the other pots were broken in a similar fashion?" When he nodded, she shook her head. "Some people have no respect for history. You only have to break the lid. See?" Turning the pot upside down, she tapped the lid on the tile floor. It cracked at first, which allowed her to tap on it until she broke through enough to pull the scroll from its encasement.

"We don't have a lot of time left," Jesse said, sensing the other side was on the move. "They know it's open."

"Shush!" Angel reprimanded him. Handing the scroll to the Colonel, she placed the precious pot back into the foam-packing slot it was originally housed in in order to hold the scroll for the remainder of the century.

As everyone watched in anticipation, they got their pens and paper ready. If it was only opened once every hundred years, they had better take good notes.

"Why do you only open it every hundred years?" Felipe, Rico and Leah's son asked, as the Colonel unraveled the scroll.

"Because as soon as the box is open, it's like a beacon to the other side of its location," Mark explained. "We need to do it quickly. You guys have to write fast so we can get outta here."

"What is this?" Angel asked after a minute, as everyone scribbled as fast as they could. "It lists names, dates, and what, city or town names?"

"Exactly," the Colonel said, pleased she figured it out so quickly. "It's a NOC list."

"What's a NOC list?" Antonia asked.

"It's a spy term," the Colonel explained. "It stands for 'non-official cover' list. Basically, a NOC list has one list with the spy's name, and the other list has their real name. When you put them together, it tells the other side what the real name of the spy is, painting a target on that person. Now, in this case the apostles were pretty smart when it came to thinking outside the box, even for back then. You see, this list contains only the *last* name of the A.N.G.E.L.-to-be, along with the approximate date of when they can be found, and in what city. The other half contains their *first* name, along with the approximate date of when they can be found, and in what *country*. Now, this makes it a bit of a struggle for each side to find the person when the lists are separate. The idea is when you get them together you have a complete road map until the year 5000. As you see, the years 3000 and 4000 have yet to be opened. It's reexamined once every hundred years, and the previous list is destroyed after each hundred years until the turn of the millennium."

"So, what are the brackets on here?" Angel asked. "These are broken into sections."

"Those are broken into every generation. That's why the box is only opened every hundred years. This is what is left of the 1900's list," he said picking up the scroll from the vacant slot where a pot used to be. "We haven't destroyed it yet, because we wanted to show the next generation. Now that you have seen it, we have to burn it."

"You have to *what*?" Angel asked, stunned. "That has historical value beyond belief!"

"No. It's only kept in order to check every hundred years, and to show the next team how to use it. Look here's how we found your mom and uncle," the Colonel pointed out in a section of the 1900 scroll toward the end. "It has their last name, about the time they moved to the Denver area, and the city of Denver. We found Jack there, and thought that's who we were supposed to recruit. Little did we know it was supposed to be Casey."

"It may very well have been Jack," Casey pointed out. "He was the one who recovered the box, remember? I'm just along for the ride."

"You brought in the next generation," the Colonel countered. "We'll never know until we find the other scroll exactly *which* one of you it was supposed to be."

"True," Casey agreed.

"Point is, we actually found you both in Denver at that time."

"I see."

"Now," the Colonel said, turning back to the scroll, "here's the current section of this scroll. If you notice, there are three with the last name English, meaning all three of you. There are also two with the last name of Sullivan in…this can't be right." He shook his head, confused.

"What's wrong?" Derek asked, glancing over his shoulder, as he kept an eye on the front of the house, while Rico kept an eye on the back.

"This is in Australia. This doesn't make sense. Then these two are in Russia. Look, these three are in Ireland. These three are in Jordan. These two are in Egypt. This one's Japan, and this one's China. Then there's this one in England. Outside of you three, the only ones listed in the U.S are from Dallas and New Orleans. This doesn't make sense."

"Let me see," Angel said, scanning the section. "These are four teams of twenty, not the ten that you guys had. Look, they're all over the world too. Here, the second list is you guys, South America, Portugal, and Spain," Angel said, showing them to Pablo, a member of the younger Mexican crew. He was the son of Mauricio and Ariel, and the trainer of the upcoming generation of the Mexican A.N.G.E.L.'s children. "This third set is mostly middle-east and Africa. And the fourth is more from the remaining countries in Europe, Asia, and Canada."

"You're right. They're combined. It's like the apostles knew the world would be more accessible come the turn of the century," Pablo agreed. "We'll write only the second half of these sections," he told his team.

"We'll write the top. Do *not* lose these lists," Angel said sternly. "We need to pass them down. You adults write the third and fourth sections. We can divide the third and fourth lists, in order to make sure they're all found. I would hate to lose any part of this."

"Exactly," Pablo agreed.

Pleased at how well the next generation was picking up the ball, the Colonel felt confident they would be more than capable of handling the divine legacy passed down to them. While he knew it wouldn't be easy, he also knew the Lord would protect and guide the new team every step of the way. He was grateful to have been a part of the plan, and the opportunity of seeing it fulfilled thus far.

"Move it, people," Jesse warned, bringing them back to reality after several moments. "We need to clear out of here as soon as possible. We can't wait until morning. We're down to minutes."

"We're going as fast as we can," Jon said, writing feverishly.

"You don't understand," Jesse said, feeling the hair on the back of his neck stand on end as tingles filled his body. "We've run out of time."

"How close?" Derek asked, joining the others in writing.

"Throw the what's left into the vehicles. We have less than ten minutes," he warned.

"I'm starting to feel them closing in," Antonia agreed. She didn't want to see the American A.N.G.E.L.s leave. Over the years the group had become close. As the older children got married and had children of their own, the English children were like an aunt and uncles to them. "Here, I'm finished with my section," she said, getting up, helping Jesse and Mark load the two vehicles and made sure they were secure.

"Done," Angel announced. As soon as Jon, Casey, and Derek finished, they handed theirs to Angel while the Mexican crew handed theirs to Pablo.

"We need to get out of here," Juan hurried them. "We'll follow you to the border, but we have to move."

Angel helped the Colonel quickly, but gently, place everything back in its spot before they latched the box, placing the locks on either end. While Mark and Juan carried the box to the truck, Angel and Pablo exchanged information.

Grabbing the lists, they ran to their vehicles and sped out of the area as fast as they could, pushing the limits of their vehicles, while keeping an eye in every direction. The four oldest Mexican team members, along with four of the new team members, sandwiched the American A.N.G.E.L.s between their vehicles, sending the remaining Mexican A.N.G.E.L.s into hiding until their return.

"Are we going to make it?" Angel nervously asked her dad, as they rode with Jon and Derek, while Casey rode with

Jesse and the Colonel. Separating the group by experience and expertise, they decided this was the best combination.

"We have to," Mark said, putting his foot down heavier on the gas as they were now out of the city. "There's a whole world counting on us to do our job. Many are called, but few are chosen. You guys were chosen before you were even born. He'll protect you. If your job isn't done, you're not going anywhere."

"Once we get to the U.S., how will we know where and when to start?"

"What's the first date on the list?"

Checking the papers, she gulped. "Five days from now in Australia."

"Better brush up on your Aussie," Mark warned. "Looks like you guys are heading out."

"What about graduate school in Nevada?" Angel asked, panic taking over. "I'm supposed to go to graduate school in Reno. This is *not* how I had things planned out."

"Who said *you* were the one making the plans?" Derek asked.

"That's not funny," she snapped.

Derek shrugged. "I'm not laughing."

"Look, we can't control the timing, honey. You've been chosen. What are you going to tell God?"

Angel thought for only a moment before she decisively said, "Here am I, send me."

# Chapter 2
# For Everything There Is A Season

Deep in the heart of the Outback stood Serenity Wells Station, owned by Nico and Kit Sullivan. This over five-hundred-acre station was home to a myriad of animals, centering on cattle and sheep. The many ranch hands were like family to the owners and their four children. Containing two sets of twins, the family took on many battles over the years, including keeping a successful station in the Outback for generations.

The older of the set of twins were twenty-five-year-old boys. Joshua and Caleb Sullivan topped respectfully at six-five and six-three, with Josh being the taller of the two. Both of the strapping young men grew up on the station, and it showed in their stocky, well defined builds. With jet-black hair and sky-blue eyes, many young ladies in the territory admired these two gentlemen. Caleb, by this point, was married to his love, Willow, and they had four children, two out of four of their children were twins as well.

Twins were all over the Sullivan family tree, but not as evident as in this generation. The second of the set of twins were spunky, smart, feisty young ladies. Twenty-three-year old Rachel and Leah were often a topic of admiration of the young men in the territory. Standing at five-ten and five-eight, the blond-haired, sapphire-blue-eyed, well-toned duo kept most men at a distance. The four children knew at a young age that two of them would become an A.N.G.E.L. one day, and didn't want to start a relationship only to be pulled away when the time came.

Once Josh and Rachel got the call, Caleb and Leah were more relaxed in the relationships they found themselves in.

While Caleb was married, Leah had found a young man she was with for over six months, Finn Walker, before she told her sister and older brothers. This caused a bit of a stir amongst the close-knit clan, but Josh and Rachel set it aside to refocus on their training while they waited until the appointed time. When that would be, was only known to the Lord. Their job was to recognize it when it came.

*   *   *

When Rachel and Josh stepped out into the blistering sun of the station from getting an afternoon snack, they looked toward the road to see a jeep bouncing down the drive toward them.

"Interestin'," Rachel commented before glancing toward Josh to see his reaction.

"It's time," Josh simply said. Taking his radio off his belt, he said into it, "Mum, Dad, they're here."

"Who's here?" Nico asked.

"*Them*," he enunciated.

"Got it. We're helpin' Willow with the little ones while she feeds the baby," Nico said, referring to Caleb and Willow's children.

"Get here as soon as ya can. Not sure how much more time we got."

"Be there as soon as possible."

"Copy that," Josh said, and replaced the radio on his belt as the jeep pulled up to the house. While the dust settled, three young people got out of the vehicle. Stunned by the beauty of the young lady, who had a thin build, sparkling green eyes, and chestnut hair that hung to her mid-back, Josh had to catch his breath at the sight of her. "Welcome t' Serenity Wells Station."

"Thank you," the young lady said, shaking his hand. "My name is Angel English, and these are my brothers, Jon and Jesse," she introduced them.

"I'm Josh Sullivan, an' this is my blood-n-blister, Rachel," Josh said, as everyone shook hands in greeting. "How can we help you?"

"Pretty sure you know why we're here," Jon pointed out.

"We do. How did you find us?"

"That's the interesting part." Angel smiled. "We were led here."

Leaning against the porch post, crossing his arms, Josh asked, "What do ya mean?"

"We could show you, if you'd like?" she offered.

Struck by her demeanor and her laid-back nature, Josh felt himself instantly attracted to her. "Sure. Curious t' see how you came about findin' us."

As they made their way to the back of the jeep, Nico and Kit came out of Caleb and Willow's house to see the group. "We're losing them, aren't we?" Kit said somberly.

"No. They're just moving on to another season in their life," Nico corrected her. "By the looks a' the tanks with the young lady, they'll be pretty well protected."

"Let's hope they had good training," Kit said, walking up to the group.

After introductions were made, with a twinkle in her eyes and a smile on her face, Angel pulled the tarp off the dark-green metal box, three-foot in length, by two-feet in height.

Glancing into the back of the jeep, Rachel asked, "What's in the box?"

"It's something that's been handed down for generations, dating back to the apostles," Angel explained, excitement unmistakable in her voice. "The history behind it is incredible."

"What do ya mean the apostles?" Rachel raised an eyebrow. "Are you talking Matthew, Mark, Luke, an' John type apostles?"

"Actually, it was Paul, John, Peter, and Peter's apprentice Timothy," Jesse corrected. Rachel caught his eye as soon as he saw her. Doing his best to hide his feelings, he explained, "You see, back in those days it was a dangerous time for any follower of Jesus, let alone one of His inner circle. Praying one night, they were given a massive list and began writing, filling multiple scrolls. Now, these scrolls contain a NOC list of sorts. A NOC list is –"

"Trust me. We know what a NOC list is," Nico, a former FBI agent said, crossing his arms. "How are the lists written, and what information is on them?"

"Well," Jesse nervously cleared his throat. Knowing he was Rachel's father, and noting his massive size, he said, "The lists *we* have contain the last names of those destined to be A.N.G.E.L.s, along with dates and the cities they can be found in. Before you say anything, know this particular box also contains a copper scroll with the book of Revelation, and the towel Jesus used to wash the apostle's feet at the last supper."

"Okay," Nico said, hesitantly. "And what does the other box hold?"

"Don't be so suspicious," Kit said, resting her hand on Nico's arm. "They're definitely one of the Lord's. And with as bright as they are, I'm sure they're A.N.G.E.L.s as well."

"What's the code?" Nico challenged.

"A.N.G.E.L. stands for Available to Nurture God's Eternal Love," Angel jumped in, sensing Jesse's nerves.

"Okay. And what's in the other box?" Nico pressed.

"It's the first names of the A.N.G.E.L.s, along with dates and the *country* they can be found in," Jon explained. "We have the more revealing list as far as location, but are unsure of the first name. For this location, we have two with the last name of Sullivan. We're letting the Lord guide us. Interestingly enough, these were the first two we ran into."

"Imagine that," Nico said, studying them.

"How is it *you three* have possession of it?" Kit questioned.

"It was passed down to us," Angel explained. "As the next generation, the legacy, or in this case the box, is in our possession. My parents, along with the Colonel and Derek are now resting. They're getting older and aren't quite up to running missions anymore."

"And, who are your parents?" Kit asked, sensing a familiarity with the trio.

"Mark and Casey English."

As soon as she said the names, Kit gasped as she covered her mouth in shock. "Your dad is *Mark*?" she asked, and then got a better look at the boys. "I should have figured it out sooner. You're the spitting image of him."

"How do you know our dad?" Jon asked.

"He helped me many years back. I thought you guys looked familiar. The resemblance to your father is uncanny."

"Ya know, just out of curiosity, that Colonel you talked about?" Nico asked, resting his elbow on the back of the jeep. "Seth mentioned that he ran into a Colonel Ethan O'Donnell on one of his trips here."

"That's the Colonel," Angel said, excitement running rampant as chills ran through her body. "I *know* we're in the right place now! Wow. The Lord sure works in mysterious ways." She sighed, looking toward the heavens. "Thank You, Father!"

"So, yer tellin' me that we're all connected?" Nico asked, not really believing the nature of the connections between their families.

Pulling his wallet from his pocket, Jon showed Kit and Nico a photo of their family, Derek, and the Colonel. "This was about five years ago."

Shaking her head, Kit looked at the photo, stunned. "It's him. He was quite a bit younger when he helped me get to Nico when I was in trouble. He said he was an A.N.G.E.L., but we never saw him after that night. He saved my life. I half wondered if he was real or not."

"I'll bet if we show this picture to Seth, he would say this is the Colonel who led him to the Lord. I'm sure of it. How many Colonel Ethan O'Donnell's can there be?"

"He's the one and only as far as we know," Angel said.

Under his breath, Jesse added, "Think the world can only *handle* one Colonel."

"Not a fan?" Rachel observed.

"Oh, I like him. He's just used to being in charge. I'm closer to Derek," Jesse clarified. "He understands me better."

"The Colonel and I are closer," Jon explained. "He often pushes me, but it's to make me better."

"Have you three been trained?" Nico asked.

"By the best," Angel acknowledged. Turning to Josh and Rachel, she asked, "What about you two?"

"Ethan Carson an' Charlie trained us," Josh explained.

Wide-eyed, Angel asked, "Ethan Carson? As in Australian A.N.G.E.L. Ethan Carson?"

Josh sighed as he crossed his arms. "Another connection?"

"He saved my mother from her injuries when Jackie kidnapped our mom and dad. She tortured my mom beyond measure. She still has the scars on her back to prove it. He helped nurse her back to health."

"Jackie?" Nico asked, furrowing his brow. "As in Jackie Monroe?"

"Yes," Angel said, color draining from her face as she remembered the horrific stories told to her by her parents. "Did you know her?"

"She used t' own Akoonah Station. It's the station adjacent t' ours," Nico explained. "She died quite awhile ago, taking out some good friends before she did, Shawn O'Brien an' Victoria Stanton."

"Umm," Angel nervously tucked a portion of her hair behind her ear as she explained, "They died saving my parents from Jackie the first time. This is too weird. Things do *not* connect this heavily from one side of the world to the other. There is *no way* this is happening."

"Afraid so." Nico nodded. "There's no such thing as a coincidence when it comes t' God." Looking toward Rachel and Josh, he added, "There's a reason our families are so intertwined. This was meant t' be. Make sure t' look out for your sister or you'll catch it from me."

"Yes, sir," he promptly responded.

"Go pack yer bags," Nico instructed. Once Rachel and Josh disappeared into the house, Nico asked, "Are you plannin' on stayin' for dinner or do ya need t' jet?"

"Whoa!" Jon said, wide-eyed, when Caleb walked up to the group. "Didn't you just go into the house?"

"Seein' double?" Caleb asked with a grin as he shook their hands. "Name's Caleb Sullivan. Yer probably referring t' my brother, Josh."

Confused, Jesse asked, "Are there more of you?"

"Hey, Dad?" Leah rode up to the group on her horse from the south field.

"Hey, Leah." Nico stood. "This is Jon, Jesse, an' Angel English. C'mon down an' meet them."

"I would love to, but you have t' come with me t' the south field. One a' the big bulls broke his leg an' he's ticked. I can't get t' him."

"Where's Barwon?"

"He's the one who sent me for *you*. He can't do it on his own."

"Got it," he said. Jumping on the back of the horse with Leah, they rode out to the south field together.

As they disappeared in a cloud of dust, Jesse remarked, "And my mom thought she had it bad with *one* set of twins. I couldn't imagine *two*."

"Seeing double is frequent," Kit admitted. "Once you know them, though, you can recognize them on sight."

"I'll bet."

"So, are y'all staying for dinner?" Kit asked. "I'm asking for selfish reasons, but I understand if y'all have to leave."

"Is this safe here?" Angel asked, referring to the box.

"I can find a good hiding spot for it," Kit agreed, with a thrill of excitement. Knowing she would have to give Rachel and Josh up for the adventure of a lifetime, she wanted to know those they would be with on a daily basis.

"Yeah. She's got this place wired," Caleb agreed, resting his elbow on his mom's shoulder. "Besides, Felix is an amazing cook. Can't find anythin' better in Australia."

"Nice! We haven't had a good meal in a while," Jesse explained. "We just moved back to the States, and then had to help unpack and renovate the house a bit before we hopped a plane here."

"Moved *back* to the States?" Kit asked. "Where did you move from?"

"We grew up in Mexico," Angel clarified.

"Where you had a big battle," Kit finished, remembering the story Charlie told her.

"Yeah. My parents were involved in that," Angel explained. "That was actually the day these guys were born," she said, gesturing toward her brothers. "How did you know about that?" Before Kit could answer, Angel said, "You know what? Never mind. I'm going to just accept there is quite a bit about each other's history that we know, and many connections."

"I'd say that's a wise move," Kit agreed. "Caleb, can you tell Felix there'll be three more for dinner? In the meantime, we're fixin' to find a good hiding place for your box."

"Make it the best one you can think of," Jesse said. "There are a lot of bad people looking for it."

"I have the perfect place."

*   *   *

That night at dinner, the ranch hands and family got to know the new visitors. While they were cryptic in answering some of the questions asked, Kit was used to that by the A.N.G.E.L.s, but it irritated the others. Kit cherished every moment that night, and made sure to write down everything she could remember about the new A.N.G.E.L.s she met in her journal, and how they were connected.

Astounded by the complexity of the connections, the Lord never ceased to amaze her in making good things come out of tragedies. Before going to bed that night, she bathed the group in prayer, and committed to doing so every night from that point forward. Knowing she may not have much communication with her son and daughter, she would trust the Lord to take care of them. Confident He didn't do everything He did for her, Nico, and the family, just to send them out to get killed, she prayed for their lives, whatever the length, to make a difference.

*     *     *

The next morning, there were many hugs and tears as Rachel and Josh said good-bye to their family and ranch hands that had become family over the years.

"Be blessed and be safe," Kit said, tears streaming down her face while she hugged her children.

"We will," Josh promised. "I'll look after the girls. I'm sure those other blokes will too."

"Definitely," Jon and Jesse agreed.

With that, they loaded into their jeep. Pete drove the truck with Josh and Rachel inside, along with their bags, while the others rode in the jeep. The jeep didn't have the room. While Kit and Nico wanted to drive their children to Carnes, they didn't have the heart to say good-bye to them again, so Pete drove instead.

"You ready for adventure?" Pete asked when they were almost there.

"Pretty sure," Josh said confidently.

"I'll be honest," Rachel confessed, "I'm nervous."

Putting his arm around Rachel, Josh gave her shoulders a squeeze. "Yer strong. You can do this."

"I know it's what we've been trained for," she agreed, "but I'm still nervous."

"While you do seem nervous, I *did* notice you checkin' out young Jesse at dinner last night," Pete teased Rachel. Then he made a quirky face, as he asked, "Or was that Jon? Too many twins runnin' around the station yesterday."

Josh chuckled. "Yeah. You'd almost think it was a requirement for an A.N.G.E.L. to be a twin. We're goin' t' confuse quite a lot of people."

"Not really. *Our* twins aren't comin' with us," Rachel reminded him.

"Too true."

"I've never been apart from Leah this long. I feel like I'm losing a piece of me."

"I'm here for you," Josh encouraged. "I know how it feels. Caleb's been married for several years. I've been without him pretty much since he an' Willow hooked up."

"Right. Finn is Leah's first steady boyfriend. While they've been together for a while, she's still around the station on a regular basis, so I haven't had to deal with that permanent separation yet. While I understand life goes on, it just seems weird."

Trying to change the subject to refocus her, Josh mentioned, "The Lord seems to have provided us with a good group."

"I know. I'll still miss everyone."

"You'll be okay," Josh encouraged. "Like Mum says, it's just another season."

Rachel sighed. "Yep. For everything, there is a season."

# Chapter 3
## A Cross To Bear

That night, after Pete took back off for the station, the group got hotel rooms close to the airport. With the guys in one room, and the two girls in an adjoining room, they unloaded and met in the girl's room before going out to dinner. As they were trying to figure out where to go, there was a knock on the door.

"Are you expectin' someone?" Josh asked.

"No." Angel shook her head. "As far as we know, no one knows where we are."

Going to the door with Jon and Jesse behind him, Josh peeked through the peephole and exclaimed, "Yes!"

"Who is it?" Rachel asked.

Without answering, Josh flew open the door and threw his arms around Ethan Carson. Also with him were Danny Hawk and Charlie of the Australia A.N.G.E.L.s.

"G'day!" Ethan said, walking in, giving Rachel a hug before he shook hands with the trio from America.

"Welcome t' Australia," Danny Hawk, the leader of the Australian A.N.G.E.L.s said, shaking everyone's hand.

When Charlie came in and hugged everyone, he had a grin ear to ear. "This is excitin'!"

"How did you find us?" Angel asked. When Hawk gave her a look, she just rolled her eyes. "I get it. Never mind."

"Let's have a seat an' chat." Hawk gestured toward the beds. While they separated by families on the two beds, the other three A.N.G.E.L.s pulled over the chairs from the table. When they were settled, Hawk started, "First off, where's the box?"

"Funny you should mention the box," Angel said, with a sly smile.

Cocking his head to the side, Hawk asked, "What did you do with it?"

"We hid it. You see, Kit had the best idea so we left it on the station."

"That's actually a good place for now," Hawk agreed. "Serenity, Akoonah, an' Koala Pass are triangulated and run by Christians, so that means it's in a safe place. Can I ask where?"

"Well," Angel grinned, "Kit came up with a brilliant idea. You see, Jon and Jesse helped unbury the casket of Nick Locke. Then we dug a little more and placed the box under the casket."

"That *is* brilliant. She's not worried about anyone noticing a freshly dug grave?"

"Nope. There's no grass over it. The dirt only had a few damp areas left when I checked it this morning. By tomorrow, there'll be no evidence the grave was dug up at all."

"Why would she think it's okay to dig up our uncle's grave?" Rachel asked, horrified.

"Your parents haven't talked t' you about that yet?" Hawk questioned in shock.

"Dad told me," Josh confirmed. "He fessed up about three years ago t' me an' Caleb. He said Mum would tell you two once you graduated college."

Narrowing her eyes as she crossed her arms, she demanded, "Tell me *what*?"

"Remember when Mum said Mark English helped her get away yesterday?"

"Yeah."

"Well, at the time Mum's name was Katie MacKenna, an' Dad's name was Nick Locke."

"I don't –" she shook her head, confused. "I thought –"

"Shhhh, don't hurt yourself," Josh teased. "Just know the body in the casket *isn't* our uncle Nick Locke. Nick Locke is our dad."

Dropping her head in her hands, Rachel groaned. "I don't understand."

"Just sort through it in your mind," he encouraged.

"Okay. So, the box is under some dead body that *isn't* our dad, but has our dad's name on the gravestone."

"Right."

"Then, who's in the casket?"

"Uncle Seth's sister is a doctor, an' she got Mum an' Dad cadavers t' burn in order t' get away. Since the bodies were supposedly burned, the funerals were closed casket. There are sandbags in the caskets that are about the same weight Mum an' Dad were at the time of their death."

Rachel let out a slow breath of air. "This is *so* wrong."

"Okay, since that's sorted, back t' the reason for our visit," Hawk said, taking over the conversation again.

"Didn't think it was a social visit," Josh quipped. "You never seem t' pop up when it's just a social call."

"Sorry, mate. Some day I may pop up for a social call."

"But not t'day." Josh shook his head. "Go ahead."

"You five are startin' a journey that will take you into dark places, but know while it seems dark, you need t' focus on the light. You also need to remember the long game. Sometimes you can get there in time, sometimes you won't. You were all taught t' sense the Spirit. Stay focused on Him. He'll guide you if you stay focused."

"Where do we start, though?" Angel asked. "We've found these two, but where do we go from here?"

"As you locate the others on your team, I'm sure the Lord will send you on missions. It's up t' you t' listen an' follow."

"Until then we just follow the list?" she asked.

"Yep. Here's my mobile number in case you have any questions," he said, passing a card to both Angel and Rachel.

"So, you're just going to cut us loose? There are no further instructions? No one coming with us?" Angel asked, stunned.

"Look, you've all been trained. You have actually had more trainin' than we did when we started. When the world wars went on, the A.N.G.E.L.s took a major hit. Without someone t' pass the list to, it called for a different plan of action in recruitment."

"Meaning?"

"Well, both the Colonel an' I were recruited at the same time, an' given our portion of the list from a *real* angel, the archangel."

"How were you recruited at the same time?"

"We were in a joint trainin' venture," he said, thinking back to that day…

*   *   *

…Scattered throughout the outback in the dead of night, groups of eight men shared stories of their experiences in the field.

"I kid you not!" Then twenty-eight-year-old Captain Ethan O'Donnell said, laughing, as they sat around the fire. "They just stared at us while we had our weapons trained on them, literally trying to put their pants on. Seems we woke them from a deep sleep."

"How did ya keep a straight face?" Then twenty-nine-year-old Flight Lieutenant Danny Hawk asked, between fits of laughter.

"It was difficult, but at that point we were –" suddenly cut off by a sound in the distance, as everyone's ears perked up, an immediate silence fell over the group.

Hawk pointed, sending out a U.S. team member each with Australian team member in different directions. Then he and O'Donnell headed out in the fourth direction to find the source of the noise, leaving the fire going as a source of reference in the vast Outback.

Moving silently through the brush, they suddenly found themselves in an area of rocks with a cave. Ducking into the musty, dirt cave, they found an iron pot, along with the remnants of a fire that looked to be a day or so old. Seeing footprints leading down a tunnel jetting from the interior cave, they cautiously followed it, until it opened into an enormous interior cavern, which contained a small, greenish-blue lake that didn't seem to have a bottom.

As they stood there, stunned by the find, a streak of light flashed right before them, landing on the small island in the middle of the lake. Uncovering their eyes from the shocking brightness of the form, they saw a man standing there in clothes that looked as if he were from ancient Greece. Pulling the flaming sword from its sheath, he lit the cavern around them even brighter. His wings spread out behind him, showing all his glory. "Do not be afraid."

"Now he tells us. 'Fraid it's a bit late for that, mate," Hawk said, heart racing faster than he ever thought possible.

O'Donnell gulped. "Who or *what* are you?"

"I am the first of many new and fascinating things you will see. You are part of a bigger plan from the Lord God Almighty," he said, his voice echoing off the walls of the cavern.

"Are you seeing this?" Hawk asked O'Donnell. "Or have I gone troppo?"

"Not unless I've lost sanity with you," O'Donnell assured him. "I'm seeing it too."

"Okay then." Taking a deep breath to keep his emotions under control, Hawk asked, "Why are you here? Why us?"

"Many are called, but few are chosen," the archangel said. "*You* are among the chosen. I will give you directions to find a list located in two different boxes in order to locate others."

"You're serious?" O'Donnell's jaw dropped. "We're military. We get in trouble for going A.W.O.L.!"

"If you choose to follow Him, it will work out."

"How do we follow Him when we get our orders from our superiors? We're not in charge of our schedule...or lives for that matter. They *own* us."

"Do you trust in the Lord?" the archangel asked.

"Yes," both men said in unison.

"Then trust Him."

"How will we know what t' do?" Hawk questioned.

"Follow the leading of the Spirit. The more you stay focused on the Spirit, the more prominent His voice will be to you."

"Cryptic. I like a challenge," O'Donnell said, crossing his arms with a smirk.

"You *like* cryptic?" Hawk turned to O'Donnell. "I always *knew* you were twisted." Turning back to the angel, he explained, "I like clear. I deal in black n' white."

"I don't mind reading between the lines." O'Donnell waved him off. "I live in a world of gray."

"That is why you two were chosen together. Your strengths are both needed to help others," the archangel explained.

"Help others *how*?" Hawk probed. "You need t' be more specific than this."

"At this time, I cannot." Gesturing toward the ground near them, the archangel explained, "Here are others you need to find. As your numbers grow, you will find more to help carry the load. United you stand, divided you fall."

Looking to where he pointed, the men found a scroll on the ground. Picking it up, O'Donnell unrolled it. As Hawk looked over his shoulder, O'Donnell mentioned, "This list looks a little thin."

"You will need those men and women to help you find the boxes."

"What *exactly* is in these boxes?" O'Donnell asked. "They seem very important."

In a split second, the archangel was suddenly standing beside the men. Standing around seven feet tall, his blue eyes stood out on his fair skin. His blond hair was kept short, showing the etched features on his face and his ruddy cheeks.

Hawk gulped. To offset the seriousness of the situation, Hawk said, "Yer a tall one, aren't ya?"

The archangel chuckled, his face softening for the first time since the meeting started. "You have amused me many times over the years."

Hawk raised an eyebrow. "What do ya mean by that?"

"You have been protected through the years for such a time as this."

"Who's protected us?"

"We are many."

"More cryptic," Hawk said, rolling his eyes. "*Who* is *we*?"

"Haven't you figured it out yet?" O'Donnell smacked Hawk's arm. "He's an angel…as in a *real* angel. Pretty sure a high up one at that. *Look* at him! What? Do you think he was some sort of magician by making this appear out of thin air?" he asked, holding up the scroll. "And, I don't see any lines for a harness for when he was over there one second, and right here the next."

"Prove it," Hawk demanded.

"When you were nine, your father died on the field in battle," the archangel started. With each statement, the color from Hawk's face continued to drain. "When you found out, you cried and cursed God. On that day, the Lord's heart broke with you. Through the next few years, you struggled to find out more information on the death of your father. It wasn't until you joined the military and gained connections, were you able to finally read the report regarding your father's death. I could go into the details of your father's death if you want me to?"

"No," Hawk groaned.

"Okay, then in the meantime, you skinned your knee while learning to ride a bike in Kindergarten. You had your heart broken by Robin Marks in the eighth grade. You cheated on an exam in the tenth grade by looking at Angela Thompson's paper, but never got caught. You –"

"Okay, okay. Enough." Hawk raised his hands in surrender. "I get it."

"So, what's the deal with the boxes?" O'Donnell pushed.

"That is a long story," the archangel responded.

Sitting on the ground, he said, "We got time."

As the archangel and Hawk sat down, the archangel started, "Paul, Timothy, John, and Peter were in hiding one night, shortly after the transfiguration, when they were Spiritually inspired. Grabbing scrolls, they scribbled as fast as they could to get down every piece of information given them. When finished, I visited them to explain the lists."

"What *are* the lists?"

"One list has the first names of future A.N.G.E.L.s, along with the approximate date you can find them, and the country of their location at that time. The other list has the *last* names of future A.N.G.E.L.s, along with the approximate date you can find them, and the *city* of their location at that time."

"Like a NOC list?"

"Precisely."

"That night, after the lists were completed, they made the boxes. John produced the copper scroll of Revelations, while Peter had kept the towel Jesus used to wash the apostles feet the night of the last supper, along with the cup. Meanwhile, Paul had the thirty pieces of silver from where Judas threw it at the temple before taking his own life. Peter gave Timothy the cup to put into the box he and Paul were responsible for. John and Peter put their articles in a box, while Paul and Timothy placed their articles in the other box. The men then made pots with a Roman Numerals of each century up until the year 4000, the list of names until the year 5000. These pots are only to be opened on the century mark. I placed a marker within the items, so if they are opened too early, or become lost and then opened, my A.N.G.E.L.s will know it and be able to locate the items."

"So, what you're tellin' me is since your A.N.G.E.L.s have somehow lost the scrolls, that if someone opens the pot it's contained in, that we'll know it?" Hawk asked.

"Yes."

"So," O'Donnell nervously cleared his throat, "you're telling us we don't have a choice in being one of *your* A.N.G.E.L.s?"

"You always have a choice. That is the free will granted to you by the Lord."

"So, we can say no?"

"Yes."

"But you know we won't," O'Donnell said in understanding.

The archangel only nodded in response.

"So, if the pots are only opened every thousand years, how do we get our hands on the list? How do others get the list? While people are living longer nowadays, I'm pretty sure I won't make it that long," O'Donnell pointed out. "And, my job actually dictates a much shorter life than the average person."

"You are to find those on the list by the dates. Once they are trained and ready to take missions, you are to pass the list to them to continue the legacy. You are to burn them on the hundred year mark after you show the next team how to use the list."

"Wait! What missions? Where did missions come into this? You *do* remember we're military," Hawk reminded him. "We get our missions from *them*."

"You will receive them from me as well."

"What *kind* of missions?" O'Donnell questioned.

"Missions that will help people on many levels. Whether it is everyday help for their needs, or to save their lives, your missions will be a blessing to them…and to you. There are many long-range plans that may never come to fruition if you do not fulfill them."

"But, if we don't get there, I'll bet you have a back-up plan," O'Donnell said knowingly.

"Yes, but the initial person will always be the best."

"What happens if we can't locate the scrolls?"

"You will find them in time. In the meantime, you are to find the individuals on that list."

"But, what if –"

"Yours is to take each step in faith, even if you cannot see the entire plan. Are you willing to take that step?"

"We're t' find these people t'gether?" Hawk asked.

"Until you find those on your unit, yes. Once they have been found, it will be your mission to look for the others, allowing them to connect and begin their journey. I will also be giving you assignments as you go. If you choose not to accept this assignment, the balance of power may shift, and not in a good way. What is your decision?"

Hawk looked to O'Donnell, who shrugged. When he looked back to the archangel, the archangel was gone, and they were sitting in the middle of an open patch of the Outback, with a scroll sitting near their feet.

Picking up the scroll, O'Donnell said, "Hmm, think we need to get started. We have a lot of work ahead of us."

*   *   *

"Wow," Rachel said, shaking her head, as everyone intently listened to the story Hawk shared. "That's crazy."

"The Colonel told us that story," Angel explained. "I can't imagine what it was like, but thank you for not saying no."

Hawk chuckled. "While we had a choice, we really couldn't say no. The balance of power in the world was at stake. And, now that legacy lands on your shoulders."

"So, we start in Dallas," Angel said, scanning the list. "Mason is the last name. We have to be there within the week."

Hawk stood. "Then, may God bless your steps and guide you in your missions."

Before they left, everyone joined hands in prayer. As they prayed, there was a light around them that lit every corner of the room in a warm glow. By the time Hawk said, "Amen," the group of young people were charged and excited. "The Lord be with you," Hawk said before he and his men left.

As Angel locked the door behind them, her eyes went straight to the list. Picking it up again, she said, "We have a legacy to protect."

"And protect it, we will," Josh agreed. "The balance of the world is at stake. This is our cross t' bear, an' I accept it with honor."

# Chapter 4
# A Double-Edged Sword

As the plane finally touched down in DFW International Airport, a thrill ran through Rachel. Never having been out of the country, going through customs in Atlanta, Georgia was a unique experience. Knowing travel would be the call to order for their new position, it only reaffirmed her decision to let the Lord handle everything, and to take things one day at a time.

"Okay. Where to?" Jesse asked, as they stood there with their backpacks on. Jesse and Josh each also carried an extra bag. They only checked two bags in order to transport their weapons. "It said Dallas, and we're in Dallas. Where do we go next?"

"Food," Jon said decisively. "We need food. *Real* food, not airplane food."

"Always thinking about your stomach, eh?" Jesse teased.

"Well, it's talking to me in a rather belligerent tone of voice, and I really didn't want to have to tell it to wait again," Jon admitted with a grin.

"What about a hotel first, an' *then* dinner?" Rachel offered. "We don't have a vehicle, nor do I want t' carry those two bags everywhere. I would *much* rather have those *on* me if you know what I mean."

"Agreed. Let's get a taxi to a hotel and then dinner," Angel said, decisively.

"Where are we gettin' the money for this stuff?" Rachel asked. "I mean, I know we have a callin', an' I know we are going t' do a lot a' travelin', but *where* is the money comin' from? I don't get it."

"That, my dear, is being taken care of by two former A.N.G.E.L. teams. You see, the American A.N.G.E.L.s joined the Mexican A.N.G.E.L.s for thirty years in order to build their crew. Since that group is already intact, the Mexican A.N.G.E.L.s are sending money to help us grow our crew. The Mexican crew's first date isn't for at least five years, so the teams pulled together once again. They'll still go on missions, but they don't need to locate anyone for a while, so they're confident in their amount of support."

"I see."

"*And* your parents made a hefty donation as well," Angel mentioned before hailing a cab.

Grabbing her arm, Rachel spun her toward her. "They *what*?"

Shrugging, she turned back to hailing a cab. "They gave me money."

"Why would they give *you* money when they gave *us* money as well?"

Leaning down near her ear, Josh quietly said, "Maybe because they believe in what we're doin'. Let-it-go."

"I just want t' know why they gave it t' both a' us."

"Relax. Trust them. We need t' be able t' trust them, as much as they need t' trust us."

"Look, in paying cash it allows us to maneuver around without leaving a trail. Your parents understand that more than the average person," Angel said as a van pulled up to the group. While they loaded up, Angel gave him the name of the hotel where they were to be dropped off. On the way to the hotel everyone sat in silence, lost in their own thoughts.

Once there, they checked in and headed up to their adjoining rooms. Arming themselves by hiding weapons on their person before they left the hotel, they walked over to a local restaurant.

After they were seated, Angel started, "The dates for 'Mason' in Dallas start today."

"Dallas is a large area," Jon pointed out. "How are we supposed to locate one person in this giant city? It's not like it's a small town."

"Welcome, I'm your server for the evening. The name's Joe," their waiter said, appearing at the table only a moment after they sat.

"Are there any specials?" Angel asked.

"Sure. They're listed right here for your convenience," he said, pointing them out on the menu.

Rachel sat back in her seat with her arms crossed. Covering the smile on her face, she sat there with a twinkle in her eyes.

After they ordered, Joe disappeared to get their drinks and put their order in. Once he was gone, Josh turned to Rachel and demanded, "Fess up."

"Fess up what?" Jesse asked. Getting a good look at Rachel, he asked, "What's so funny?"

"Ohhh," Rachel laughed, shaking her head. "Blind Freddy coulda seen it. Are ya tellin' me that y'all didn't see it?"

"See *what*?" Jon asked.

Returning to the table, Joe gave everyone their drinks. When he got to Rachel, she asked, "Joe, I know this is an odd question, but would you mind if I asked you your last name?"

"We're not supposed to share that," Joe said, narrowing his eyes at her. He looked to be about twenty-five years old. Standing around six-foot-two, his medium brown hair and brown eyes blended with his tanned skin from living in the south. What stood out to Rachel the most were his dimples when he smiled.

"The reason I'm asking is because we're looking for a young man named Joe Mason," Rachel said, filling in the first name, as she rested her chin on her hand. "He lives here in Dallas, Texas. That wouldn't happen t' be you, would it?"

"Ya know? Under normal circumstances I would be thrilled to have a beauty such as yourself to be looking for me, but knowing I have never seen you before, it's a little unnerving. And by the accent, I'd say you're not from around here."

"Aussie, born an' bred," Rachel said, batting her eyes.

"Nice."

"My name's Rachel Sullivan," she said, shaking his hand. "What's yours?"

"Well, you already seem to know it. Not sure why you're looking for me, though."

"Well, pull up a chair an' let's talk," she gestured toward an empty chair at a close table.

"Unfortunately, I'm on shift. Aaaaand, it looks like your salads are up," he said, glancing at the pager on his hip. "I'll be right back."

"You sure?"

"Trust me. I'm *definitely* intrigued by those beautiful blue eyes," he said, flashing a smile before disappearing into the kitchen.

"How did you know?" Angel asked, stunned, when he was out of earshot.

"I know how," Josh said, shaking his head in disbelief. "Why didn't you tell Mum?"

Shrugging, Rachel simply stated, "She never asked."

"Asked *what*?" Angel demanded. "What aren't you telling us?"

"She has Mum's gift," Josh explained.

"Which is?"

"She can tell by lookin' at someone whether they are one of the Lord's or not. She can also tell if they are an A.N.G.E.L. or not by the amount of brightness she sees in them."

"Is this true?" Jesse asked.

"Yes," she admitted.

"That's cool!"

"So, now you know how I knew he was Joe Mason," Rachel explained. "Looks like we didn't have t' look very far."

"Okay, here ya go," Joe said, setting his tray down on the stand. Passing out their salads, he then ran the tray back to the kitchen for their meals before returning. After handing out their meals, he slid into the rounded booth next to Rachel. "So, mind explaining to me how you knew my name?"

Rachel had taken a sip of her water right before he sat down. When he did, she inhaled the wrong way and started coughing. Once she got it under control, she asked, "What, um," she coughed again, "I thought you were on shift."

"Taking a break," he said, sitting back in his seat. "I'm curious to find out how a beautiful Aussie knows my name."

"When is your shift over?"

"I've got another hour."

"Tell ya what. We'll eat slowly, an' when you're done we'll buy your dinner an' explain why we're here," she offered.

"Why would you do that?"

"Because I don't want ya t' miss out on your tips, an' it may take us a while t' explain how we know your name."

"Sounds intriguing."

"Oh, it is," she said, flipping her hair with a playful smile on her face. "Are ya interested?"

"I am," he agreed. "For some reason, I feel relaxed around you. All right. I'm game. Have to admit that I'm curious. Let me go finish my shift and I'll be back."

"Sounds good," Rachel agreed, and he dashed off to let the manager know he wasn't going on break. "That was fun," she said with a smirk.

"I have a feeling there's already a plan in place to find the others on our list," Angel said, pulling the current list from her pocket. "After we recruit Joe, our next destination will be New Orleans."

"Well, let's eat," Jon said, "I'm hungry."

As they joined hands, Jesse prayed over the meal, making sure to thank the Lord for providing them guidance in finding Joe. After he said amen, they dug in, grateful for non-airplane, non-hotel food.

"Never thought I would miss Felix's cookin' as much as I do now," Josh said, and sighed. "I actually miss the station an' those blokes out there too."

"I miss all of my family, blood *and* spiritual family as well." Angel sighed. "I have to admit it's kind of weird not having them around."

"We're all on our own. We have t' trust each other," Josh pointed out.

"Trusting a complete stranger is not normally in my playbook," Jesse admitted. "Looks like we'll have to all use a completely new playbook until we're all used to each other."

"We're going to have to learn each other's strengths and weaknesses," Jon explained. "This will either be an epic fail –"

"Or the best thing the Lord put together," Angel finished.

*   *   *

After his shift, Joe went back over to the table and sat down beside Rachel. "So, beautiful, wanna tell me a story of how a sweet thing like you found little ol' me here in the middle of Dallas?"

"It's an interestin' story. Is your dinner ordered?" she asked.

"Yes, ma'am. It's on its way. They'll buzz me when it's ready."

"Good. So, where do ya want us t' start?"

"I'd imagine the beginning, because I already have an idea of how it ends…with me and you. Want to ditch this crew and go out for dessert on our own?"

Rachel cringed. "Not tonight. I have t' give my frog a haircut."

"Ouch!" Joe laughed, as Jesse stiffened. "Look, I'm just sayin' I really dig you."

"I'm not in this for a date."

"Then why *are* you here?"

"Where do I start?" Deciding to start with his heart, she asked, "Joe, are you a Christian?"

"Oh, so busted." He blushed. "I *knew* you were going to ask me that."

"How?"

"I have a feeling the next thing you're going to ask me is if I believe in angels."

Rachel looked at him, wide-eyed. "How'd you know *that*?"

Sighing, he explained, "I saw it."

"Cool!" Jon grinned. "You have visions?"

"You believe me?" he asked, stunned.

"I have dreams," Angel said, pleased to have a connection. Deep inside, though, she was starting to resent Rachel for getting all the attention from the guys.

"I don't get them often, but when I do, they're extremely accurate."

"Mine too. Mine are usually violent as well."

"Well, I'm okay as long as mine lead me to a beauty, such as this enchanting young lady," he said, turning back to Rachel as Angel rolled her eyes.

"Easy on, mate. That's my sister," Josh shot.

"Well," Joe nervously cleared his throat, sitting upright. "Sorry, friend. Nothing personal. To be honest with you, though," he looked back to Rachel, "you have the most beautiful blue eyes I have ever seen. Where have they been hiding you?"

"You'd better watch that silver tongue of yours," Josh snapped, crossing his arms, making him look bigger than usual.

"No problem, brother." Raising his hands in surrender, Joe added, "Her eyes are just so mesmerizing. I'll be good, though, I promise."

Angel clicked her tongue in irritation before she asked, "So, you knew we were coming?"

"I knew *she* was coming," Joe corrected, pointing to Rachel. "It was *her* face I saw. When I came to the table and saw her, it didn't surprise me when she asked me to stay."

"Would it surprise you if we asked you to join us on a journey?" Rachel questioned.

"Not if it's to New Orleans."

Stunned, Angel asked, "How do you know about New Orleans?"

"I saw it. I was walking down a street in New Orleans with Rachel, when we stumbled into a small shop. There was a guy in the shop not too much older than us with the name 'Val' on his name tag."

"A *guy* named Val?" Jon asked. "Are you sure your dream was accurate? That doesn't sound right."

"You have to remember there are a lot of Creoles in New Orleans," Joe pointed out. "It's probably short for something else."

"What does he look like?" Jesse asked.

"Val has dark skin. While his skin dictates potential African American decent, his voice has a bit of a French accent to it. He's about six-foot tall, has dark brown eyes, and has short, dark curly black hair that's shaved on the sides, but higher on the top, kind of like a flat top haircut. His body is fairly thin, but I would be willing to bet he's deadly if pushed. It's usually the thin ones who are underestimated, but are the deadliest – kind of like me. Oh! And he deals a lot in spices and herbal medicines."

"You got that from this vision?" Angel asked.

"Actually, *that* was from the shop he was in."

"I see. And who all found him?"

"Everyone split off in two teams. Rachel, that guy," Joe said, pointing to Jesse before he pointed to Jon, "or maybe that guy. It was one of the two of you, Rachel, and I who found him."

"Well, *that's* not goin' t' happen," Josh said, anger laced in his voice. "Where she goes, I go. I'm supposed t' protect her. Dad made her my charge."

"Calm down, big boy." Joe chuckled. "I'm not gonna do anything inappropriate. The Lord wouldn't like it very much. Personally, I don't want to face Him if I was inappropriate with one of His A.N.G.E.L.s."

Angel's jaw dropped. "How did –"

"How do you know about the A.N.G.E.L.s?" Jon demanded.

"Had a visit from our friend about a week ago," Joe admitted. "You know him. He's about seven-foot tall, has blond hair and blue eyes. *Definitely* intimidating, but a decent sense of humor."

"You *knew*?" Jesse asked, shocked.

"Of course I knew. Oh! Hold on. My dinner's ready," he said before dashing back to the kitchen for his food.

"Seems we don't have to worry too much about sounding crazy to those we find. Looks like the Lord is already a step ahead of us," Jon said, and then sipped his soda. "We just need to follow the list."

"Kind of like our walk with the Lord," Jesse pointed out. "If we follow His lead, He'll lead us through."

"Ready?" Joe asked, showing up at the table with his meal in a bag.

"For what?" Jesse asked.

"We're fixin' to go to New Orleans in the morning, right?" Joe asked. "I figured we'd be heading to the hotel to set up where to meet. All of my stuff's in my truck. It's only a couple bags, but it's ready."

"How did you know to do that?" Angel asked, irritated.

"After all these years, you gotta ask?"

"What does *that* mean?"

Bursting out in laughter, he shook his head. "You thought you would get the jump on me, but the Lord had other plans. You would be *amazed* by what I know. And now that I know it's true, things are finally making sense."

"I *knew* there was a reason you were so bright," Rachel said, things lining up in her mind.

"I already paid your bill. Let's go to the hotel," Joe suggested. "You guys have camped here long enough."

"What does that mean?"

"The waiter who took over this station wants his table back. This is a big table. Big tables tend to leave big tips," Joe explained.

"But, *we* were supposed to pay our bill," Angel objected. "Yours too."

"Don't worry. I already paid it. Let's get out of here. I've already quit. They tend to not like former employees to hang out either."

"You *quit*?" Angel tilted her head. "Why would you do that?"

"I told you. We have to go to New Orleans and find Val. I would imagine we'll be going to find the others afterward," Joe challenged.

Angel rolled her eyes. "I'll never get used to this."

"That's because you're used to being in control," Jesse pointed out. "And you're learning that you're not."

"I never was, was I?"

"It's a double-edged sword, babe." Joe shook his head. "You have to follow a path, but you don't know where it leads. Yet, you have to be able to still have an element of control in order to get out alive from some of the situations we'll be facing."

"You *know*?"

"I get flashes." He nodded. "C'mon, let's blow this popsicle stand. I'll catch y'all up on who I am when we get to the hotel."

"All right." Angel sighed, giving up. "Let's go."

* * *

Settled in the guy's room, the group split by families on the two beds while Joe pulled a chair over from the table. Resting his crossed feet on the bed with Josh and Rachel, he asked, "So, what do you want to know about me?"

"Well, first off, what does your family say about you bailing on them?" Angel asked.

"I don't have a family. I grew up in the foster system. I was emancipated at the age of eighteen because no family adopted me. In their defense, that was more than likely my fault. I was very angry as a youngster."

"How old *are* you?" Angel asked.

"Twenty-four. You?"

"Twenty-three."

"What happened to your parents?" Jesse asked.

"A stupid skiing accident took my mother when I was two. She broke her neck when she slid into a tree headfirst. My dad did what he could for the next two years, but stress was often the order of the day. One night after work, he stopped off at a bar while I was with the sitter. On his way to the car, he was robbed at knifepoint, and didn't come out on the good end of the fight. He was killed that night by a knife through the neck. When the police came to the house, they found me with the sitter, and I was thrown into the foster system. I was furious. All I wanted was my dad. After losing my mom, my dad was my only family."

Curiosity getting the better of her, Angel asked, "What about other family?"

"They didn't want me. Their lives didn't have room for me. My mom's sister travelled a lot for her job, and she was a single woman. She considered it, but decided she wasn't ready to give up her lifestyle. My grandmother was the only grandparent left on my mom's side. She's handicapped and been in a wheelchair since she was forty due to a car accident. That's the same accident that took my grandfather. She never recovered physically *or* mentally from that one. On my dad's side, my grandparents tried, but I was too much for them, and they decided they couldn't handle me. So, they sent me back to my caseworker. When I was a teen, I bounced between my friend's houses, but it didn't end well. When I turned eighteen, the state cut me loose. I worked and slept on the streets until I saved up enough money to stay in an extended stay hotel. Our *friend* came to me about a week ago. I have to admit that while I was terrified of him, his message not only gave me hope, but also the shot at a real family again. You see, one of my high school friends was a Christian. He had me come to some of his youth outings. He was one of the guys I stayed with for a bit. Being a part of his family life felt foreign, but really cool. He was a rodeo rider, where he and I paired up for team roping. It was the happiest in my life I had ever been. I even felt relaxed enough to try the church thing out. I felt the call of the Lord about a year after I moved in with them, and quickly fell in love. Jesus was something I never had, and I didn't want to lose that either."

"So, what happened?" Jon asked, sensing there was something he wasn't saying.

Sighing, he looked toward the ceiling for a moment, praying to get through the next section without crying. "About two years after I started living with them, they started the paperwork for adoption. Three days before they were to sign, the summer before our senior year, we went to a rodeo. Kevin wanted to try something new, and had been working with a guy in bull riding."

"Oh no," Rachel groaned, dropping her head in her hands.

"You got it. We got third in our event, and then he headed over for bull riding. He held on for five seconds before he got thrown. He broke his neck in the fall. The family understandably wanted me to go, because I reminded them of him. We were best friends…inseparable. I not only lost my brother that day, but also lost my family. I spun out of control. Lost on the streets for months. While I didn't know which way to turn, I knew I wouldn't get anywhere without a diploma. So, I went to see my social worker. She got me hooked up in a shelter for teens without foster families. We had extremely strict rules. The three couples who ran the home wouldn't give anyone an inch. It was run like a military academy. I followed their rules and kept my head down because I could stay there until graduation. I had a bed, food, and shower every day. I was responsible for my clothing and keeping my area clean. The day I got my diploma was the day I was sent away. During that year in the home, I worked my behind off in order to set money aside. I wasn't comfortable moving into an extended-stay hotel until two months after graduation. At that point, my finances were stable enough that I knew I would be able to stay there for at least a little bit. That's the reason all my stuff fits into those two bags," he said, nodding toward the two bags on the floor beside him. "When you don't have anything, and you are given the opportunity the archangel gave me, you don't have anything to lose. I had a vision about you," he said to Rachel, "the day after the archangel's visit. I knew instantly when I saw you who you were and why you were there. Seeing you meant my life was changing once again. This time, it was in a good way."

"So, no one's going to miss you?" Rachel asked.

"No. I only heard from my real family for the first couple of months in the foster system. After that, they had trouble keeping up with what foster home they placed me in that month. My grandparents tried. I got a Christmas and birthday present for the first five years. Then it was only a Christmas present, which only lasted for another two. After that, I didn't even get a card. That's why when Kev said he talked to his parents and I could live with them, I jumped at the chance. When I lost him, I felt alone once again. It took a girl I used to work with at the restaurant, Joy, who pulled me out of it. Her name was fitting for her. She *was* full of joy and kindness. While others shoved me aside, because to them I was angry and shut down, she refused to give up. She chose to love the unlovable. In doing so, I found the Lord once again. Jesus never left me through it all. *I* was the one who turned my back on *Him*," he admitted, "but He *never* left me. She helped me find my way back."

"What happened to her?" Jon asked.

"She went to college out of state. Look, everyone has a story. Some are a little rougher than others. But my understanding from the archangel is that we have an opportunity to help others find Jesus, and bless them as well. He said we're going to do it as a family. We need to understand each other in order to do so, so he encouraged me to be open about my life to y'all. Having said all of that, it will be my honor to work with y'all for as long as the Lord allows me to do so. I know our days are numbered in doing what we're about to do. I also know what we are about to do will be huge for the Kingdom, and that's what I care about. My blood family is gone or doesn't care, but I learned long ago that family is not necessarily dictated by blood. There are friends who stick closer to us than blood family. To me, those are my true family."

"Well said." Josh nodded. "Thank you for sharing your life, and becoming a part a' ours."

"If we're fixin' to be family, we need to know about each other."

"Then, let's *all* share," Josh said. "I'll start."

*   *   *

After everyone shared their stories, it was around one o'clock in the morning. They split up with the girls in one room, and the guys in the other, with the doors closed between the rooms for the night.

The next morning, they loaded up in Joe's SUV, which was an old Ford Expedition. With plenty of room in the vehicle for their baggage and eight individuals, they took off for New Orleans to pick up their next team member. Joe filled them in on his vision regarding Val, as well as some of the history of New Orleans.

By the time he finished, Rachel prayed for safety of everyone in New Orleans. To her, it sounded like a scary place. Grateful that her brother, Jesse, and Jon were as massive as they were, she was curious to see what skills their new team members had. While she wasn't sure where or when they would be able to do it, she knew they had to assess each other's strength and weaknesses. She also knew the Lord had a plan for everything, and she would trust in Him.

# Chapter 5
# The Wisdom Of Solomon

After checking into a hotel for the night, the group went to a restaurant right next door. Jesse sensed the evil all around them as soon as they crossed into the city, so they didn't want to venture too far in the dark. While it was a city known for jazz, art, and its unique cuisine, especially the Creole, it was also known for its high crime rate. The distinctive area known as New Orleans was as diverse as its inhabitants. To Jesse, though, it was just dark, and made the hair on the back of his neck stand on end. He knew the darkness of the city, and wanted out as soon as possible.

"So, we find him in the mornin'?" Josh asked while they were eating dinner.

Right before she took a bite, Angel said, "Yep."

"Do we go out in teams?"

After finishing the bite in her mouth, she asked, "Joe, do you know what shop Val works in?"

"Unfortunately no." He shook his head. "Looks like we're going to have to split the list and into teams."

"Teams of three?" Rachel suggested. "Two guys and a girl?"

"Sounds fair," Angel agreed after swallowing another bite of her Chicken-Andouille gumbo. "Jon and Jesse are with me, and Joe and Josh with Rachel."

"Why don't we mix it up a bit and trade out Josh for Jesse?" Jon suggested. "We need to start blending and not stay with just what we know. I think a day in the city would be a good way to get to know each other."

"No. We'll do it the way I said."

"Controlling much?" Joe shot.

"Fine," she huffed. "We'll do it *your* way, Jon."

Joe chuckled. "Wow. You *are* controlling."

"No. I just like organization."

"We'll see. I have a feeling we're going to end up butting heads here shortly." Joe added, "I don't care for bossy people."

Setting her spoon down, she narrowed her eyes at Joe. "We can always take you back to Dallas."

"No you can't," Rachel objected. "You don't get t' decide who goes with us. He was chosen. The *Lord* chose him. If you can't get along with him, that's something you'll have t' work out on your own. If you're goin' t' be selfish about who *The Lord God Almighty* chose for *our* team, then you'll have t' deal with the *Him* on your own as well. Until then, the unit stands."

When everyone froze at the table, Angel asked her brothers, "Aren't you going to defend me?"

"Oh no," Jesse chuckled. "A control freak like you having to deal with people she can't control? Yeah, this'll be more fun than watching people shopping on Black Friday from the safety of the security room. You're on your own for this one. I'm just going to sit back and enjoy the show," he said before taking a bite of his roll.

"What about you?" she asked Jon.

Sitting back in his seat with his arms crossed, he shook his head. "No one has said anything disrespectful toward you. I agree with Jesse. You're on your own."

"Fine," she huffed, crossing her arms.

"Are you normally this obstinate and immature, or is this one of your good days?" Joe snapped.

"I don't like it when people are rude."

"Rudeness is relative. If calling you out on your controlling behavior and selfish attitude is rude, then I have to let you know that your controlling ways are offensive to me."

"Seriously?"

"Seriously," he said with a straight face.

"Fine," she growled. "Looks like we're going to have to operate without a leader if you guys don't want one."

"I *want* a sister who will fight *beside* me. All of us equal."

"What about organization?"

"Tell ya what. If that's your strong suit, then run with it. Not as a boss, though. We live in a constitutional republic. We all have rights. We *all* should have input. If organizing is what you're good at, then so be it. That's working with our strengths. Just don't be rude about it."

"I have strengths other than that. I just feel we need to be organized in our operational abilities."

"That's understandable. Tell ya what. What if we wait to slide people into positions until we have everyone? That way we can figure out everyone's strengths and weaknesses in order to combine in the best possible way," Joe suggested. "In the meantime, you have the list and most of the money. What if you keep us focused on our goals? As far as how we go about doing it, though, we should work together."

"I agree," Josh put in.

Angel clicked her tongue. "Fine."

"I think he's right," Rachel added. "It sounds fair."

"I said *fine*," Angel growled. "Let's just eat so we can find Val in the morning."

"Can you do it without those ugly feelings?" Jon glanced at her as he took a sip of his soup. After he swallowed, he reminded her, "Remember, I can feel what people are feeling. Your attitude is suffocating me."

"Fine," she huffed. Taking several long deep cleansing breaths, she picked up her spoon to eat once again.

Eating in silence for the remainder of the meal, they were all lost in their own thoughts. As they finished, Rachel said, "The archangel never said it would be easy, but he *did* say with the Lord *all* things are possible. We jus' need t' follow Him. If we're goin' t' work together, then we need t' do it in a civil way. We're goin' t' have our fights. Any family does. It's how we handle them that make us different. We need t' focus on Jesus, not on ourselves. This isn't about us. There are people out there countin' on us t' make it t' them on time."

"Are you always this chipper and positive?" Angel grumbled.

"Seriously, Angel!" Jon snapped. "Knock it off!"

"I agree with Rachel," Jesse said. "The Lord chose us way before our time for such a time as this. Think about it. He knew we would be here at this time, in this place, centuries ago. If that doesn't convince you to focus better on our goals, I don't know what will. He chose each of us for these missions. We all bring something different to the table. We all complement each other. As the body of Christ, we're all one. Just like it describes the body of Christ in the Bible, we are just as diverse and gifted. It's our gifts that will allow us to achieve the goals He's already placed before us."

"I give," Angel relented. "I'm sorry for my behavior, and will do my best to do better."

"That's all we ask," Joe said. "Rachel's right. We're going to have our disagreements, but it's how we handle it that'll make the difference."

*   *   *

The next morning after breakfast, the group downloaded all the herbal medicine shops in the area. Knowing it would take them a day or so to wade through the list, they set out in two groups of three.

Rachel sighed as they walked into what she figured to be the tenth shop they had been to within two days. As spread out as they were in the city, it took them some time to get through their list by walking to them. They left Joe's vehicle in the shelter of the garage of the hotel, figuring it was the safest option for their only vehicle.

The bell rang above the door, signaling their entrance into the old, dim-lit wooden shop. With various herbs drying, and jars and small bags of dried herbs, spices, and oils on the shelves, Joe reminded them, "Only two more on the list."

"Good. I can't wait to get out of this city. There is so much darkness, I can't even get to sleep. My body is constantly on edge," Jesse grumbled.

"Isn't there *any* light?"

"There's some, but not a lot. Let's just find Val and get out of this place," Jesse said, staying near the door to keep an eye out for any unwanted visitors.

Walking up to the counter with Joe behind her, Rachel asked, "Is Val working t'day?"

"Yep. He's in the back on break," a young African American girl said, who was scanning a magazine before they walked in. Looking up, she asked, "Can I tell him who's asking?"

"Please tell him it's Rachel, Joe, an' Jesse," Rachel said.

Cocking her head to the side, the girl asked, "Where are you from?"

"Australia."

"Why is an Australian looking for Val?"

"We were sent by a friend t' give him a message. Not a bad one, mind you, just a message. Is he available?"

"Who's the friend?"

"Inquisitive little thing, aren't you?" Joe asked, flashing a smile as he leaned on the counter in front of her.

"Well, I need to look out for my friends."

Seeing light glowing from a room in the back, Rachel wandered off into the store while Joe flirted with the girl, distracting her. Slowly making her way to the back, she ducked into the opening marked "Employees Only."

"Can I help you?" the young man Rachel figured was Val, asked. He was just as Joe described, even down to the hint of French in his accent.

"Hi," she shook his hand, "I'm Rachel. My friends an' I are lookin' for Val. You wouldn't happen t' be him, would you?"

"With a looker like you looking for him, I definitely *could* be. Why *exactly* are you looking for him?"

"We have a message for him," she said, sitting down on the stool next to his.

"What's the message? I'll give it to him when I see him."

Feeling the Spirit's leading, Rachel said, "Here's the message: *"God gave Solomon wisdom and very great insight, and a breadth of understanding as measureless as the sand on the seashore."*"

"First Kings 4:29. Interesting choice for a message."

"What do you think Val will say when you give him the message?"

"Val isn't a girl?"

"I don't think so," she said knowingly.

"What kind of a name for a guy is Val?"

"I think it's short for his first name."

"Such as?"

"Valentine would be a cool name."

"You think so?"

"I do."

"What about Valentin Mathieu Thibodaux?"

"I think it's cool."

"What's your name?"

"Well, since you told me yours, I'll tell you that mine is Rachel Elizabeth Sullivan. So, what is your response to the message?"

Leaning back against the wall, as he sat on his stool, he said, "Well, '*Solomon's wisdom was greater than the wisdom of all of the men of the east, and greater than all the wisdom of Egypt.*' You see, wisdom is a virtue that many do not possess. It is the ability to combine understanding, knowledge, experience, common sense, and insight in such a way as to guide and direct one's thoughts and actions to the benefit of those around them. You, my dear, are very insightful. You *do* use wisdom beyond your years. Yes, I am Val. Now it's my turn to ask why you are looking for me, and how you found me?"

Rolling her eyes, Rachel groaned, "This was so much easier with Joe. He already knew we were coming."

"Coming for what?"

Deciding the best way to go about it with Val was honesty, she asked, "Val, do you believe in angels?"

# Chapter 6
# A House Divided Against Itself Cannot Stand

When he was off work that night, Val met the group at the restaurant near the hotel for dinner. While they ate, they got to know their new recruit. "I know this may sound odd," Val started, "but I feel comfortable around you guys."

"Not odd." Angel shook her head. "We were led together by the Lord."

"So, let me see if I got this straight. We're going to be getting assignments?"

"Yes."

"And, what do we do when we're not going out?"

"We have a long list of other people we still need to find, along with some training. You have your passport, right?"

"I do. For some reason, I felt compelled to get it about six months ago. I've had this feeling of something big coming. I didn't realize it would come in the form of such beautiful people," he said, looking into Angel's eyes. "Stunning."

"Thank you." Angel nervously cleared her throat at the attention. "So, um, are you going to join us?" she asked

"I believe I will. I need to load up on oils, along with dried herbs and spices before we leave. We may need them in the field. I'll do that tomorrow when I talk to Adelaide."

"Your boss?"

"Yes, ma'am. She took me in when I was a street kid. Living on the streets of New Orleans is not safe for an adult, let alone a child."

"How did you end up on the streets?" Jesse asked.

"I ran away from home."

"Why?"

"Because I was being abused by my mother's boyfriends."

"And your dad?"

"My mother was a prostitute. She didn't know who my dad was."

"Oh! Wow! I'm so sorry."

"Don't be." He shrugged. "It was the best thing that could've happened to me. If not, I would have never run across Adelaide. She took me in and taught me how to use oils, herbs, and spices for medicinal purposes. Nothing nefarious. I promise."

"I know," Rachel said. "The light within you is bright. The Lord is your guide. I don't see any dark."

"That's the thing. She is very consistent and strong in her walk with the Lord. When she took me in, she also took me to church. As I said, running away was the best thing that could have happened to me."

"I can see that. Is she going to be okay when you leave?" Rachel asked. "Are *you* going to be okay to leave her?"

"Yes, and yes."

"Okay then." Angel smiled. "We leave in the morning. Agreed?"

"Agreed," they all said in unison.

*   *   *

The next morning, the group of seven took off for Reno, Nevada to regroup, and talk to the Colonel, Derek, and Mark about guidance in where to go next.

With a faraway look in his eyes, sitting in the passenger seat, Joe said, "We need to stop in Dallas."

"Why?" Jon asked, as he was driving. "I hope it's for food."

"Is that all you think about?" Rachel sighed. "There's more to life than food."

"But, I can't function without it."

"Okay, what's the real reason we're stopping off in Dallas?" Angel asked.

"We need to help someone," Joe explained.

"Who? Wasn't Dallas where we got *you* from?"

Rolling his eyes, Joe explained, "Dallas is bigger than you think. I know where we have to go. Take this exit," he said, directing them to a hotel. After they checked in, they gathered in the boy's room.

"Okay, what are we doing here?" Angel asked impatiently. "I kinda want to get home."

"We would *all* love t' go home, but we can't," Rachel reminded her. "You at least get t' see your parents soon. Ours are all the way over in Australia. We all have t' give up somethin'. Pretty sure Joe had a vision?" she asked, turning the attention back to Joe before she got angry with Angel. To her, Angel had an attitude, and she hoped to not have to give her an attitude adjustment, but would if it came down to it.

"Yep. We can eat first, though. We have plenty of time."

"What do ya mean?" Josh asked.

"It starts around eight o'clock tonight. We'll need our strength."

"That sounds ominous. Wanna share?"

"Yes, and no. I remember where, but I don't remember exactly what happened."

"Who are we looking for?" Rachel asked.

"Two young ladies. C'mon, let's go eat."

*   *   *

Later that night around eight, Jesse, Joe, and Rachel went out, much against Josh's objections. Dressed in standard jeans, t-shirts, and light jackets, they headed into East Plano to a grocery store.

67

"Okay, you're seriously gonna tell me that we're here t' go grocery shoppin'?" Rachel chuckled as they made their way through the Mexican-themed grocery store.

"Yep. It's for a single mom and her children. What else will they need, Jesse?" Joe asked. "You lived there."

"Yes, I did. Here, they'll need some of these too," Jesse said, putting some vegetables in the cart.

When they finished, they walked next door to the apartment complex. "Which one?" Jesse asked Joe.

"That one," he said, pointing to one of the apartments. "How do you want to do this?"

Jesse shrugged. "Let's take it up."

"How will we talk t' them? I hear a lot of Spanish," Rachel pointed out as they made their way upstairs.

"Ohhh, mi amigos de poca fe," Jesse said with a smirk.

Rachel furrowed her brow. "Meanin'?"

"Oh, my friends of little faith. There's a reason I'm with you. Watch," he said, and then knocked on the door.

A young Mexican mother of four opened the door. When she did, they saw the small children looking at them curiously, as one of them held onto their mother's leg. The oldest couldn't have been more than six, with her brothers and sister sitting on the couch. "¿Quién eres?" the mother asked. "¿Por qué estás aquí?"

"She asked who we are, and why're we here," Jesse said before he responded. "Estas provisiones son para usted." He then turned back to Rachel and Joe, and said, "I told her these groceries were for her."

"¡Qué Dios te bendiga!" she exclaimed with tears in her eyes as they passed the bags to the woman.

"She said 'God bless you,'" Jesse explained. Then he turned back to the woman, and said, "Recuerde Jeremías 29:11. Dios tiene un plan para ti." And then they left.

As they walked away, Joe asked, "What did you tell her? She burst out in tears at the last thing you said."

"I told her to remember Jeremiah 29:11, and that God has a plan for her."

Catching someone running out of the corner of her eye, Rachel asked, "You blokes see that?"

"What?"

"Look," she said, pointing to where a young boy of about thirteen or fourteen scaled the fence of the grocery store. As they ran around the fence, they saw three more boys scale the fence and run after him. "Oh no!"

"You guys go that way, while I go this way," Jesse said, chasing the guys, while Rachel and Joe ran around to the front of the building.

"There," Joe pointed, seeing the group running through the parking lot.

Rachel and Joe ran to intercept the young boy. When they caught up to him, Joe grabbed him, wrapping his arms around the boy, while Rachel stood her ground between the boys and Joe with the other boy.

"Hey! What are you doin'?" one of those chasing the boy asked.

"I could ask *you* the same question," Rachel said, not moving a muscle as she stood there with her arms crossed.

"We just need to get to our friend," another one offered.

"Are these your friends?" Rachel asked the boy in Joe's arms, as Jesse ran up behind them.

"No, ma'am," the boy answered, his voice quivering.

Rachel turned back to the boys. "Looks like he doesn't wanna go with you blokes. Perhaps you should go back to where ya came from."

One of the boys whipped out a knife, as he said, "Maybe *you* should go back to where *you* came from."

When Jesse went to jump, Rachel held her hand up to stop him. "If you blokes don't leave, we'll have t' call the police."

"No matter. We'll get 'em later," the head kid grumbled. He went to turn away, but spun around and lunged for Rachel.

Rachel grabbed the hand with the knife and twisted it toward his thumb. When he released the knife, it dropped to the ground. Rachel then continued to twist his arm behind his back and pulled up. "This is your last warnin', mate," Rachel growled, as she stepped on the knife with her foot to keep it there. "Either ya leave the boy alone, or you're dealin' with me. I've kept myself under control, but if I find out you hurt one hair on his head, you're not only dealin' with me, but you'll be dealin' with *that* bloke," she said, nodding toward Jesse, who glared at them as he nodded. "Do we understand each other?"

"Yes, ma'am," the boy said, his voice trembling as he body shook. "We'll leave 'im alone. I promise."

"I mean it," Rachel warned. "We'll be watchin'."

"I promise!" the boy squeaked out. "We'll leave 'im alone!"

"You'll not only leave 'im alone, but you'll also stop anyone else from hurtin' him. If I find out otherwise, we're comin' back. By the way, there's another one who looks just like him," she said, nodding toward Jesse again.

"Y-yes, ma'am."

"Vete a casa y leer Colosenses 3:8," Jesse instructed.

"No tiene una Biblia en casa," the older boy responded.

Jesse sighed. Then an idea hit him. "Entonces es tu misión para averiguar lo que es. ¿Puedes hacer eso?"

"Sí," the boy agreed.

"Luego de salir de aquí," Jesse said. "Let him go, Rach."

As soon as Rachel released him, the three boys ran. "What did you say to them?" Rachel asked.

"I told them to look up Colossians 3:8. When he told me they didn't have a Bible at home, I told them it was their mission to find that verse."

"What's Colossians 3:8?" Joe asked.

"'*But now you must put them all away: anger, wrath, malice, slander, and obscene talk from your mouth,*'" Jesse recited. Then he knelt in front of the boy still wrapped in Joe's arms. "¿Estás bien?"

"Yes," he responded, weakly.

"¿Habla Inglés?" Jesse asked him.

"Yes. A little."

"Then, go back home, knowing God is with you wherever you go."

"Thank you," the boy said before he ran off for his home.

When he was gone, Jesse looked up at Rachel. "So, what else can you do?"

"Wouldn't you love to find out," Rachel said with a mischievous grin.

"Were you trained in the physical as well as the spiritual?"

"Yep."

"Don't mind me," Joe said. "I'll just stand here while you two hook up."

"We're not hooking up," both Jess and Rachel said in unison.

Putting his hands up in surrender, Joe took a step back. "Just let me know when y'all are ready."

"For what?"

"To stop the clerk over there from gettin' attacked," Joe said, gesturing toward the grocery store clerk who checked out their groceries earlier. "She's the second reason we're here. This last one was by chance."

As she walked into the parking lot, Rachel's eyes wandered toward the man hiding on the other side of her car.

"Oh! No way!" Rachel said, and ran for the car to stop the mugger, while Jesse snuck around to the other side of the attacker to take him from behind, and Joe ran up to the cashier.

"Excuse me, do you remember me from earlier?" Joe called to the cashier.

Nervously looking from Joe to the store, the cashier stood where she was. "W-what do you want?"

When he got closer, he quietly said, "I need you to go back into the store. There's a guy on the other side of your car."

Wide-eyed, she demanded, "Who?"

Once Rachel reached the car, she crossed her arms as she leaned against it. Buffing her nails on her shirt, she then studied her fingers as she asked, "Wanna tell me what a bloke like you is doin' sittin' on the ground next to a young lady's car?" she asked, and he stood, anger churning in his dark brown eyes. "You wouldn't happen t' be layin' in wait for her, would you?"

While Rachel distracted him, Jesse grabbed him from behind. The man struggled in his arms, as he shouted, "What are you doing?"

"What are *you* doing?" the cashier demanded, as she and Joe neared the vehicle. "I have protective order against you! Police are coming!"

"I'll kill you!" he spat.

"Too many witnesses," the woman said, snidely.

"This time."

Seeing the police lights in the distance, the man struggled harder in Jesse's arms, but Jesse was too much for him. "You're not going anywhere," Jesse growled.

"Watch me!"

"Ha! I'd like t' see that one." Rachel scoffed. "That bloke's at least twice your size. Good luck with that, mate."

"I'll get you too, when I'm free," he said, struggling harder in Jesse's arms.

"Fine. You asked for it," Jesse said, then put him in a sleeper hold. As the man went to the ground, the police pulled up.

Pulling his gun, the police officer aimed at Jesse, "Put your hands up, now!"

"No! No! No! No!" the woman yelled. "Is him!" she said, pointing to the man on the ground, gasping for air.

As the police officer handcuffed the man, Rachel pulled the woman aside. "You have t' get out of here before he gets out."

"I have nowhere to go. No way to do it," she said, shaking her head. Resting her hand on her stomach, she glanced at it before looking back up at Rachel.

Rachel turned to Joe, and asked quietly, "Do you have any connections for an ID?"

"I do," he said cautiously.

Turning back to the woman, Rachel said, "When we're done here, pack a bag an' we'll get ya outta here tonight. Understand?"

"You are a godsend!" the woman said with tears in her eyes. "How can I repay you?"

"By living your life for Him. In Matthew 22:37, '*Jesus said unto him, Thou shalt love the Lord your God with all thy heart, and with all your soul, and with all thy mind.*' Then in Matthew 6:33, He reminds us, '*But seek ye first the Kingdom of God, and His righteousness; and all these things shall be added unto you.*' Stay focused on Him and let Him guide your steps," Joe explained. "We'll meet you back here in three hours. Do you understand?"

"Yes," she agreed.

"I'm stayin' with her. I'm not leavin' her alone until we get her outta here," Rachel insisted.

"We can't leave you," Joe argued.

"Yes. You can an' you will. We'll meet you back here in three hours."

"Fine. Josh isn't going to like this, though," Joe warned.

"Just get her an identity," Rachel insisted. "We're goin' t' go t' the police," Rachel said, pulling her over to a police officer to give her statement, while Jesse and Joe finished up before they left.

* * *

While Joe and Jesse were gone, Rachel and the woman, Daniela, talked. Daniela explained her story of how she and Javier had gotten together three years ago. The relationship started just fine, until he asked her to marry him. The week after their wedding, she said it was like he was possessed, and his personality suddenly shifted. He would question her every move, and set his friends to watch her when he couldn't be around. His behavior quickly escalated from verbal abuse to physical abuse over the next six months.

When Daniela showed Rachel the bruises on her arms and lower back, Rachel shook her head, beside herself. "How can someone who's supposed t' love you, hurt you like that?"

"I do not know," Daniela said, shaking her head. "He told me over and over again that he loved me. I wish I had seen it before I married him." The more upset she became, her English became more broken.

"Are you married still?"

"No. When I divorce him, it got much worse!" Daniela exclaimed, wide-eyed. "And now, I pregnant with his child."

"How far along are you?"

"Four months. He not know," she admitted.

"Good. Let's keep it that way. When you have the baby, put down that you don't know who the father is. You are t' raise this baby for the Lord. He'll be strong in Him."

"Is a boy?"

"Yes. Don't let the cycle of abuse carry on into this generation. Raise him for the Lord."

"I will. You are truly an angel," Daniela said, wiping the tears from her eyes.

"C'mon, it's time. Joe an' Josh should have your papers ready by now."

* * *

After the trio got Daniela on a bus with a thousand dollars in her pocket, they headed back to the hotel, exhausted. Flopping on her bed, face down, Rachel let out a slow breath of air.

"Long night?" Angel questioned, sitting up while resting on her arm.

"Definitely, but worth it," she said, rolling over to face the ceiling, her hands resting on her stomach.

"We're heading out here in a few minutes," Angel said, watching Rachel for her reaction.

"Have fun. Where are ya goin'?"

"Don't know. *Josh and I* are leaving in about fifteen minutes."

Rachel glanced at her out of the corner of her eye. "Is there a particular reaction you're expectin' from me?"

"No." She shrugged. "Just thought you'd like to know that your brother and I are heading out together. Who knows when we'll be back?"

"Ya know, yer soundin' like yer braggin' over there. We're supposed t' be a team."

"Not bragging. I just think he's cute. I find it interesting that *I'm* the one who gets to go out with him *again*."

"Wow. Maybe you should rein that attitude in a bit. You can't be head of this team with an attitude like that. I'll make sure t' let him know *exactly* what I think of you *an'* your attitude," Rachel said, getting off the bed, temper getting the better of her.

Jumping off her bed, Angel stood in front of her with her arms crossed, cutting her off. "There's nothing wrong with what I said."

"If there wasn't, then you have nothin' t' worry about," Rachel challenged.

"Knock, knock," Josh said, walking into the girl's room from the adjoining door. "Well," he crossed his arms, "this looks interestin' t' say the least."

As Rachel and Angel glared at each other, Rachel said, "It seems that Angel here, is more than happy t' be goin' out with you t'night, an' decided t' rub my face in it."

"Really? We're not goin' out that *I* know of," Josh said, shaking his head. "Where'd that come from?"

"Josh, you, Angel, and I need to go out," Joe said, coming into the room. "I got an assignment and I need your help."

"Comin'," Josh said, not moving.

"Told you," Angel said, snidely. "I had a dream about it."

"Well, little Miss Priss," Rachel snapped, "just remember that the Lord gave ya that gift for a reason, an' I don't think it's t' rub your teammate's face in it."

"Me neither," Josh said.  Before disappearing into the other room, he added, "An' I don't care for it at all."

"Miss Priss?" Angel cocked her head to the side when Josh was out of earshot.

"Listen here," Rachel took a couple steps toward Angel. Eyes wide, Angel took a step back. Rachel took another step forward and she sternly warned her, "He's aware of your ways. Unless ya clean them up, you don't have a prayer with him."

"Time will tell."

"Watch it. You almost sound like you're doin' a fine balance between sides, there."

"What does *that* mean?"

"You an' God may wanna have a deep conversation…*soon*," Rachel shot before leaving their room for the boy's room.

Seeing Jon leaning on the doorway with his arms crossed, Angel growled, "What?"

"You know she's right. Mom and Dad aren't going to be happy with your behavior lately. Pretty sure God won't be happy about it either."

"You think you're the judge and jury around here?"

"Nope. Just pointing out the facts. I think it's good that we're going home. You could use some one-on-one time with Mom and Dad."

"You too?"

"Seriously. You were given a little power and immediately fell flat on your face. May want to take that into consideration next time you and God talk. As a matter of fact, take some time now before we go. You guys need to be on the level when you go out. And just so you know, I'm going with you on this to make sure nothing goes sideways."

"I'm fine."

"That's an order. I'm pulling rank here. If you don't, we're taking Rachel."

"You wouldn't!"

"We can't be a house divided."

"We're not in a house. We're in a hotel."

"We are a family whether you want to admit or not."

"Fine," she huffed, crossing her arms.

"*Now*," he growled before he left.

As he closed the door behind him, shutting her away from the others, Angel took a deep breath. Looking toward Heaven, she asked, "Is he right?"

Jumping when she heard a voice behind her say, "Yes." She spun, finding herself face-to-face with the archangel. "You have stumbled a bit, Angelina."

"But, she – "

The archangel crossed his arms as he gave her a look.

Angel sighed. "Fine. You're right."

"What do you think you need to do?"

"Find a way back. But how?"

"First, you must find out why. If you do not figure that out, it will happen again. That is where Satan will strike you first. He now knows he can get a foothold on you in that area."

Sitting on the side of the bed, Angel dropped her head in her hands. "It's a pride issue, isn't it?"

"Yes, it is," the archangel said, resting his hands on her knees, crouched in front of her. When she looked up, he explained, "Sometimes it takes you actually going out and doing the work to find out where your strongholds are. You have a heart issue. I know this is the first time a young man has captured your heart. In doing so, you feel you need to prove your worth to him. This is also the first time where you are in competition with another young lady who is your equal. You are used to being in charge and the one the young men looked at because you were different."

"This is true."

"Do you not know by now that you are priceless to the Lord? Do you not know the value the Lord has placed in you, and that *His* value is the One that counts. Joshua cannot find the value in your heart if you are hiding it from him, pretending to be something you are not."

"This is true."

"You are a strong one for Christ. There is a reason you were chosen. Romans 12:2 tells you, *'And do not be conformed to this world, but be transformed by the renewing of your mind, that you may prove what is that good and acceptable and perfect will of God.'* Have your actions lately been good, acceptable, and perfect in His eyes?"

"No," she admitted.

"Then, I believe that is where you need to start. You are a strong young lady, Angelina. You will lead this group, but you have to do it with God as *your* leader. If *you* take control, He cannot lead."

"I understand."

"Do you remember what it says in Matthew 5:5-9?"

*"'Blessed are the meek, for they shall inherit the earth. Blessed are those who hunger and thirst for righteousness, for they shall be satisfied. Blessed are the merciful, for they shall receive mercy. Blessed are the pure in heart, for they shall see God. Blessed are the peacemakers, for they shall be called sons of God.'"*

"Or in this case, daughter of God," the archangel reminded her.

Dropping her head in her hands, she mumbled, "I understand."

"Good. Then go forth and do the work of the Lord your God."

Angel nodded. When she looked back up, he was gone. "Ohhh," Angel sighed, shaking her head. "Hate it when he does that." Looking toward Heaven, she prayed, "Father, I'm really sorry. It seems like I can't get it right lately. Please lead my steps and guide my thoughts. In Jesus' precious name I pray, Amen."

Dragging herself off the bed, she went into the other room. When she walked through the door, all eyes were on her.

"Guys, can we start again? I've royally screwed this up. I need to trust in both you guys and the Lord more than I have been. It's not about me, it needs to be all about Him."

"Finally!" Joe threw his hands into the air. "I've been waiting since I met you to hear those words."

"I've been messing up big time. Can you guys forgive me?"

"Every time," Rachel said, walking over, giving her a hug. "We're a unit. God put us together for a reason." Taking a step back, she admitted, "I'm missing my sister, an' would welcome another one...not a challenge. We're gonna be headin' into enough challenges. I'm pretty sure we will need each other."

"I agree. My loving brother reminded me that a house divided against itself cannot stand. I don't want to be divided. We were called to a divine legacy that I want to continue to do for the Lord, in order to pass down to the next generation after us."

"I do believe that's the plan," Jesse pointed out. "It may not be to our children. Only the Lord knows who He wants on His team. Our mission is to follow."

# Chapter 7
# Faith Will Move Mountains

Amber Jones clocked out after her double-shift as a nurse at the local hospital in Las Cruces, New Mexico, with terrible news burning a hole in her pocket. Carrying the burdens of bills, caring for patients, and being a single mother to six-year-old twin girls often left her stressed and exhausted. Callie an Allie were her world, and she would do anything to ensure them a safe and happy life. The issue was that her ex-boyfriend had a gambling problem. Normally this wouldn't be *her* problem, except the collector of the debt couldn't find Eric, so he insisted Amber pay it.

After numerous threats on the lives of the girls, Amber negotiated a payment plan. In order to execute her plan, she would have to pull double-shifts for quite a while. In doing so, she also had to pay the sitter to do it as well. This was a vicious cycle Amber never thought she would ever escape.

At this point, she made too much money for medical help or food stamps, but barely enough to keep her head above water. She often cried herself to sleep, feeling like she would never be able to escape her past. While she cherished the girls, their father was another story. Their relationship started off great. After several months, though, love, acceptance, and tenderness were slowly replaced with anger, demand, and frustration. The last straw for him was when she told him she was pregnant. He acted as if it were completely her fault, and demanded she get an abortion. After multiple fights and her refusal, he threw his arms in the air and left.

Breathing a sigh of relief for the first time in months, she thought she was finally in the clear. She didn't care if Eric ever came back...until one night when she was five months pregnant and got a knock on the door.

When she went to open it, the door flew open, and a man who barely fit through the doorframe was standing there. "Where is Eric Samuels?" he demanded.

"He-he left two months ago," Amber stammered, backing against the kitchen table.

Getting in her face, he used his pointer finger. Poking her in the shoulder, he said, "Then *you* have a problem."

Looking at him in wide-eyed horror, she asked, "Why?"

"Because he owes my boss. Since Eric used your car and belongings as collateral, guess who owes him?"

"He can't do that!"

"He did," the man said, with an evil smile. "*You* owe him seventy-five g's."

"I...*what*? I didn't do it! What he did was illegal. That was *my* stuff, not his."

"Then, you lose it all and *still* owe fifty g's."

"How is that fair?"

"Nothing is fair, sweetheart. The money is owed and *you* are payin' it."

Sliding from in front of him, she struggled to keep herself from crying. Sinking onto the couch, Amber dropped her head in her hands. "What am I going to do? I'm five months pregnant. I can't do this."

"You can make payments. As long as the payments are made, you can keep everything," the man suggested, as he stood there with his arms crossed. "As long as my boss is happy, I'm happy. If he's not happy, I'm not happy. If I'm not happy, *you won't* be happy."

"Understood."

After setting up a payment plan she could afford, Amber set to reduce as much debt as she could, until she found out at her five-and-a-half-month ultrasound that she was pregnant with twins. She considered adopting them out, but soon realized they were the only thing holding her together.

When she was around eight months pregnant, her friend Carina started working with her. Carina was married and had two children, one of which was a fifteen-year-old daughter. After going back-and-forth, Amber hired the daughter for when the twins were born to watch the girls after school. During school hours, Amber's neighbor offered to watch them for her. Unfortunately, the neighbor had children of her own. Her concern was that it would be too much once her kids got home to watch the twins at that point. After Carina's daughter stepped in to watch the babies, relief flooded her body. Something in her life finally worked out.

One day, a couple of years after the twins were born, Amber confided in Carina about all of her problems in a babbling mess. With the lack of family support, Amber's concerns centered around surviving the whole ordeal. After a while, Carina felt comfortable enough to ask Amber to go to church with her. At first Amber resisted, until she really didn't have any reason not to.

Once she did, she instantly found a family who would love and support her. Carina was a godsend as far as Amber was concerned. While her problems were still there, she found a support and encouragement in Carina's family, as well as her new church family. After a few months, Amber even started listening intently to the pastor's sermons and started asking questions. *Who was this Jesus? Why would He care what happened to her? Why would He give His life for her? And, what was the deal with this salvation stuff?*

Carina had Amber over after church one Sunday to hopefully answer some of her questions. After dinner, Carina's kids, along with Amber's five-year-old twins, ran off to do their own thing, while Carina and her husband, Art, spoke with Amber.

"Amber, you've been a part of our family for several years now," Carina started.

"And I have appreciated it more than you will ever know."

"I do know," she said with a smile, "but I know you have some questions too."

"I do. Can you explain who this Jesus guy and God are? And, who is this Spirit that Pastor mentioned today. I'm a little confused. I understand they're all interconnected, but I have no idea how."

"They are. Art, would you like to handle this one?"

"Sure," he said, as he sat at the end of the table with Amber on one side and Carina on the other. "That's a mighty tall order, but if you have time I'm pretty sure we can sort quite a bit of it out for you."

"I would appreciate it."

"All right. Let's start from the beginning. You see, it started pretty close to the beginning of time when God created the world. There was an angel, Lucifer, who was a strong angel, and thought he was better than God Almighty. He convinced a myriad of other angels that he was better than God as well, and a rebellion started…but it didn't last very long. God was going to have none of that in His realm. He kicked Lucifer, now commonly referred to as Satan, and his followers now commonly referred to as demons, out of Heaven. Pretty much landing here, where Satan made the Earth his playground.

So, when God created man, Satan took the opportunity to get revenge. You see, when God created Adam and Eve, they were good. He gave them reign over all of the animals of the planet, all of the fruit in the Garden of Eden, with the exception of one tree. They were not to eat from the Tree of Knowledge of Good and Evil. Well, of course Satan took that opportunity and exploited it. He tempted Eve, and she fell. Then Eve gave the fruit to Adam, and he fell. From that point forward sin entered the world. Now," he held up his hand to stop Amber from interrupting for a moment, "a lot of people get angry at Adam and Eve when they hear that part of the story, but keep in mind, they were human. They had human curiosity as well."

"I see," Amber said, taking it all in. "So, what happened when God found out?"

"He kicked them out of the Garden of Eden, leaving two angels with fiery swords to guard it, barring anyone else entry. And, as punishment as well, from that point forward women would have pain during childbirth and man would have to work for food. The worst punishment, though, was that man was separated from God. For atonement of sin, there would have to be a blood sacrifice of an animal on an alter. Not just any animal either. It had to be perfect, without defect or spots."

"Wow."

"Yeah. Through the next several hundred years, man and God went head-to-head until God couldn't handle the amount of sin that was in the world any more, and decided to start over. Finding only one righteous man, Noah, He had Noah build an ark. He gave him specifications on how to build it. Noah followed every instruction to the letter, even amidst the laughter and harassment of those around him.

Finally the day came. God had Noah, his wife and sons, his son's wives, along with two of every animal board the boat and God closed the door. Then, the heavens opened and it rained and poured for forty days and forty nights, flooding the world, killing every land dweller not on the boat. It took quite a while for the waters to recede. And when they did, God placed a rainbow in the sky as a reminder of His promise to never destroy the world by water again."

"Cool. But, where does Jesus fit in?"

"Well, for many generations after that, good and evil battled each other daily. God had His chosen people, the Jews, and He protected them. Through those years, it was prophesied that there would be a Messiah who would come and save the world. That Messiah was Jesus. Born of a virgin in Bethlehem, He grew up feeling everything humans do, but remained sin-free. He began His ministry early. If you read through Matthew, Mark, Luke, and John, it explains about His baptism from John the Baptist. It tells of His temptation in the wilderness by Satan himself, and how He battled and won. It explains of how He drafted His inner circle of apostles, and who was in it. It wasn't the cream of society either. The Gospels also share of all of the miracles and wonders Jesus did during His time here on earth. And, through all of that, people still fought the idea that Jesus was the true Son of God, the Messiah. As a matter of fact, the major players in the religion of society at the time set out to destroy Him. They convinced one of His inner circle to betray Him in order to get close enough to take Him into custody. Before Judas betrayed Him, Jesus had one last meal with His men. He told Judas he would betray Him. He told Peter that he would deny Him three times before the rooster crowed the next morning. Both men were horrified, but that's exactly what happened. Want to know the really cool part of this story?"

"What?" Amber asked, hanging on every word.

"Jesus knew everything that would happen to Him regarding the crucifixion and the betrayals, but He did it anyway."

"Why?"

"Because He wanted to share the inheritance of being a child of God with us. He wanted the communication to be restored between God and man, and there was only way to do it. Remember the blood offering of the perfect animal for sin? The one without spot or blemish?"

"Oh no," Amber groaned, dropping her head in her hands.

"Jesus was the only One who could do it. Being the Son of God He was the only perfect man who could do the blood sacrifice for the sins of the entire world…past, present, and future. He was sent out from Heaven to pay atonement for the sins of every one of us. The debt's been paid. We only have to accept the gift.

Now, back to our story. You see, that gift came at a hefty price. As I said, He was not only betrayed by two of His inner circle, but also had to suffer at the hands of man. They took Him and beat Him within an inch of His life with this evil thing called a cat of nine tails. His flesh was shredded to the bone. They then placed a purple cloak on Him. You see, back then purple signified royalty, and since He professed to be King of the Jews they put it on Him after they finished beating Him. This was their way of mocking Him. They also jammed a crown of thorns on His head as well just to top it off. Once the blood from His wounds dried, they ripped the cloak off and shredded it, creating a lottery for those who wanted a piece of it."

"That's horrific!" Amber exclaimed, eyes wide.

"They weren't done yet. You see, Pilot didn't think Jesus should die, so he found the worst person of that day, offering to set one of them free. Believe it or not, they didn't release the One who was performing miracles. They chose to release Barabbas, the murderer, instead. So, Jesus was to be crucified against Pilot's better judgment. He was a Politian and didn't want to lose his position.

During all of this, Peter was in the courtyard hoping to get a view of His Master and friend. While there, he was recognized. Fearing for his life, he denied he even knew who

Jesus was…three times. Just as he did it the third time, the rooster crowed and Jesus was brought through the courtyard. Catching the eyes of Jesus, Peter was reminded of what Jesus told Him earlier that night.

Finally the day arrived. Jesus was so beaten and battered by that point, He struggled to carry His own cross through the city to the hill where He was to be sacrificed. The soldiers ended up pulling someone else to carry it while Jesus stumbled His way through the town to face His death through a crowd that mocked and spit on Him.

Once they reached the hill, they fashioned crosses out of the wood, and then secured the condemned men to the crosses by three-inch spikes. That was all that held them there. Above Jesus's cross was a sign that read, 'King of the Jews,' and they made Him keep the crown of thorns on His head that was shoved on earlier."

"I don't know what to say to this. That's horrible!" Amber said, feeling heartbroken.

"Story's not over yet. This is where some of your questions will be answered. You see, while up there, Jesus made sure one of His closest friends named John would take care of His mother, Mary. Then, while a criminal on one side of Him made fun of and antagonized Jesus, the criminal on His other side yelled at the one chastising Jesus, and then asked Jesus to remember him when He got to His Kingdom. Do you know what Jesus said to that man?"

"No. What?"

"He said, *'Truly I tell you today, that you will be with Me in Paradise.'* Even though Jesus was going through what He went through, He *still* had a heart for others. It was a long day, and after a while one of the soldiers jammed a spear into His side to speed up the dying process."

"Cruel," Amber remarked.

"But efficient. So, from noon until three that day a darkness fell over the land. Then, around three in the afternoon, Jesus cried out, *'My God, My God, why hath Thou forsaken Me?'* You see, there was so much sin on Jesus, that God the Father couldn't even look at His own Son anymore."

"That's horrible."

"Someone thought Jesus was calling for Elijah, so they ran and got Him a sponge full of vinegar to quench His thirst, thinking He had lost His mind."

"*Vinegar*? How is *that* quenching His thirst?"

A smile crossed Art's face at the intensity in which Amber was following the story. "I'm afraid they weren't very nice back then. Anyway, back to our story. After the soldier gave Jesus the drink, Jesus cried out one more time before He died."

"Died? I thought Pastor said Jesus was alive."

"Just be patient. We're almost to the end of the story."

"You mean His death wasn't the end?"

"Oh, far from it. Yes, He did die on that day. When they buried Jesus in the tomb, the religious leaders made sure to post two guards by the door. No one was to go in or out until the women brought spices three days later."

"Why would they do that?"

"Because it was prophesied that the Messiah would raise from the dead. This Jesus guy was claiming to be the Messiah. In order to debunk that, and stop His apostles from stealing the body in order to claim He rose from the dead, they placed soldiers at the entrance. And, as extra security they rolled a giant boulder in front of it as well."

"I see," Amber said, feeling agitated. "So, they thought Jesus' followers were going to pull a fast one?"

"Yep. So, for two days things were quiet. Jesus' followers were even in hiding, fearing for their lives. And, do remember Judas?"

"Yeah."

"He was so upset for what he did to Jesus, he threw the thirty pieces of silver on the temple steps he was given to betray Jesus before he went and hung himself."

"Whoa!"

"Yep. So, on the morning of the third day, Mary and some women went to Jesus' tomb to put spices on His body. That was the practice back then. When they arrived, they were met with a wild sight."

"What happened?"

"The soldiers were passed out and the stone was rolled away from the doorway. The wild part of it was the two angels who appeared by the tomb. The angels told Mary and the women with her that Jesus was no longer there – that He was risen from the dead just like He said."

"But, couldn't people say they still made it up?"

"They *could* have, if not for the five hundred other people who saw Him *after* Jesus' resurrection from the dead. They all knew He died on the cross. There were hundreds who saw it."

"So, what did Mary and the women do?"

"As soon as the angels told them Jesus rose from the dead, they ran and told the apostles, who immediately took off for the tomb. Of course, it was exactly as the women said it was. In the meantime, the soldiers had recovered and took off to the chief priests, not wanting to get in trouble. The chief priests in the meantime cooked up this story that the apostles stole Jesus' body. Kind of like what you said."

"Right."

"Despite that story possibly spilling out, Jesus had to correct something before anyone else saw Him."

"What?"

"He went to Peter. You remember, the one who denied Him three times in the courtyard?"

"Yeah. I'll bet he felt like a jerk."

"I'm sure. Well, when Jesus appeared before Peter, Jesus asked Peter if he loved Him. He said of course he did. Jesus then responded for Peter to feed His sheep, meaning take care of His followers as well as tell others. Jesus didn't do this just once. He followed the same statements three times in the same conversation. In doing it three times, it negated Peter's denial. He cared so much for His friend's heart that He wanted to heal that first."

"I'll bet Peter was relieved. Talk about being given a second chance."

"Exactly. Well, after a short period of time, as I said, Jesus appeared to five hundred others. Just before He left for Heaven —"

"Wait! Why would He leave? How could He leave His friends? Who was going to teach and guide them?"

"That is where The Spirit you were asking about comes into play."

"I'm confused."

"Just listen," Art said, enjoying their conversation. "Before Jesus left, He made sure The Spirit was with His apostles so *they* could continue the work Jesus started. Only thing was, they were doing it while being hunted. Due to all of the buzz, people were following Jesus at alarming rates. They would need the apostles to teach and train them. With The Spirit as their guide, the men did many signs and wonders in the name of Jesus. This was an exciting time, but a scary one as well. There was a lot going on around them. But they also understood that whatever happened, they didn't need to worry. Jesus set them up for success.

Now, as far as Who everyone is? God is the Father. He's the Lord God Almighty. Jesus is His son. Being in human flesh allowed others to know that He understood them. And the Spirit is our guide. We only have to listen."

"So, if all of this is supposed to be good, why do Christians face bad things? Why wouldn't He stop it?"

"That's where sin and free-will come into play. God isn't up there maneuvering us like puppets. He wants us to make our own choices. He wants us to choose Jesus."

"Wait. What do you mean? I thought Jesus already died for my sins."

"He did, but *you* have to make the choice to ask Jesus to forgive you of your sins and choose to follow Him for the rest of your life."

"Wait. Confused again."

"Okay, let's put this into a perspective you will understand. That collector guy who's after you, what's his name?"

"Andre Mathers."

"Okay, so Mathers says you still owe him a little over fifty thousand, right?"

Amber groaned. "Yes."

"Sorry, we don't have secrets," Carina apologized when Amber glared at her.

"We don't," Art confirmed. "Anyway, so Mathers says you owe him that money. Money you didn't borrow, right?"

"Right."

"For this example, that money will represent sin in our lives, and Mathers will represent Satan."

"That's a fair comparison. He *is* Satan."

Art chuckled. "Not really. Satan is way worse. Anyway, just like you didn't create the seventy-five thousand dollar loss, neither did you create the sin that entered the world, but you're paying for it either way you look at it, right?"

"Right."

"What if you knew someone who had the money to pay for that debt and he was only waiting for you to ask?"

"Why would he pay for it at all? It's not his debt."

"Well, for sake of argument, we'll say that Jesus heard about your issues with Mathers. A friend of a friend told Him, and sent a message to you telling you that He would pay it. Would you?"

"I don't know. I don't know this Jesus."

"I realize this. However, if He paid your debt then you could go on living, not owing Mathers any money. You also could raise your girls without fear, right?"

"Right."

"So, in this case, Jesus has the money to pay the debt, just like He's already paid the debt for your sin. As soon as you ask Him to forgive you of your sins, and claim Him as your Savior, then Satan has no hold over you anymore than Mathers would. Does it make sense now?"

"Actually, it does. But the part I don't understand is why He would do it?"

"Because He cares about you. In the story, Jesus may not know you by sight, but in reality He does. Just like God knew you before you were even in the womb, Jesus knows you too. In the beginning of Jeremiah 1:5, it tells us, '*Before I formed you in the womb, I knew you. Before you were born, I set you apart.*' He *does* know you. If your friend were in the kind of trouble you were in, and you could afford it would you not help?"

"Of course I would."

"So will He. He's already done it. You only need to ask. He's waiting to help you, but He wants you to ask for it."

"That's all I need to do?"

"Well, if Jesus paid the debt to Mathers, what would you do?"

"I would be relieved and excited at the same time. The first thing I would probably do when I left him would be to call Carina, because I know she's praying for me."

"Exactly! That's what Jesus wants you to do too. He wants you to tell others what He did for you, so He can help them as well. He just wants to save everyone."

"From what?"

"Hell."

"That place is real?"

"Yep, as real as Heaven is. If there's Heaven, there's a Hell. If there's good, there's bad as well. Tell me what you know about Hell?"

"When I think of Hell, I see in my mind the devil with the horns and a pitchfork surrounded by fire."

Opening his Bible, Art flipped to the back. "Right here in Revelations 21:8, it tells us, *'But the cowardly, the unbelieving, the vile, the murderers, the sexually immoral, those who practice magic arts, the idolaters and the all liars – their place will be in the fiery lake of burning sulfur. This is the second death.'* This is what Hell will be like," he said as he flipped to Matthew. "Matthew 13:20 says, *'And throw them into the fiery furnace, where there will be weeping and gnashing of teeth.'* Then over in Matthew 25:46, it says, *'Then they will go away to eternal punishment, but the righteous to eternal life.'* In Mark 9:43," Art continued, flipping over to the reference, "it says, *'If your hand causes you to sin, cut it off. It is better for you to enter life maimed than with two hands to go into hell, where the fire never goes out.'* These are just a few examples. What do you think about Hell now?"

"I *think* it sounds terrifying!"

"Well, there's a way out of it. All you have to do is ask."

"So, if I ask, how can I trust I won't go there? How do I know I'll go to Heaven instead?"

"In Matthew 17:20, it says, *'Jesus said, "Because you have so little faith. Truly I tell you, if you have faith as small as a mustard seed, you can say to this mountain, 'Move from here to there,' and it will move. Nothing will be impossible for you.'* You see, it's a matter of the heart and faith."

"I see. How big is a mustard seed?"

While Carina went and got her a mustard seed, Art said, "Faith is a funny thing. It can make you strong or weak."

"What do you mean?"

"If you have faith and hope, not much can break you. If you lose your faith and hope, you're done for."

"True."

"Here," Carina said, sitting back down at the table. "This is a mustard seed. I put it in a baggie for you to keep to remind you of this discussion."

Accepting it, Amber said, "Thank you."

"Amber, you're going through a lot. You've got family support at the church. Do you want to join it officially?"

"As miniscule as this little mustard seed, huh?" Amber said, looking at the seed in the baggie.

"Yep."

"Well, I do have a better understanding of this. Let me do a little bit more research."

"If you were sick and dying, and the doctor told you there was only one medicine that could help you, and he was giving you free samples of it, would you take it?"

"Well, yeah. Without it, I'll die."

"Without Jesus, you'll die forever."

*     *     *

Pulling the envelope from her pocket as she made her way to the car from working that day, Amber ripped it open to find the letter she had been dreading for weeks. She heard the rumors, but hoped with everything in her heart that it wasn't true. This letter was confirmation of her worst fears. There was an overtime freeze. With the overtime freeze, there would be no way for her to make the payments to Mathers.

Sitting in her vehicle, Amber dropped her head on the steering wheel. *What was she going to do? How could she care for her two little girls, pay her bills, and keep up with the collections without overtime?*

Deciding to head off any trouble, she called the collectors muscle, Terrik. After she explained her situation, she heard the aggravation in Terrik's voice, "How are you going to make the payments? My boss isn't going to be happy."

"I-I don't know. That's why I called you."

"If you expect me to help, you've lost your mind. Mathers will have none of that," Terrik warned.

"Just for a couple of months. If I can get six months ahead of payments, I can make the payments, overtime or not."

"Look, you're a sweet girl. I don't want to see you get hurt, but I can't cover you for *six months*."

"What am I going to do?"

"Let me talk to my boss. He won't like it, but I'll do my best. I *may* be able to squeeze out a couple months for you."

"Please don't let him hurt my girls. I'm doing the best I can. I haven't missed a payment."

"I know you haven't. I'll do my best. And for the record, I wouldn't hurt your girls."

"Thank you. That's all I ask."

Hanging up the phone, Amber threw it against the passenger's side door. As it hit the floor, she dropped her head on the steering wheel again. After a moment, she glanced toward her purse, where the baggie holding the mustard seed was sticking out. Pulling out the baggie, she held it in the air. Seeing the mustard seed, she remembered the verse Art said on that day a year ago at Carina and Art's house, *"He replied, "Because you have so little faith. Truly I tell you, if you have faith as small as a mustard seed, you can say to this mountain, 'Move from here to there,' and it will move. Nothing will be impossible for you."*

"Faith as strong as this itty bitty mustard seed, huh?" Amber asked aloud. Looking toward Heaven, she prayed, "They tell me You are the Lord God Almighty. They tell me to trust in You. They tell me that You said with faith even as little as this mustard seed that I can move mountains. I know my faith has to be in You, though. You gave up Your one and only Son for me. Jesus, You sacrificed everything for me. You even loved me enough to provide me a guide in The Spirit. I know You're real. I know You did what they say You did. Please forgive me? I've done nothing to earn Your salvation, and there is nothing in this world that I *can* do. You are the only One who can and *did* do it. Please forgive me for that situation having to be done in the first place. I am so sorry. Please accept me as a child of Yours? Please direct my steps? Please protect my girls? They are innocent in this. Please forgive me most of all for my sin? I am evil in Your sight. I only want to be pleasing to You. Thank you. In Jesus name I pray, Amen."

Opening her eyes to see the sun as it rose in front of her, she was in awe. The spectacular gold, yellow, pink, and blues painted across the morning sky never ceased to amaze her. With something so beautiful before her, she had a difficult time imagining the evil that surrounded her.

"Excuse me?" Val asked, knocking on her window.

When Amber gasped and jumped, Angel crouched beside Amber's car window. "I'm sorry to scare you. Please don't be alarmed." Seeing Amber calm down, Angel continued, "Hi. My name is Angel. We were sent to help you."

"By whom?" Amber asked as suspicion, fear, and anger coursed through her body.

"God," Angel simply replied. "Look, you prayed and we were sent."

"How are you going to help me out of this mess?"

"The Spirit has a plan. You just have to have faith."

Clutching the baggie with the seed, Amber mumbled, "As small as a mustard seed."

"Tell you what," Val said, looking around, as Amber rolled her window down, "there's a restaurant over there. What if we meet over there, keeping everything in public until you're comfortable?"

"That'll work. Just let me call my sitter."

"Do you want to get your girls off to school, and then meet us over there?" Val asked.

"I'll just have the sitter take them to school," Amber said. "I normally sleep, but this is my day off, especially since I can't have anymore overtime. What am I going to do?"

"Get a hold of your sitter, and then meet us at that restaurant," Val said. "We're buying your breakfast, so don't worry about that. We'll be waiting."

"Thank you," Amber said, sniffing, as she wiped the tears from her eyes.

Walking toward the restaurant, while Amber called her sitter, Angel asked, "How are we going to help her?"

Val shook his head. "We're not. God is."

# Chapter 8
# The Love of Money Is The Root Of All Evil

As the group waited for Amber to come to the restaurant, they ordered breakfast. Just as they were served, Amber arrived and ordered. When the waitress disappeared to get her breakfast, Amber asked, "Okay, so who are you?"

"We're a group of A.N.G.E.L.s. 'A.N.G.E.L.' stands for Available to Nurture God's Eternal Love," Angel explained. "The Lord sends us on special missions to help those who are His. In this case, you prayed for help and He sent us."

"*All* of you?" Amber asked, amazed. "Am I in that much trouble?"

"You very well could be. Why don't you fill us in?" Joe suggested.

"Yeah, sounds like we may need t' catch up a bit," Josh commented before taking a bite of his scrambled eggs.

Taking a deep breath, Amber went through the entire story, starting from the point of where she met Eric, all the way through until that morning where she said a prayer to the Lord. "What am I going to do?" she groaned. "Without the overtime, I can't pay him, and he'll hurt my girls."

"What's the name of the collector?" Val asked.

"Terrik said it was Andre Mathers," Amber explained. "I'm pretty sure if it were up to Terrik, I wouldn't be in this mess."

"Sounds like he doesn't agree with his boss's decision," Joe said, thinking through their options.

Hearing her cell phone go off, she fished it out of her purse, "Hello?" she answered. As she listened to the voice on the other end, the color drained from her face. The various emotions were evident, landing on pure terror by the time she hung up the phone. "That was…um…my sitter. She took the girls to the park before school. She said she only turned her back for a moment, when the girls suddenly disappeared. She heard them screaming, and barely got a glimpse of them being thrown into a van. She called the police as the van's tires spun out, and the van took off. The police want to meet me at the park. I-I need to go," she explained as she stood.

"You're not going alone." Angel stood as well. "Val, Josh, and I will go with you, while Jesse, Joe, Rachel, and Jon figure out where the girls are and how to get you out of this mess."

"Thank you," Amber said, still in shock. "I–I want you to know that I'm grateful you all came into my life and are going to help me. I don't know what I would do without you."

"Wanna give me your keys?" Josh asked. "Nothin' personal, but you don't look like you're in shape enough t' drive."

"And *you* don't have a license to drive in The States," Val said, taking the keys from Josh that Amber gave him. "Why don't you guys take the Expedition while we go with Amber?"

"Sounds good," Joe agreed.

As the trio left with Amber for the park, the others paid the bill before heading downtown to see if they could find information on Andre Mathers. Without any information, they would be flying blind.

*   *   *

"So, you have no idea who would take them?" the Officer asked Amber, as they stood in the middle of the park.

"I don't know for sure," Amber explained.

"Tell him," her sitter encouraged. "That will at least give them a place to start."

"Fine." Amber huffed, crossing her arms. "Andre Mathers –"

"The bookie Andre Mathers?" the Officer asked, stunned.

"Yes. He said it was my responsibility to pay the debt of my ex-boyfriend."

"That doesn't sound right."

"That's how he operates. Anyway, I called his security guy this morning to tell him my overtime was cut off. I did it in order to prevent this. Looks like I may have escalated it."

"That gives us a place to start. Anyone else you can think of?"

"Well, if you can find my ex-boyfriend, that may be a possibility as well."

"Who is that?"

"Eric Samuels."

Writing the names down in his notebook, the Officer mentioned, "If anyone contacts you for a ransom, please contact me immediately."

"I will," she said, tucking the Officer's card he gave her into her purse. "What do I do now?"

"You go home and wait."

"You're kiddin', right?" Josh asked, appalled. "You can't seriously think she's just gonna sit around an' wait, do you? Those girls are her life."

"And, who are you again?"

"He's a friend of mine," Amber explained. "We were eating breakfast when I got the call. They're here for moral support for me."

"I see," the Officer studied the trio. "And, what are your names?"

"They're fine," Amber insisted. "Just go find my daughters."

Closing his notebook, the Officer nodded before he and his partner disappeared. As they left, the sitter turned to Amber and asked, "Seriously, what are you going to do?"

"Obviously *not* sit around," Amber said, watching the Officers pull away. "While I trust they will do what they can, those are my girls. I *will not* sit around and wait."

"And we won't either," Angel encouraged.

*      *      *

Angel texted the remainder of the group Terrik's number, as well as the name of Amber's ex-boyfriend, Eric Samuels. They decided Rachel would be the one to call and set up a meet with Terrik, thinking he would be more likely to show for a girl than a guy. As they sat in the restaurant waiting, Rachel was nibbling on her nails.

"Why are you so nervous?" Joe observed.

"There are two little one's lives at stake if we mess up," she explained. "That's an immense amount of responsibility."

"Let's just hope Amber's assessment of Terrik is correct, or we could be making things worse," Jesse pointed out.

As they watched Terrik walk through the door, momentary fear crossed all of their faces at the sheer size of him. Jon and Jesse would probably be the only ones of the group who could hold their own against him. Josh would be a close second, but it would be close.

Sliding into the booth, Terrik sneered, "Where's Amber? I understood she was going to be here."

"She's lookin' for her daughters," Rachel said, testing how much he knew.

Narrowing his eyes, he demanded, "Where are her daughters?"

"They were kidnapped from the park this mornin'."

"*What?*"

"Ya know, you almost look genuinely shocked," Jesse said, sitting back in his seat, crossing his arms. "Are you trying to tell us you know absolutely nothing about it?"

"I don't. If her girls were taken, please let me help get them back?" he asked with a sense of almost desperation.

"You serious?" Joe furrowed his brow. "You really have no idea what happened to them?"

"Look," Terrik growled, "I love those girls. I've been around them since before they were born. I admire Amber. Truth be told, I wish we met under other circumstances. I would have personally put her ex in traction."

"I like your style," Jesse said, with a grin. "Are you willing to check around for us in your boss's place to see if anyone has seen the girls? Or if they know anything about the kidnapping?"

"I will. Call me in an hour. I'll do what I can, but Mathers can't know I'm helping you."

"Completely understand," Rachel said, grateful. Getting pushed by The Spirit, she asked, "What are you willin' t' do t' help Amber an' her girls?"

"What do you mean?"

"Are you willin' t' help them escape Mathers grasp?"

"What are you asking?"

"Will you help her get away with her girls?"

"If I do, Mathers will kill me!"

Still feeling the push, Rachel asked, "Do you love her?"

"I-I do," he admitted after a moment. Then he asked, "How did you know?"

"I just know. Look, in order t' save her an' her daughters from this mess, you need t' play a vital role. I needed t' know how strongly you felt for her."

Terrik stood, and said, "Call me in one hour. In the meantime, see if you can find her ex-boyfriend. If Mathers isn't responsible for this, pretty sure Eric Samuels is."

"Do you know where he was working before he disappeared?" Jon asked.

"He worked for Sanders Construction. It's a commercial construction company. Every time I got close to catching him, he'd disappear. I would imagine they would know where to send his paycheck, or at least have a record of his last known address."

"Okay. That's where we'll start."

*     *     *

"Is Harold Sanders available?" Rachel asked, when she, Jon, Jesse, and Joe walked into the manager's trailer at the construction site.

"Not at the moment. The foreman is here, though. Will he work?" the secretary asked.

"Sure."

After ushering them into the office, the secretary closed the door behind her, leaving the group in the empty office. "Keep an eye out," Rachel said, making a beeline for the filing cabinet.

While the guys watched the secretary walk out to the site, Rachel picked the lock of the filing cabinet and dove into the files. Relieved to know they were in alphabetical order, it didn't take her long to locate Eric Samuels's folder. "Got it. Do we just want to get out of here, or go ahead and meet with the foreman?"

"Give that to me." Joe stuck his hand out. When Rachel gave him the file, he tucked it into the back of his pants and covered it with his shirt.

"They're coming," Jesse announced. He and Rachel took the two chairs opposite the desk, while Joe and Jon leaned against the wall.

When the foreman walked into the office, he shook hands with everyone as he introduced himself, "I'm Kent Shepard. Mary said you wanted to talk to me?"

"Yes, sir," Jesse said, taking control. "You see, my father has a decent amount of land. He wanted to build a building for his farm equipment business, along with a warehouse. He also wanted to know if you built homes as well. We're checking into several companies, so if you have any brochures, that would be a huge help."

"How big are we talking here?" Kent asked, intrigued.

"Well, he was talking about a warehouse around sixteen thousand square feet. The main building used for sales would be around five thousand. Then he was thinking the brick home would be around three thousand square feet. He also wanted to know when you would be available to meet. He's in a lot of meetings, so he sent us to filter through all of the construction companies in the area."

"How are you filtering?"

"That depends on how good of a feel we have for the company."

"He trusts you that much?" Kent asked, raising an eyebrow.

"Considering we grew up in the business, and the various talents we all possess, he has the utmost confidence in us."

"You're quite an interesting group. What talents do you possess?"

Jesse chuckled. "Like we'll really tell you."

"Gotta tell ya, right now yer not doin' well," Rachel added.

"Are you an Aussie?" Kent asked. "Why are you with these guys? That one over there doesn't even look like he belongs with this group," he said, gesturing toward Joe. "Why are you here and not your father?"

"My mother's an Aussie. Is there somethin' wrong with that?"

"You offending our family?" Jesse stood, pretending to be angry. As Jon took a bold step forward, Jesse put his hand up to stop him. "Pretty sure this would fall under the category of not getting our business. In this day and age, when someone comes representing a company, it may do you well to take them seriously."

"Why isn't *he* here?" Kent asked, upset.

"You have to get through the son to get to the father," Joe pointed out before he left the office.

"And for the record, *that* was the son you needed t' get through," Rachel said, and left with Jon and Jesse behind her.

"Wait!" Kent scrambled from around the desk. Catching the group just outside the trailer, he asked, "What do you mean by that?"

"The warehouse is being built for our brother," Jesse said, gesturing toward Joe, who climbed into the passenger's seat and slammed the door. "You had to get past him in order to even be considered. Now, considering you offended him, you're out."

"I didn't know. Can I have a second chance?"

"Not everyone gets a second chance in life," Rachel said. "Just like in Christianity where you have t' get through the Son, Jesus, in order t' get t' the Father, God, you have completely blown it. The only way to get t' the Father is through the Son."

Running over to the Expedition, Kent knocked on the door. When Joe lowered the window, Kent asked, "Can I have a second chance? Will you forgive me for insulting you and your family?"

"While I do forgive you, I will have to seriously think about doing business with you."

"You dismissed the power held by the son," Rachel pointed out as Jon got in the driver's seat. Jesse opened the side door of the SUV and climbed in, waiting for Rachel. "If you want access to The King of Kings, you have t' go through the Son, Jesus."

"How do you know I'm not a Christian?"

"I can tell. You have t' get your heart right with the Lord, Kent. He holds *way* more power than Joe. Jesus holds your eternal security. He's just waiting for you t' make that choice. Don't be fooled though, you could lose that choice in the blink of an eye. You may not even make it home today. If that's the case, an' you were t' die t'day, an' go t' Heaven, what would you tell the Lord when He asks you why He should let you into Heaven?"

"I don't-I don't know," he admitted.

"*That's* a *bigger* mistake than anything you have ever done in your entire life. If I were you, I would make it my mission t' find out the answer t' that question. Your eternal life depends on it," Rachel said, and got into the SUV, closing the door closed behind her.

As they pulled away, Rachel's heart broke for Kent. The look on his face was one of pure shock and bewilderment. It was a real life application regarding eternal life. It was one she prayed he would not ignore. Knowing by looking at him that he was searching for that answer, she prayed it would be enough.

"What's the file say?" Jon asked, as he entered the highway on the way to Amber's apartment.

Flipping through the paperwork, Joe explained, "Looks like they don't know where he lives."

"How do you know that?" Rachel asked.

Pulling a piece of paper out of the folder, he passed it back to Rachel. "That's where they're sending his paychecks. We just need to sit and wait for him to pick it up tomorrow."

"This is a P.O. box," Rachel explained. "This post office is over there," she said, pointing to the street name for the post office located off the next exit.

Taking the ramp, Jon headed toward the post office. Putting the SUV into park, he asked, "Who's going in?"

"We will," Jesse volunteered, as he and Rachel got out. "What number are we looking for?"

"Box 2771," Rachel said, scanning the boxes just inside the door.

"What do we do when we find it? How are we going to know when he'll pick it up? We don't even know what he looks like."

"Yes, we do. His photo is in the file. The box is right here," she said, pointing it out. "We could get here early in the morning an' sit where we can see this box from the Expedition." When she waved to Jon from next to the box, he waved back. "See? It can be seen from there."

"Nice."

"Now onto Amber's house t' see what they came up with."

Glancing at his watch, Jesse reminded her, "Yeah. We have to call Terrik in about twenty minutes. I would rather have all the information we can before we get a hold of him."

"Good thinking."

*  *  *

"I can't believe this man is putting money before the lives of two little ones," Angel grumbled.

"The love of money is the root of all evil," Josh pointed out. "This guy doesn't sound like he has a whole lot of light in 'im."

"Here, drink this," Val said, handing Amber a cup of chamomile tea, as they were at her apartment. "This may help you relax. Also, rub this on your temples," he said, handing her a tiny vial of liquid. "It lavender oil. Again, it should help you relax."

"I don't think anything will help me relax at this point," Amber pointed out, taking the cup and vial from Val, "except seeing my girls again." Glancing at the photo of the two little girls, smiling, having fun at the park, she added, "*If* I ever get to see them again."

"We'll find them," Angel said confidently. "I highly doubt God would have sent us to you if we were never to find them."

"I'm actually wonderin' exactly *why* God sent us t' her," Josh pointed out.

"Meaning?" Val asked.

"Well, I'm wonderin' if there's somethin' deeper goin' on."

"Deeper than *what*?"

"Deeper than just a bookie who wants his money."

Pulling Josh out into the living room, Val demanded, "What are you talking about here?"

"You know there's evil in this world. I'm sure you've felt it."

"I have."

"You've seen how God works in bringin' people t'gether."

"I have."

"What if I told you just as angels are real, so are the demons?"

"You're serious?"

"Very much so. We don't fight against flesh an' blood."

"We have so far."

"Ohhhh," Josh chuckled. "You have no idea what we're *really* fightin', do you?"

Eyes wide, Val gulped. "Are you telling me it's all real?"

"Yes. An' I'm wonderin' if there's somethin' goin' on here that's unnatural."

"What do you mean by unnatural?"

Resting his hand on Val's shoulder, Josh said, "Hold your breath, mate. We're traveling into uncharted territories for you. Once you see the reality around you, spiritual warfare will take on a whole new meanin'."

# Chapter 9
# Even The Demons Believe And Tremble

When the small group arrived back to Amber's apartment, Amber greeted them with a hug. "Please tell me you have something?"

"We've got some irons in the fire," Jon said, noting the sitter was not there. "Have the police found anything?"

"They're looking for Samuels and Mathers," Angel explained. "What did you find out?"

"Well, in about ten minutes we're going to be calling Terrik," Jesse said, glancing at his watch. "In the meantime, we've found the P.O. box for Eric Samuels. He should be picking up his paycheck tomorrow. This is what he looks like, though, for reference," he said, holding up Eric's photo.

"Why are you calling Terrik?" Amber asked.

"He cares about you. Did you know that?" Rachel asked.

"I...*what*?"

"He's checking out things on his end to see if Mathers has your girls," Jesse explained.

"What do you mean he cares about me?" Amber pressed.

"Can you not tell how much he cares for you?" Rachel asked. "Really?"

"I guess I never thought of him like that."

"He admires you."

"I never thought of him in that way."

"I know it's a bit early, but why don't you go ahead an' give him a call?" Rachel asked Jesse.

When Jesse went outside to call him, Amber asked, "What are you going to do if you find Eric tomorrow?"

"We'll cross that bridge when we get t' it," Josh dismissed her concern. "In the meantime, I'm goin' t' another room t' pray. Anyone wanna join me?"

As they prayed, Jesse talked to Terrik on the phone. "Hey, what did you find out?" Jesse asked when Terrik answered his phone.

"If he has them, no one knows about it. Were there no cameras in the area?"

"I don't know. There may have been, but we never went to the park. The others would know."

"I'll find out about those. We have connections in the police department. Is this a good number to get a hold of you?"

"Yep."

"Great. I'll give you a call when I find out anything. Please don't leave Amber alone."

"We don't plan on it. We'll probably bring her to the hotel with us for tonight and be back to the apartment tomorrow in case the police find anything."

"Good idea. What hotel are you in?"

After giving Terrik the hotel and room numbers, Jesse hung up and headed back into the apartment. Together, the group prayed for safety for the young girls, protection for all involved, and for the Lord's guidance and wisdom to complete their mission successfully.

*   *   *

Instead of calling them, Terrik met them at the hotel that night.

"Terrik, why are you here?" Amber asked when Jesse let him in.

"I'm here to help."

"Why? I don't understand."

"Do you really not know?" he asked, stunned. Kneeling in front of her as she sat in the chair, he took her hands into his. "At first, you were another mark. The more I stopped to pick up your payments, the more I looked forward to it. I enjoyed seeing your smile and talking with you. Have you not noticed that I would hang around and talk with you?"

"I did. I just didn't connect –"

"Do you really think Mathers gave you those gifts when the girls were born or for their birthdays? All you are to him is an unpaid debt," he explained, tucking a portion of her hair behind her ear.

"But…why?"

"Knowing I get to see you makes me smile. Watching those little girls running around, giggling, makes my heart happy. Hearing about your little ones being kidnapped makes me angry. I will do everything in my power to find them and get them back to you safely."

"What will you do once they're brought home?" Angel asked.

"What do you mean?" Amber looked at her, furrowing her brow.

"Do you really think once they're found that the three of you will be safe?"

Dropping her head in her hands, Amber groaned. "I'm so scared and confused, I can't even think straight."

Resting her hand on Amber's shoulder to comfort her, Angel said, "Just rest. Do you want some more tea?"

"Yes. Thank you."

As Angel went over to Val so they could make tea for everyone, Rachel asked Josh and Terrik to step outside to talk. When they were in the hall with the door closed behind them, she said, "We need a plan for when the girls are found."

"What are ya thinkin'? I can see the wheels turnin'," Josh said, crossing his arms as he leaned against the wall.

"Well, we've placed people into other lives before, but in this case she's goin' to have t' go deep." Turning to Terrik, she asked, "What can you do as far as hidin' her?"

"I can get us new identities if that's what you're asking?" Terrik confirmed.

"Is that goin' t' be deep enough?" Josh challenged. "This guy sounds downright terrifyin'. Are she an' the girls goin' to be safe in this country?"

"Probably not," Terrik grumbled. "I have a couple of ideas, but first I need to go find Mathers."

"What are ya goin' t' do once you find him?" Josh asked.

"We're going to have a little chat," he said and left.

"What do you reckon he meant by that?" Josh asked, watching Terrik storm off.

"I don't think I wanna know," Rachel said with a smirk. "He's kinda big."

"Too true. Jus' glad he's on our side."

"Me too."

*   *   *

The next morning, Rachel, Josh, and Jesse were at the post office watching for Eric to retrieve his paycheck. "What do we do when we see him?" Rachel asked.

"We treat him to a meal," Jesse said, getting out of the van when he saw Eric walk into the post office. Resting his hand on Eric's shoulder, Jesse asked, "You wouldn't happen to be Eric Samuels, would you?"

Fearing by his size and youth that this was one of Andre's guys, Eric swallowed hard. "Don't know what you're talking about."

"Then, why are you holdin' his paycheck?" Rachel pointed out.

As he turned to run, he ran right into Josh. "Well, you're a big one," Eric nervously chuckled.

"An', you're comin' with us," Josh ordered, crossing his arms.

"Well," he gulped, "do-do they make all of you this big where you come from?"

"Yep. So, are you goin' to come with us or do we have t' get rough?"

"Brother, dear," Rachel slid in between Josh and Eric, putting her hand on Josh's chest to stop him, "I think Eric will come with us willingly. Won't you, Eric?"

"Why would I do that?"

"Because we're currently the only thing standing between you an' Mathers. He's mighty angry with you. What do you reckon he'll do when he finds out you've been here the entire time?" she challenged. "I'm pretty sure he'll be livid once he finds out that little tidbit of information. I'll bet he may even want t' charge ya some *major* interest on the seventy-five thousand dollars you owe him. Ya know, since he's had t' use alternative methods t' collect your debt. As a matter of fact, pretty sure you owe Amber every penny she's ever paid him in your name. She's been the one carryin' you. Did you know that?"

"N-no. No, I didn't."

"You're goin' t' come with us t' go have a chat with 'im," Josh said.

"Dear brother, even though I know you could probably tear his limbs off, an' scatter his parts throughout New Mexico, I don't think that'll be necessary. I'm *sure* he'll come willingly. Won't you, Eric?"

"Are *you* coming with us?" Eric asked, hopeful.

Josh reached around Rachel and grabbed Eric by his chin, "Easy on there, mate. That's my sister. She may look innocent, but she's just as lethal as we are."

Glancing at her out of the corner of his eye, he squeaked, "Lethal?"

"She makes Terrik look like a kitten," Jesse confirmed.

Putting his hands in the air, Eric said, "I give. Let's go to…wherever it is you're taking me."

"Knew you were a smart one," Rachel said with a smile, and then added, "I would feel bad for the postal worker that would have t' clean up all that blood. Besides, I just got my nails done, and would *really hate* for all that work t' go t' waste."

Shoulders slouching, Eric didn't say another word. Silently following them to the van, his heart rate was racing beyond belief. He didn't want to be with these people, but he knew by the size of them that resistance would be futile. His hope was that they weren't with Mathers. He flew under the radar for six years where he was, and didn't want to have to move. In Las Cruses, he could easily slip into Mexico or EL Paso, Texas when things got too hot in New Mexico. He liked the convenience of that, and didn't want to have to find alternative methods of disappearance.

*   *   *

When the group walked into Amber's apartment with Eric to begin interrogation, they were stunned to find Mather's tied to a chair in the middle of the dining room. "Table for two?" Terrik asked, sitting at the table, gesturing toward an empty chair next to Mathers.

Struggling to talk through the duct tape on his mouth, Mathers wiggled and squirmed, trying to get free of the ropes.

"Oh no. You don't have the option to talk yet," Terrik mentioned, not moving from his seat.

"What-what's he doing here?" Eric stammered. "Are you *trying* to get me killed?"

"No. We're trying to find two little girls. The only ones we can think of who may have taken them is *you* and *him*." Terrik gestured toward Eric and Mathers. "So, have a seat." As soon as Eric sat down, Terrik tied him to the chair as well. Then he took his chair, and sat in front of both men with his arms crossed, studying them.

As soon as Terrik ripped the tape off Mathers, Mathers hissed, "Do you not know what I can do to you? I will kill you where you sit! Release me now!"

"Really? Don't you see who this is? Have you forgotten what Eric Samuels looks like?"

"What does it matter?" he growled. "You have me tied like a common criminal! I am your boss. You will not live to see tomorrow if you do not release me now!"

"You, sir, have already gotten a rather large chunk of change from Amber, but it's the wretch sitting beside you who owes you the entire seventy-five thousand dollars. Now, considering he hasn't paid you a dime, pretty sure you should be able to get it all from him. He's here right beside you, wrapped in a pretty little bow. I'm sure he'll be more than willing to negotiate payment. Right, Samuels?"

"Wait! Amber's already paid you money! Shouldn't that count toward lowering it?" Eric asked, desperate.

"Actually you owe *her* the money she has paid," Terrik reminded him. "You still owe Mathers your entire debt."

"Our bigger concern, though, is for the twins," Rachel reminded them. "Which one a' you blokes has them?"

"Twins?" Eric asked, stunned. "She had twins?"

Terrik rolled his eyes. "Like you didn't know?"

"I didn't!"

Turning to Mathers, Terrik demanded, "Did you have the twins taken?"

"No. Why would I? She's making payments," Andre Mathers pointed out. "The girls were leverage. That would be asinine to take them. They were the only way to make her pay. She doesn't care about herself as much as she cares for those little girls. If I took them, and something happened to them, then she would rather die than pay."

"Look, I don't care *which one of you took them*. We need to find those girls!" Rachel snapped. "They're in danger an' have been missin' for more than twenty-four hours!"

"Untie me and I can help," Mathers offered.

"Nope." Terrik shook his head. "Not until the girls are safe."

Mathers swore. When he did, his eyes shifted to pure black before shifting back to his hazel eyes. "You want those girls found safe? Releasssse me now!"

"What was that?" Terrik tumbled backward, falling out of his chair, landing with his hands behind him. "What did you just do? What *was* that?"

"What was *what*?" Mathers demanded.

"Your eyes…" his voice trailed as Mathers stood.

Snapping the ropes, Mathers' eyes shifted to pure black, as his body transformed in front of them. His skin turned to black scales, and his nails changed into talons. He practically doubled in size as black wings fanned out behind him.

Terrik scrambled off the ground, and then backed into Jesse and Josh. "*What is that?*"

"Your worssssst nightmare!" Mathers hissed. "I *told* you to let me go."

"I *knew* we were fightin' an unnatural in this!" Josh growled. "Do you know who we are?"

"Pitiful excuses for human flesh," the demon said, before he laughed a maniacal laugh that filled the room with terror. "You are *so* in trouble."

Suddenly, a streak of bright light flooded the room for only a moment before the archangel appeared between the demon and the group. "Stop," the archangel warned.

"Um, is someone going to get me out of here?" Eric asked, voice shaking.

The demon turned and glared at Eric.

"Okay. Never mind. I'm good right here. Carry on."

Turning back to the archangel, the demon hissed.

While Rachel, Josh, and Jesse got on their knees in prayer, the archangel began to glow. Pulling out his sword, flaming with a glorious light, the archangel braced in front of the demon, otherwise not moving a muscle.

"Pray," Rachel whispered to Terrik.

"I don't know how," he admitted.

Grabbing his hand, she pulled him to the ground next to her before Rachel whispered, "Close your eyes an' listen t' my prayer, agreeing in your mind. Prayer is what is giving the archangel the edge. The power is in the prayer."

As they prayed, the archangel asked, "Where are the children?"

"They are hidden," the demon admitted.

"Where *are* they?" the archangel demanded, getting stronger by the minute.

Crossing his arms, an evil smile appeared on the demon's face. "You will never find them."

"Yes. We will."

"You will *never* find them. They are now a part of *our* side. We have begun to find those on *our* list, starting with them. And there is not a thing you can do about it."

"Do you not remember Who we serve? Your audacity and insolence will only be rewarded with eternal death in the pit of Hell," the archangel warned, his sword glowing brighter by the second.

"Ha! Right now we are winning. We will find more. We *will* win in the end."

Rachel looked at him, stunned. Standing, she said, "Have you not read the end of the Bible?"

"Shut up, you filthy piece of human flesh! Get back on your knees where you belong!" the demon snapped.

"Leave her alone! She is a child of The King!" the archangel shouted. "She is under the protection of The Lord God Almighty!"

"Ohhhh," the demon said, registering who was in his company, "you are His new A.N.G.E.L.s? Awww, they *are* cute. How old are they? Fifteen? This is the best you can find to fight us? Consider your fight lost. Pitiful!"

"I have had just about enough of you!" the archangel warned.

"If you destroy me, you will *never* find them."

"Oh, ye of little faith," the archangel chuckled. Then his face hardened as he demanded, "You are to surrender the children, or face Jesus Christ Himself."

Fear momentarily flashed before the demon's eyes before he narrowed his eyes and hissed, "I will *never* tell. Good luck finding them. If you remotely believe you will find them without me, then you are more naïve then even *I* gave you credit for. Cassius has them, and he will *never* releasssssse them!"

"*For we must all appear before the judgment seat of Christ, that each one will receive the things done in the body, according to what he had done, whether good or bad,*" the archangel quoted 2$^{nd}$ Corinthians 5:10. "And *yours* will be swift and harsh!" he shouted before he sliced into the demon. As soon as the sword touched the demon's skin, its body flashed into flames before disintegrating. While the ashes fell to the floor, the archangel turned to the group behind him, and said, "Gather the others. Amber and Terrik have a trip to take. There is yet another who will help find the young ones. You must hurry to him. There is not much time."

"What do we do with him?" Jesse asked, pointing to Eric.

Glaring at the man who sat in the chair shaking in fear, the archangel calmly informed him, "He will face his own demons."

# Chapter 10
# Well Done Thy Good And Faithful Servant

Jerrod Lucas sat in his home at the kitchen table with the 9 mm sitting on the table in front of him. Working at the hospital, he hoped it would help heal his heart from the wounds of serving in Iraq as a Navy Corpsman. While he was able to save many young men and women through his tours, there were many he lost as well. Those were the ones who haunted him night and day.

When he got out of the service, he struggled to fit into civilian life. Working as a nurse gave him the sense of camaraderie he had in the service, but his past still haunted him. Every night when he closed his eyes, he would see the young men they attempted to evacuate, even in the middle of a firefight. Many days and nights he put his life on the line just to get to them. Making split-second decisions, with their lives in his hands, he questioned some of his choices as the faces of those lost floated through his nightmares.

During the day, when places he would go were crowded, his body was on edge. Watching every person, keeping track of them with a fear in the back of his mind that one of them could potentially be carrying a weapon of some sort. He almost found it easier to hide in his home. He knew his home was secure. He could breathe there.

Saying goodbye to one of his best friends at work yesterday, Amber, he felt her pain knowing her circumstances. Knowing she called in sick the next day, he knew there was only one reason for her not going to work. It had something to do with her little girls, but what, he didn't know.

Mind racing the entire drive home, once he got there, he sat on his couch, wondering if he could take Mathers out himself. He knew he could, but would he get arrested was the question. Surviving in the cage of a jail cell was not an option, even if it broke his heart to know Mathers was using Amber's girls against her to make her pay her scumbag ex-boyfriend's debt.

When he finally fell asleep on the couch after hours of laying there, his mind flew him back to Iraq. As a Navy Corpsman, he served the Marines as their medic. In this instance, it was the middle of the night when he was woken from a sound sleep.

"Doc, we gotta go!" the pilot woke him. "Got a CAS-EVAC in a hot zone."

"Coming," he sleepily mumbled. Grabbing his gear, he ran to the waiting helicopter and strapped himself in before it took off.

"Got two down, sir," the pilot mentioned over his shoulder as they flew into the night. "Going in hot."

Jerrod just nodded in understanding. He had done this very thing multiple times. As the apache helicopters flanked them, they pushed into the area to the unit surrounded by gunfire.

Once landed, they scrambled to evacuate the alive and wounded. "You have to save this one," the Gunney Sergeant shouted as they loaded his Marine into the helicopter.

"I do my best with every one," Jerrod explained, and began his quick assessment.

"*This one* is important. He needs to get back to his wife who just delivered their first yesterday."

"Gunney!" Jerrod snapped. "Let me do my job!"

"I mean it, Lucas!"

"Let him do his job, Gunney," one of the other soldiers coaxed. "You know Doc will give his all. He always has."

Once the helicopter was in the air, Jerrod worked feverishly on 'Pickett.' "Pickett, can you hear me?" he asked.

Pickett grabbed Jerrod's shirt, pulling him toward his face as he whipped the oxygen mask off. "Tell Kayla I'm sorry and to take care of Aiden."

"You'll take care of them yourself," Jerrod said, trying to put the mask back on before exposing his other arm to start another IV, while the blood soaked through the abdominal wound dressing where he was hit.

Pickett reached up and grabbed Jerrod's chin so he couldn't help but look at him. Tearing at the mask, while breathing heavily, his face strained from the immense pain, Pickett growled, "Tell her! Tell her I love her!"

"You tell her!" Jerrod shouted before turning back to the IV. "Don't go anywhere. Fight this."

"I-I can't. I…" Pickett's voice trailed as his body slowly let go.

"Pickett?" Jerrod's head snapped back to the face of Pickett just in time to see his face relax, as his eyes got a faraway look in them as they dilated. "Pickett! No! Pickett!" Jerrod tapped his face. "PICKETT!"

*     *     *

Bolting upright on the couch, breathing heavily as he grabbed the sides of it, Jerrod looked around to see where he was. Noting he was in his own home, he dropped his head onto his hands and groaned. Tears slipped down his cheeks as he remembered the look on the Gunney's face when he told him Pickett passed on the way back. At first it was anger, which was quickly replaced by grief that Jerrod felt deep in his own gut.

The nightmares were so crisp and vivid, he wasn't sure how much more he could take. It wasn't only at night when he saw them. Certain sounds would trigger memories. Certain smells would trigger other memories. It was like he would never get away from them. Even while driving, he was on edge.

Pulling his loaded 9 mm from the safe in the closet, he went to the kitchen and sat down at the table, staring at it as it lay in front of him. He spun it once, debating whether to really do it this time or not. *Could he take his own life? He swore to protect life. Did that count his own?*

Remembering Pickett's blood covered body, and Gunney's anger at the loss, he shook his head. Picking up the gun, he made the decision. "I can't do this anymore."

Placing the cold barrel in his mouth, knowing the magazine was full and was loaded with one in the chamber, tears slowly crawled down his cheeks. "I-I can't," he looked toward Heaven, praying for the Lord to understand his choice. "I can't do this anymore."

Taking a deep breath, he squeezed the trigger…click! Nothing happened. Jerrod checked the gun, everything looked okay, so he placed it in his mouth again.

Suddenly there was a knock on the door. He tried to ignore it as he took another deep breath and squeezed the trigger again…click! Nothing happened, just a click.

The knocking turned to a fierce pounding as Angel, Rachel, Jon and Josh were at the door. "Move!" Josh ordered, and then kicked the door in.

They ran into the house to find Jerrod standing there, aiming his gun at them. "Who are you? Why did you kick my door in? Make one more move and I will kill you where you stand!"

As the group threw their hands in the air, Rachel calmly asked, "Are you Jerrod Lucas?"

Cocking his head to the side, he narrowed his eyes. "Why?"

Taking a brave step forward, Rachel explained, "Amber Jones sent us t' find you. She needs your help. Someone took her girls."

Eyes popped wide, Jerrod demanded, "Who took them? What happened?" Relaxing his weapon to his side, he asked, "Where's Amber?"

"Amber is with Terrik, my brother, and our boss. They're guarding her until they get her to safety," Angel clarified. "The girls were taken from the park yesterday morning. The police have no leads. We do, but need your help to find them."

"Why didn't you tell the police your lead so they can get the girls?"

"Sir," Jon stepped forward, "we were directed by the Lord God Almighty to find you at this moment in time to help us."

"We know what you were going t' do," Josh confirmed, nodding toward the gun. "Your skills are what's needed t' help those two little girls. You were spared for such a time as this. Will you answer the call?"

"You know where Allie and Callie are?" Jerrod asked.

"Yes. We need your help to get them," Rachel said, taking another step toward him. Slowly lowering her hands, she put her hand toward Jerrod. "Can I have that?"

Looking toward the gun, Jerrod shook his head.

"Then, will you please put it away?"

"Do you not like guns?"

"I prefer knives, but when guns are necessary, they're necessary," Rachel confirmed. "Of course, there's always just blowing whatever it is up as an option as well."

A smile slowly formed on Jerrod's face. "I think I like you."

Rachel smiled. "Good. We like you too. Does this mean you'll help us?"

"Yes."

*   *   *

"Why exactly are we in…what town is this?" Jerrod asked, groggy-eyed, as he woke in the Expedition. To get to the English home as quickly as possible, the group took turns driving through the night.

"We're going just outside of Spanish Springs, Nevada," Jon explained. The others left earlier that day in a rental, while Jon, Josh, Rachel, Angel, and Jerrod took the Expedition back to Jesse, Jon, and Angel's parents house out in the middle of the high desert, outside of Spanish Springs, near Reno.

"What's out there?"

"Nothing," Jon said with a smirk. "They like it that way. It makes training easier without people questioning."

"Training?"

"Our Dad's former Air Force Spec Ops," Angel explained.

"Interesting," Jerrod said, mulling this new piece of information through his mind.

"Just trust us," Jon said. "We won't hurt you. You may get yourself hurt, but I promise you it won't be from us."

"You have to understand that trust is not high on my list."

Turning down the long dirt road onto his parent's hundred-acre property, Jon announced, "Here we are."

Seeing the two-story, three thousand square foot, stucco home with a three-car garage, Jerrod's jaw dropped. The home looked to be built around the turn of the nineteenth century, with a tile roof and old fixtures. Jon mentioned all the remodeling that was done prior to them moving into the house, bringing it into the current century. Slowly letting out a breath of air, under his breath Jerrod said, "Here we go."

As soon as they pulled up, Amber ran out of the house with Terrik not far behind her. Throwing her arms around Jerrod as soon as he set foot outside the van, she exclaimed, "I'm so glad you're here."

"I kind of had no choice."

"I know. They can be quite persuasive."

Jerrod looked up to see an older couple walking out of the house, hand-in-hand. "Who are they?"

"That's Mark and Casey English. They own this house. There's actually two more who are here as well, but one is…um…really sick," Amber said quietly.

"Jon?" Casey said, giving her son a hug. "I'm really glad you made it. Derek's in with the Colonel, but he's not doing well at all. I'm afraid the Colonel doesn't have much time. Truth be told, I think he's waiting for you. We've already said our good-byes and can't do it again. Go see him."

"What happened?" Jon asked, feeling like he got punched in the stomach.

"He had a stroke just after you left, which left his left side paralyzed. We thought he was doing better once he was released from the hospital, but he never really recovered. You know him and how strong he is."

"Yeah."

"He couldn't handle being paralyzed. He even stopped eating a couple of weeks ago, and refused to drink about five days ago. I've been praying he would last until you got here."

"Okay," Jon said, looking toward the house. "Let me get in there."

"Please. I'm going to meet our newest arrivals," Casey said, turning to Jerrod, Rachel, and Josh, while Jon ran into the house.

Flying through the atrium, Jon wasted no time. Taking the steps two at a time, he hoped to get to the Colonel before it was too late. Growing up, Jon and the Colonel were close. He wasn't sure what he was going to do without him.

Jon flung the door open to see Derek and Jesse standing beside the bed. Angel practically ran into Jon as she ran up behind him.

"Are you going in?" she asked.

"I don't know if I can do this," Jon whispered, shaking his head.

"He needs to see you," she coaxed. "Go." When he didn't move, she shoved him in.

Stumbling into the room, Jon stopped short when he saw his strong mentor looking extremely weak. "Colonel?" Jon asked, voice shaking.

"Come here, son," the Colonel reached up with his hand.

Derek and Jesse each gave the Colonel's hand a squeeze, and then moved near the door. Angel gave the Colonel a kiss on his forehead before returning to her place beside Derek and Jesse.

"I don't know what to say," Jon said, taking a seat on the chair beside the Colonel's bed. "The room is heavy, but –"

"You don't need to say anything. I wanted to say something to you." As the Colonel continued, tears slowly fell down Jon's cheeks, but he didn't wipe them away. "It has been a privilege and an honor to help raise you and your siblings," the Colonel explained. "You know, though, as do they, that you and I are close. If I had a son, I would want him to be just like you. You are strong and brave, and have the heart of a lion. You are a leader in your own right. You will do amazing things for the Lord if you keep Him first."

"I will, sir."

"I'm proud of you. It was my distinct privilege to train you and care for you, your brother, and your sister. Do your best, because your best is….your best is *always* good enough," the Colonel said, and took a staggering breath of air. "I don't think I have much left in me."

"Colonel, you gave your all to help raise and take care of us. You have passed the baton on to the next generation. It's now our turn. Go home to the Father. Hear His praise of 'well done, thy good and faithful servant,' because you've earned it. Please go be by His side, and watch over us from Heaven. We will see you when it's our time."

"I can go?"

Running his fingers through the Colonel's hair, Jon could only nod in response. Holding back the sobs, he didn't want the Colonel to see him cry.

"I can feel His peace," the Colonel whispered. "God is good, all the time."

Knowing her brother couldn't talk anymore, Angel stepped back over to the Colonel's other side, and took his other hand into hers, as she responded, "And all the time, God is good."

With that, the Colonel took his last breath. Jon noticed the peace that covered the Colonel's face, and gulped. "I-I can't," Jon said, and bolted from the room.

"I'll call the doctor," Derek said, stepping out of the room, as Angel covered the Colonel's body with the blankets from his bed.

"He was a good man," Jesse said, somberly.

"He was the best," Angel said, wiping the tears from her eyes. "He was the one and only Colonel. And he will never be replaced."

# Chapter 11
# All The Time, God Is Good

"Hey," Derek said, taking a seat by Jon on the rock he was sitting on out in the desert behind the house. "Mind if we talk?"

Looking toward Heaven, Jon admitted, "I don't know if I can do this."

"You know he's not in there anymore. Right?"

"I know. How am I supposed to do this without him? He started this."

"He did. And, he got the privilege to train the next generation as well. He has seen and done more than any of us."

"I know. I just…I feel like I just lost my dad."

"In a manner of speaking you did. We're all close. However, once Angel came along, your parents had their hands full, so the Colonel and I stepped in. We all had a hand in raising you three. That's a privilege most in our line of work don't get to have. We were blessed to have that opportunity, and wouldn't change it for the world. And now, knowing you three are all A.N.G.E.L.s? Don't think that hasn't added immense stress and years to all of us. You guys are our family. We worry for you, but pray and leave your lives in God's hands. It's an honor to be an A.N.G.E.L., but it's also a life sentence."

"What does that mean?"

"While you will do wondrous and amazing things for the Lord, you will be lucky to find love and any sort of life outside of that. The English name may stop with the three of you, but that's only known to God. If you notice, neither the Colonel, nor I, have any other family."

"I have noticed that."

"Then you'll also agree that a family as an A.N.G.E.L. may be a major risk?"

"It is, but it is also possible. The Mexican A.N.G.E.L.s made it work."

"They did," Derek agreed. "Just keep in mind the dangers you'll face. Do you really want to bring a child into this, knowing they may lose a parent?"

"They may not," Jon countered. "Only God knows, but I'm not going to concentrate on that. I'm going to focus on the work God has for me."

"Good idea."

"Right now there are two little girls whose lives are in our hands," Jon pointed out. "I don't think I have time to mourn the Colonel right now. At least not in the way he deserves."

"Well," Derek started, holding up the bag he brought with him, "What if we do it in our own way?"

"What's that?"

"This is something he gave to me for you about a week and a half ago. I know you don't want to be in there when the coroner comes, so let's stay out here and see what he left for you while the others take care of his body."

"Is that fair?"

"The Colonel was close to all of us. However, he was closest to you in particular, and we all know that. They'll understand."

"Before he passed, he said if he had a son, he hoped he would be like me."

"The way you were raised, he was like a second father to you. Mark may be your Dad, but the Colonel was your godfather. Now, even though he was military, and has earned and deserves a full honors burial, he's not going to get it, mainly because he's already supposed to be dead. So, they'll cremate him, and we'll do our own memorial right here."

"Will he at least be able to have an American flag on it?"

"Of course. We'll drape it over the urn and table it's on during the memorial."

"Okay. Then, what is that you have?"

Pulling a tiny box out of the bag, he opened it, showing Jon the contents. With each one Jon pulled out, Derek explained why it was there, "This is a corner of your blanket. The Colonel held you in that many times through the night when you were younger." When Jon set it aside and picked up the next item, Derek explained, "Those are the Colonel's medals. He didn't care to show them off, but they should go with him, with the honor that he served and those who served with him."

"Do you mind if I keep these?" Jon asked. "When and if I have children, I can tell them about the Colonel."

"Sure. You'll probably want this too," Derek said, pulling the Colonel's Air Force Academy ring out of the box.

Taking his St. Christopher necklace off that the Colonel gave him on his first mission, Jon placed the ring on it before returning it around his neck.

"Fair enough," Derek agreed. "The rest are photos of you guys through the years. There's only a few, so you still have quite a bit in the house, but these were special to him." Some of the photos were also of the unit through the years, including Casey's brother, Jack.

"Thank you," Jon said, accepting the box. "I'll keep it with me in order to share his story with others. His name will not die with this generation. His story will be passed down to the other generations as well."

Derek sighed, looking out at the vast desert land before them. "I never thought this day would come. I always thought the Colonel was indestructible."

"So did I. I thought sure he would outlive even me."

"He is a legend, and his name will live on when the stories are told through the ages."

"I can't help but think of the many lives he touched and saved."

"I know. I also know we're about to get flooded with A.N.G.E.L.s here soon. We'll see some old and new. Our ranks have grown through the years, but this last generation started with the Colonel and Hawk. When the Colonel died, the A.N.G.E.L.s took a spiritual hit."

"I know," Jon admitted. "I felt it."

"I think we all did. We'll feel it when Hawk goes as well. As a matter of fact, when we lose each one, we'll feel it."

"But the Colonel's death was as if a nuclear bomb went off in front of me."

"So will Hawk's. You're feeling each of the A.N.G.E.L.'s mourning his loss. Time has a way of taking those closest to us. Don't let his death hurt you to the point of immobility. You're needed. You need to continue to fight the good fight and not lose faith."

"I know. I'll do my best."

"That's all we ask."

*   *   *

That night, Casey sat everyone down in the living room with an idea. "There's a giant boulder out back that Mark and I want to fence in."

"For what purpose?" Derek asked, confused.

"For a memorial," Mark explained. "As each of the A.N.G.E.L.s pass, we'll paint their name on the boulder. Since the Colonel already has a gravestone in the military cemetery from before –"

"Wait. What do you mean from before?" Val asked. "How many times has he died?"

Mark chuckled before he explained, "The military killed us off a long time ago. In doing what we did, we needed not to exist."

"So, does the military even know if y'all are alive right now?" Joe asked.

"Nope."

"Then, what are we fixin' to do with his ashes?"

"We're going to sprinkle them around the boulder. I would like it if Jesse, since you're the graphic artist, would you paint the Colonel's name on it?" Mark asked. "Don't make it massive, but make it how the Colonel would like it."

"I think it's a great idea," Rachel said. "I just hope my name won't be on it anytime soon."

"We *all* hope to not have to add names to that rock any time soon," Derek pointed out.

*   *   *

It was a rough few days in the English household as they prepared for and attended the memorial service for Colonel Ethan O'Donnell in their back yard, along with the gathering of the A.N.G.E.L.s who could attend.

Listening to Colin O'Malley, one of the A.N.G.E.L.s from Ireland, do the service for the Colonel, Mark's mind wondered toward the Colonel…

"Are you Mark English?" the Colonel asked a young, eighteen-year-old Mark.

"Yes, sir," Mark said, shaking his hand after saluting him.

"No salute necessary. Come, have a seat and talk with me."

"What about, sir?" Mark asked, cautiously.

"I have a proposition for you."

"That sounds ominous," Mark said, as he sat on the bench of the base overlooking one of the training fields.

"Have you ever thought you were on this Earth for a greater purpose?"

"That's why I'm in the military."

"What about something greater than that?"

"What are we talking about here?"

"I run a special operations group, and am looking for some good men. You were recommended by a recruiter friend of mine, and I watched you through training."

"I see."

"Humanity has gone astray. We are a lost species. God has given us a gift, though, and it's our job to spread the word and protect those who are His."

"Are you talking literally or figuratively?"

"Both."

"What *exactly* are you talking about here?"

"Mark, do you believe in angels?"

*   *   *

"Colonel!" Mark yelled, as they were running, deep in the Middle East, dragging three other military members with them. "We need to get them out of here or none of us will make it!"

"Have faith, Lieutenant!" the Colonel yelled back, just as they crested the hilltop to see three waiting helicopters.

With all of the explosions around them, Mark didn't hear them. A smile of relief crossed his face when he saw them. "Nice!"

"Have a little faith, will ya, Lieutenant," the Colonel said, as they loaded their charges onto the helicopter, and took off into the air, away from the firefight below.

*   *   *

"We have to get closer to her," the Colonel explained. "You need to go to her and let her see who you are."

"Is she ready for this?" Mark asked, referring to Casey. It was just after Jack died.

"She doesn't have a choice. The other side knows who she is…and where she is. She's being hunted. We have to step in and protect her, whether she's ready or not."

Rolling his eyes, Mark commented, "Oh, this is going to be fun."

"Jack was one of our own," the Colonel snapped. "We *will not* abandon Casey just because Jack left to go to Heaven. He served with distinction. We will honor his memory and continue to look after Casey. She's now one of ours too."

"Yes, sir," Mark said, and then disappeared for Casey's apartment to meet her for the first time.

* * *

Deep in the Outback, Mark marched down to the river, angry with himself for letting Casey not only get caught, but also be tortured, when the Colonel came and sat down beside him on a rock. "Ya know, you're beginning to scare me with all of that anger. The other side only needs a tiny foothold before they have you."

Mark sighed, looking up at the vast sky, filled with more stars than he had ever seen before. "I know. I just don't know what to do with it. I love her, Colonel, and I let her get caught. Not only that, but you saw what Jackie did to her! How could I have let that happen?"

"You're not superhuman," the Colonel reminded him. "You are limited in what you can and cannot do. The Lord is the One who gives us our strength and power."

"I know."

"You know here," the Colonel said, pointing to Mark's head. "But, do you know that here?" he asked, pointing to his heart. "Psalm 27:7 and 8 tells us that, *'The LORD is my strength and my shield; my heart trusts in Him, and He helps me. My heart leaps for joy, and with my song I praise Him. The LORD is the strength of His people, a fortress of salvation for His anointed one.'* Now, I'm not a scholar by any stretch of the imagination, but I'm pretty sure that verse didn't say our strength is in *you*, Mark English. It's in the Lord God Almighty. The One who made us. The One who knows what we can handle."

"I know."

"And, what is it you told me your favorite verse was?"

"It's Isaiah 40:29 through 31."

"Which says?"

Mark sighed, shaking his head. "You're going to make me do this?"

"Yep. You know we fight our fights the best when we lean on God's words for our strength. Now, what does Isaiah 40:29 to 31 say?"

Sighing again, Mark quoted, " *'He gives strength to the weary and increases the power of the weak. Even youths grow tired and weary, and young men stumble and fall; but those who hope in the LORD will renew their strength. They will soar on wings like eagles; they will run, and not grow weary, they will walk and not be faint.'* "

"Then know that He will never fail you, Mark. Trust in Him to carry you through this. Trust the Lord to carry Casey through this."

"Will she make it? She's got serious injuries."

"That's known only to the Lord, but I have a feeling she will. And when she does, He has some really big plans for that young lady."

"I hope so."

"Know He won't let you down either. Come on, let's get back to the others."

"Yes, sir."

As they stood, the Colonel put his hand on Mark's shoulder. "He *will* carry us all through this. You just have to put your trust and faith in Him."

"I will, sir. I will."

*     *     *

"Mark English will be the first to speak about our beloved Colonel," Colin said, bringing Mark back to the funeral services.

"I put my trust and faith in You, Lord," Mark whispered, as he stood. "I need *You* to carry me through this."

As Colin stood to the side, Mark set a rose on the boulder where the Colonel's name was already painted. As each person got up, they would place a rose on the ground around the boulder, surrounding it with white and red roses.

Taking a deep breath, and slowly letting it out as he returned next to the table where the urn was, Mark started, "What can you say about a man like Colonel Ethan O'Donnell? His life was one marked by many ups and downs. He handpicked me to be on his unit way back when I was only eighteen. Through the years, we have faced many battles, saved many people, yet lost others. Sometimes we were able to get to them in time. Sometimes we were not. But we knew whatever was before us, our strength was not in man, but in God." Taking a moment before he continued, Mark sighed. "As A.N.G.E.L.s, we all know the price we pay in doing what we do. There was not a finer man to serve under than the Colonel. He was a man after God's heart. He followed the Lord with everything that was in him, whether he understood it or not. I thank the Lord for providing such a strong leader in him, and look forward to seeing him once again when I am called home. Thank you for your good and faithful service, Colonel.

Your leadership will be missed," he said, and took his place back beside Casey.

As each person got up, the tears flowed, along with the stories. Sometimes there was a chuckle or two, but mostly there was heartache and pain. The Colonel had a strong influence on the battles around the world, and while his presence would be missed, his life counted, and that was something everyone knew the Colonel held dear to his heart.

Jon was the last to speak. As he got up for his turn, he could feel his heart in the pit of his stomach. Being such a big guy, most expected he didn't have a heart, which is why he buried it so deep. If they knew the truth, they would know that his heart was his Achilles heel. God gave him the gift of feeling what others felt around him, which at this point almost suffocated him. He felt the pride, the sorrow, the anguish, and the concern of what this would do to the future of the A.N.G.E.L.s. Jon knew, however, that the A.N.G.E.L.s didn't depend on the Colonel *or* Hawk, they depended on the Lord. And, the Lord's A.N.G.E.L.s would continue to fight, even until the end of time.

Standing beside the table containing the ashes of his mentor, draped with an American flag over it, Jon took a deep breath before he said, "The Colonel and I were a lot alike. We both used our hearts in a way different than most in regards to how we operate. We use it to protect those closest to us, even if it seems to others that we have no heart. I believe I was the closer to the Colonel than anyone. He was my best friend, biggest encourager, my confidant, my godfather, and my mentor. Life without him will never be the same. He was a true man of God, and I know right now he is up in Heaven with Jesus, and has already heard the words we all long to hear, 'Well done, thy good and faithful servant,' and he deserves it. He led the American Team of A.N.G.E.L.s and even had the opportunity to train us – the next generation. I only hope and pray to be as strong a man as he was. To leave our legacy to the next generation, with the amount of strength, faith, and passion he did would be an honor." Turning toward the urn, he said, "You were an amazing man, and the loss of such a strong spirit will be felt through the Kingdom for a long time, as evidenced by those in attendance here." Gesturing toward the fifty A.N.G.E.L.s from around the world who were there, he turned to them, and looked each in the face, as he continued, "So, my charge to you, and me, as his fellow team members, is to carry on the torch that has been passed to you. Fulfill your call, teach and train others, and fight the good fight, so in the end you too can hear the words from our Father in Heaven, 'well done, thy good and faithful servant'."

As Jon went to stand beside his mom, Mark and Derek, in their dress blues, along with a couple other men from other countries who also served in their military, went over to the table. They gently lifted the American flag before folding it military style, while Colin played 'Amazing Grace' on his bagpipes.

Once they finished folding, they took the flag to Jon and saluted him. After presenting the flag, they stood at attention until Colin finished playing. When he was done, Colin set his bagpipes on the chair and opened his Bible, reading, "John 14:1-6 tells us, *Let not our heart be troubled: ye believe in God, believe also in me. In My Father's house are many mansions: if it were not so, I would have told you. I go to prepare a place for you. And if I go and prepare a place for you, I will come again, and receive you unto myself; that where I am, there ye may be also. And whither I go ye know, and the way ye know. Thomas saith unto Him, 'Lord, we know not whither thou goest; and how can we know the way?' Jesus saith unto him, 'I am the way, the truth, and the life: no man cometh unto the Father, but by Me.'"* Looking up at the group, he continued, "Peace is an ever fleeting, but cherished thing in life. In doing what we do, we are never guaranteed peace, as we are often being hunted while doing our best to help others. Jesus promises the faithful that we will have a place of peace. He told us in His word that He's gone there to prepare a place for us, and I am confident that it will be a place of tremendous peace, as we have the privilege of worshipping God every day. There are days where we question what's going on around us. We're not sure where Jesus is, as we hold the hand of a loved one or co-worker who is passing before our very eyes. It's in the midst of our deepest pain, when we are swimming in the depths of enormous amounts of grief, that we need Jesus the most. It's at those times, Jesus is the only One who can reach our sorrow-filled hearts, and can possibly give us any remote amount of peace. He brings us love, and the security of knowing that we will never be alone in this world. Colonel Ethan O'Donnell held a special place in all of our hearts. And I can say today, as we struggle between grief and celebrating the life of our beloved friend, that the Colonel is currently soaking in the peace of our loving Father. He is basking in His glorious grace and mercy, as he works with Jesus, preparing a place for us. And to that, I say, 'God is good, all the time'."

As a group, each of the A.N.G.E.L.s responded in unison, "And all the time, God is good."

*   *   *

For the rest of the day, as some tried to talk to him, Jon was lost in his own thoughts, distraught over the loss if his mentor. Clutching the flag that his dad gave him, Jon remembered what he could of the Colonel. He had been journaling everything he could over the last few days so he could pass stories of the Colonel down to the next generation.

144

The Colonel, in his opinion, was an amazing man. It was a devastating loss to the A.N.G.E.L.s, but he had faith they would recover in time.

It was his hope and prayer that he would be able to fill the Colonel's shoes and be able to lead the U.S. team in his own way. His sister tried to lead, and fell hard. He was leading by guiding. He knew his sister had it in her. However, she had to believe it herself. From what he saw, though, Rachel may be the one taking over. Her leading style was more laid back, much like the Colonel's. She let the team member's work to their strengths, and gave support and encouragement where they were weak. The team, at that point, was almost two different teams. He saw Rachel's group flourishing, while Angel's struggled. Time would tell who would really take over.

*   *   *

After the other A.N.G.E.L.s from around the world disbursed back to their missions and homes, the group left sat around the living room.

"Okay, while I feel for y'all, my bigger concern are those babies," Jerrod started. "What are we going to do?"

"They're in Australia," Joe said, and then quickly looked to Josh and Rachel for their reactions.

"How do you know?" Jerrod asked.

"He has the gift of prophecy," Rachel explained. "We each have certain gifts. Do you know where?"

"You're not going to like it," Joe warned.

"Where?"

"Do you know where Jackie was originally?"

"Is she back?" Casey asked, dropping her head in her hands. "I thought she was gone for good back in Mexico."

"She's not back, but her successor is," Joe clarified. "But if you remember, she was in Queensland – Cairns to be exact."

"Right," Casey said, anxious as to where Joe was going with this.

"Well, once she was taken out, the hive found a new home and a new leader," Joe explained. "One they call Cassius Cornell."

"An', where are they?" Josh asked, nervous as to how close to his family they were by Joe's hint.

"Black Rock."

As the color drained from both Rachel and Josh's faces, momentarily taken aback by their reaction, Angel asked them, "What's Black Rock?"

Rachel shook her head. "We can't go there."

"No way," Josh agreed.

"Why not? What's wrong with Black Rock?" Angel asked.

"That place is forbidden to go to," Rachel explained.

"Let me see if I can put this in perspective for ya," Josh started. "Imagine dark, dense, black rocks. Imagine walking into cold caves with smooth walls made of granite, and a musty stench that fills your nostrils almost knocking you to your feet. These caves are inhabited with ghost frogs, wallabies, pythons, bats, and many other creatures that you don't want to run into in the darkness. But there is one worse than all of them. They call it the Queensland Tiger. It's this cat-like creature that has been known to take out many cattle in the area."

"But what's worse is the reputation known t' those who have lived in Australia the longest," Rachel jumped in. "The Aboriginals won't go near that place. The stories our stockmen told us will make the hair on your necks stand on end."

"Such as?" Jon asked, curiosity getting the better of him.

"Pete, the stockman who runs the barns, told us this story," Rachel spoke in a low voice, hoping to make them understand the dangers of Black Rock. "Black Rock is known as Kalkajaka, translated as 'the place of the spear' or also known as the 'mountain of death.' Many people have gone in, but only one that we know of has actually come out alive."

"Seriously?" Jesse asked, on the edge of his seat.

"Seriously," Josh jumped back in. "The story that's passed down through their generations goes like this: It's said that the mountain originated from the dreamtime of a medicine man. This bloke was twisted. He was a chameleon, who had a taste for flesh. He killed a chief an' ate him. Because of this, the tribe banished him t' the mountains. They thought that would be the last they would hear of him, but it wasn't. He would sneak down an' kill a tribe man or two every so often. To escape his fellow tribesmen, the medicine man turned himself into a goanna, which is this giant lizard-like creature. When he ran for the mountains, they say he was struck by lightnin', an' his parts spread everywhere, leavin' large piles of charred rock. These rocks are now known t'day as Black Rock."

"I see," Mark said, mulling around this information in his head.

"You mean my babies are in this place?" Amber asked, horrified.

Resolve in his face and spirit, Jerrod asked, "How do we get them out?"

"We have to go to Black Rock," Joe said solemnly.

*   *   *

After a few weeks of crash-course training for those who were new, Mark, Derek, Jerrod, and Terrik got together with Jon, Jesse, Joe, and Josh to set up a plan of action. Simultaneously, Casey and Val, along with Amber, worked in the kitchen in making meals, and getting the herbs and oils ready that Val would need in the field. In the meantime, Rachel and Angel decided to take a walk into the high desert that surrounded the English home, in hopes of getting a clear head before they left.

"This is big," Angel said as they crossed the backyard, heading into the hills.

"We weren't trained for years to be given light missions," Rachel pointed out.

"I get that. I've even been on some. But, doesn't it scare you to head into Black Rock?"

"More than you know! I would rather go t' Iraq than Black Rock."

"That's saying a lot."

"It's a scary place. If it wasn't for those two little girls, I wouldn't go near it."

Climbing onto a rock where they could still see the house, yet be able to watch the sunset, Angel asked, "Do you really think we can do this?"

"I know we can. Whatever's in Black Rock, God is stronger. He made this world. I'm sure He will help protect us, an' keep us safe from whatever resides in those rocks."

Suddenly there was a loud "BOOM!" and the ground shook around them. Rachel and Angel both covered their heads from the flying debris, dropping to the ground as they each let out a scream.

"What was that?" Angel snapped, with a ringing in her ears, trying to catch her breath.

Shaking her head, hoping to clear the ringing in her ears as well, Rachel looked around. "Over there!" She pointed toward where there was still smoke rising.

Stumbling toward where the explosion occurred, they got there just in time to see someone duck behind a rock. Rachel pointed to Angel to take one direction, while she took the other. Going behind, but from two different directions, they surrounded the huddled young man.

Rachel jumped on him, while Angel blocked him from leaving. As Rachel got ahold of his ankles, he struggled and punched her, trying to get away. Angel got behind him and put him in a headlock.

"You have two choices," Angel said down near his ear. "I can tighten my grip and knock you out, or you can calm down and talk to us."

"Let me go!" he shouted, squirming even more ferociously, shoving at Rachel to get his legs free.

Noticing the light emitting from him, Rachel said, "He's one of ours."

The young man stopped and narrowed his eyes at Rachel. "What do you mean?"

"You're a Christian. We are too."

"How do *you* know?"

"Because you're bright. Look, we just want t' talk. We don't want t' hurt you. Well," Rachel corrected, "*I* don't want t' hurt you. I don't know if Angel's on the same page. She hasn't choked you out yet, so I reckon she'll ease up if you do."

Glancing up at Angel, the young man put his hands in the air. "All right. I give."

Angel and Rachel both loosened their grip on him. Rachel stayed near his feet, as he sat with his back on the rock. Angel crossed her arms, remaining where she sat, poised to take action if he changed his mind before they figured out who he was, and why he was on her parent's land.

"Let's start with your name?" Rachel asked.

"Jacob Armstrong."

"Hi, Jacob. I'm Rachel, an' this is Angel. What *exactly* did you just do?"

He shrugged. "Blew up a boulder."

"Why?" Angel asked, crossing her legs in front of her.

"Because I can. I've been experimenting with different explosives."

"What did you use this time?" Rachel asked. She was actually fascinated by this young man.

"For this one, I used a cell phone battery."

"Seriously?" Rachel asked, stunned.

"Yeah. There are a lot of things around your house that could use to blow things up."

"Are you some sort of explosives expert?" Angel asked.

"I don't know that I would classify myself *that* way."

"How old are you?"

"Eighteen."

"Are you still in school?"

"No. I'm taking a year off. I wanted to figure out what I want to do with my life."

"What are your interests?" Rachel asked.

Jacob studied her for a moment before he asked, "Why?"

"Just tryin' t' get a feel for you."

"Where are you from?"

"Australia."

"And *what* are you doing *here*?"

"*I* live here," Angel explained. "She's staying with me."

"Where do *you* live?"

Angel gestured toward their house. "Right over there."

"Really? That's a huge house."

"We have a large family."

"Do *you* have a large family?" Rachel asked.

"I have a decent sized family," Jacob said cautiously. "What about you?"

"I have a twin, and my brother has a twin. We grew up on a ranch. So, back t' my original question. What are your interests?"

"Well, I like outdoors, guns –"

"Explosives," Angel cut him off with a smirk.

"What? I like blowing things up," Jacob said innocently.

"Ya know, I'll bet we could use you," Rachel said, stunning both Jacob and Angel.

"Doing *what*?"

"We have to take a trip t' Australia. It could be dangerous."

"*Could* be?" Angel cut Rachel off. "*Could be?* Have you lost your mind? He's an innocent."

"What are you two talking about?" Jacob glared at them. "You're talking around me instead of *to* me. I don't like that. I'm right here."

"She wants you to come with us to Black Rock. That place is scary," Angel explained. "You don't want to go there. *I* don't want to go there…but we have to."

"Why?"

"There are two little girls who were kidnapped that we are going t' rescue," Rachel explained. "Wanna go with us? I think we could use your talents."

"You can't do that without talking to the rest of the team," Angel pointed out.

"Wanna bet?" Rachel smirked. "I'm pretty sure we can use him. I don't think we were here in this moment, in this time, for no reason."

Angel sighed, crossing her arms as she stood. "You *are* serious?"

"Yes. Do you wanna come?" Rachel asked Jacob.

"Actually, I'm intrigued. Can I hear the plan first? Nothing personal, but I don't want to go in there without some sort of a decent plan."

"Oh, there's a plan. As a matter of fact, there are military guys working on it right now."

"Fine," Jacob said, getting off the ground, brushing himself off from the dirt. "Let's go see what they came up with."

# Chapter 12
# A Nest Of Vipers

"So we're basically fixin' to go to a demon lair?" Jacob asked Jesse and Rachel as they sat on either side of him in the plane to Australia.

Jesse nodded. "Pretty much."

"And, y'all do this all the time?"

"This is the first time for somethin' this big," Rachel admitted.

"Then I'm glad I got some training before we left."

"We'll do our best to protect you," Jesse assured him.

"Just do your best to get those girls out of there. From what I hear, that's gotta be a nightmare for them."

"That's why we brought the extra muscle," Rachel said, nodding toward the row across from them, which contained Terrik, Amber, and Jerrod.

Resting his head on the back of the seat while the plane continued its trek, Jacob sighed. "We get to go to y'all's house first, right?"

"No. That's after," Rachel corrected. "We'll probably need a debriefing after this. My parents really wanted us t' come first, but we didn't want t' waste any more time before gettin' those kids out of that place."

"Let me stop by a grocery store then. I'll need one of y'all to get some liquor as well," Jacob said. "I have a feeling a mazel tov cocktail or two may need to be utilized."

"As long as you don't drink it, I'm okay with that," Jesse said, ruffling his hair.

"Hey!" he objected, shoving Jesse's hand away with a smirk. "I know I'm short, but I *am* eighteen years old." Jacob stood to five foot eight, respectively. He kept his light brown hair short, almost buzzed, and still had a baby face.

"You're kind of the little brother of the group," Rachel pointed out.

"Thanks. That's *exactly* the category I want to be in," he said, tongue in cheek.

Rachel waved him off. "No worries. I know you're a tough bloke."

"Who can blow this entire plane sky high," Jacob added under his breath. When they looked at him wide-eyed, he added, "Not that I would. Just sayin' I could."

"Save the explosives for the bad guys, eh?" Jesse said.

"I plan to."

After about an hour, Jesse leaned over the sleeping Jacob to Rachel, and quietly said, "I'm worried about Jon."

"Why?" Rachel whispered back.

"He lost the Colonel less than a week ago, and now he's supposed to focus on a mission where the lives of two little girls are at stake? I haven't seen him cry either. He did on the day the Colonel passed, but that was it."

"This may snap him back t' focus on our purpose," Rachel pointed out.

"It'll either focus him, or we'll lose him," Jesse said somberly. "I'm praying he'll focus and this won't be his last mission. He's strong, but the loss of the Colonel hit him hard. It would be like us losing Dad. Derek and the Colonel are like second fathers to us."

"You don't seem too distracted by it."

"I'll work through it when I'm clear of this mission. If it were Derek, Dad, or Mom who was lost, I would be hit really hard. The Colonel was like an uncle to me, but a close uncle. Life won't be the same without him. He was a legend, but I can handle it until I get back home or to your ranch. I don't know how Jon's doing it."

"Maybe he's of the same mindset, an' is concentrating solely on the little ones until he can get t' a quiet place."

"It's possible," he sighed before he looked at his brother, who was looking at photos on his iPod of their family. Looking back to Rachel, he whispered, "He's strong, but even strong people need a little help sometimes."

*   *   *

The two vehicles, one a van and the other a jeep, pulled up to the Black Mountain National Park, just south of Cooktown. The group checked into the hotel, and then decided to go check out the area of Black Rock. Knowing they wouldn't have direct access to the mountain, they could at least go to a lookout and formulate a plan for the next morning.

"Wow! That's stunning!" Terrik remarked, looking over the far-reaching landscape. There were mountainous hills of black volcanic rock with patches of green, along with areas of trees, dirt, and grass surrounding the rock with mist coming out of it.

When Jerrod went to take a step, Josh grabbed his arm. "Whoa there, mate!" Pointing toward where Jerrod was about to step, he explained, "That's a ghost frog. Don't step on that."

Crouching down, Jerrod examined the glossy frog, with speckles of purple and reddish-brown all over it. "Interesting little thing. Doesn't even look like it belongs here."

"Oh, don't let it fool you. It does," Josh assured him.

"This place is scary," Rachel said, her heart racing as soon as she set foot outside the van. "It's a terrifying place to be. You have no idea how many people have died up in these parts."

"Let's hope the twins won't be among them," Joe said, getting out after Rachel.

"Too true!"

"There are a lot of animals in this area that are goin' extinct. That's one of the many reasons why we can't go in there," Josh pointed out. "This is about as close as I ever *wanted* to get."

"It actually makes a perfect hide out for the other side if you think about it," Jon said. "No one's allowed to go there. It's protected. And, it's not like anyone would chance it either with all of the stories surrounding it."

"But, my girls are in there somewhere," Amber reminded them.

"We'll get them," Jon said firmly, as he stared at the mountain. "We won't leave here without them."

"So, y'all are saying that we're just going to take on the evil of this world?" Jacob asked.

"Pretty much," Angel responded. "For the lives of two little girls, it looks like we're going to take on the gates of Hell."

"Nothing like jumpin' into a pit of vipers with both feet," Joe sighed.

"This is a sink or swim mission," Val pointed out.

"Then we need to swim," Joe finished. "There are two little girls whose lives depend on it."

*     *     *

Early the next morning, the group got ready to head over to Black Rock. As they did, Amber wandered out to the deck, where Rachel stood, looking out at their view from the fourth floor. "So deep in thought. Care to share?" Amber probed.

"I know the lives of your girls are at stake here. That's a heavy burden. My fear is where we're goin'. Black Rock isn't known for bein' a forgivin' place. It's also not known for people comin' out alive."

"We're not going in alone," Amber reminded her.

"I know. I also know if push comes t' shove that we're all willin' t' give our lives for the Kingdom…and that includes for every person we need t' help."

"Hey Rachel?" Jacob poked his head out the door.

"Hey, Jacob. What do ya need?"

"I know this may sound weird, but do you use aerosol or non-aerosol hair spray?"

Cocking her head to the side, Rachel said, "Aerosol. Why?"

"Can I have it? I may need it today. I hope not, but I like to make sure I have more than enough."

"What are you going to do with her hair spray?" Amber asked.

"Hopefully nothing."

Smiling, Rachel told him, "It's next t' the sink. Go ahead an' take it."

"Thanks," he said, and then disappeared back into the room for only a moment before returning back to them, "What about nail polish remover and hydrogen peroxide?"

"I *do* have hydrogen peroxide." Reminding him, Rachel said, "I'm a nurse. Remember?"

"I was hoping you would. What about the nail polish remover?"

"I have that," Amber said. "Just have Angel get it out of my suitcase."

"Perfect! Thank you," he said and disappeared again.

"He's funny!" Rachel remarked. "And what he does with regular household items blows my mind…no pun intended."

"I know. Now, back to our conversation," Amber said, refocusing Rachel.

Sighing, Rachel looked back out over the town before them. "I know what I have t' do. God picked me for this job. I *will not* let Him down. I *will not* let your girls down either. There's just a major difference between knowin' what you have t' do, an' actually doing it."

"I know you won't let us down. I have faith in you. I want you to have faith in yourself. Here," she said, pulling a small baggie from her pocket containing the tiny mustard seed.

Holding it up to the rising sunlight, Rachel asked, "What *is* this?"

"It's a mustard seed. In Luke 17:6, it says, '*He replied, 'If you have faith as small as a mustard seed, you can say to this mulberry tree, 'Be uprooted and planted in the sea,' and it will obey you.'* Then in Matthew 17:20, it says, '*He replied, 'Because you have so little faith. Truly I tell you, if you have faith as small as a mustard seed, you can say to this mountain, 'Move from here to there,' and it will move. Nothing will be impossible for you.'* When things in the Bible are mentioned more than once, you're supposed to pay attention. With as little faith as this tiny mustard seed, you can do great things. I know you all have a *lot* more faith than that. Look, you guys have a tremendous task ahead of you. I want you to keep this to remind yourself that your faith in God is more than enough to do amazing things. This is not the first time you guys will see, hear, and do wonderful and marvelous things, and I'm sure it won't be the last. God has incredible plans for you. You just have to have faith."

"Faith as small as a mustard seed, huh?"

"Yep. And I *know* yours is stronger than that, or you wouldn't be in the position you're in. Now, give me the seed back when you give me my daughters back. Until then, let that seed remind you just how strong you are in the Lord."

Giving her a hug, Rachel said, "Thank you so much!"

"No. Thank *you*. You guys didn't even know me, and now you are helping me and my girls. God bless you and keep you all safe."

Standing, with her hands on Amber's shoulders, Rachel said, "He will. Now, go get that helicopter. We'll be taking off soon as well."

"Meet you there."

"Lord willing," Rachel said, watching Amber and Terrik leaving for the airport.

*   *   *

Parking a safe distance away, the group hiked under the brush and cover as close as they dared. Once they reached that point, they split up into two groups. One group was made of Rachel, Jesse, Josh, Jerrod, and Jacob, while the other containing Jon, Angel, Val, and Joe, took off in the other direction. In the meantime, Terrik and Amber went to the airport for a helicopter. They found out in the meeting that Terrik learned how to pilot helicopters from when he was in the military, so they rented one as a means of escape for when the girls were rescued to get them out quickly.

Rachel's group headed toward the left, while Angel's went around toward the right. The plan of attack was to hit it from two different sides, hoping at least one of the groups got through. As they got closer, those groups would also split up into smaller groups, allowing each person to use their abilities to their fullest.

"I have t' tell you that I'm terrified beyond words right now," Rachel whispered to Jesse.

"I know. It's written all over your face. You don't hide your feelings well," he pointed out.

"Really? I thought I did that pretty well."

159

"No, you stink at it," Jacob whispered. "And I haven't even known you that long. Pretty sure these guys would be able to read you even better."

"Unfortunately, they're right," Josh added. "You don't hide them well."

"Anyone else?" Rachel snapped, annoyed.

"Well, since I'm the only one who hasn't put their two cents in, I have to agree with them," Jerrod remarked. "Of course, at this point, pretty sure we're all feeling it right now."

"Pretty much," Josh agreed.

When they reached their appointed position, Jerrod quietly announced, "This is it. We need to break off here."

"Ya know, pretty sure this is the point in the movie where the audience shouts for everyone to run away and not go in. *Why* are we still here?" Jacob asked.

"Because there are two little girls who are living a nightmare," Rachel reminded him.

"Right. Then let's go get them." Jacob sighed, pulling out homemade C4.

Wide-eyed, Josh asked, "What are you going t' do with that?"

"Well, you know, this is for the big bangs, while these," Jacob said, showing the bottles of Vodka, "are for any uninvited guests who may try to stop me, and to make the big bang bigger. The C4 is highly unstable, and the explosion of the cocktail will ignite the fuse for these, causing it to blow pretty high. I know it's a bit of overkill, but it'll go high and wide this way." Closing his backpack after pulling his lighter from his pocket, he said, "Time to do my job." And then he disappeared into the brush.

"Where'd he go? Really?" Rachel asked.

"He's doin' his thing." Jerrod shrugged. "Time for us t' do ours. Come on, Josh. Jesse, take care of Rachel."

"Actually, Rach can take care of herself," Josh pointed out. "Let's go," he said, and he and Jerrod disappeared into the underbrush.

"Looks like it's just the two of us," Jesse said to Rachel.

"We're the distraction, huh?"

"Yep. Over there looks like a good place to give them cover. I hope Terrik and Amber are close enough when we need them."

"They will be," Rachel said confidently. "She wants her daughters out as much as we do. She's not goin' t' take any chances with her little ones."

Heading over to the area Jesse pointed out, the pair ducked behind a boulder, waiting for their cue to lay down cover fire.

*  *  *

Jon, Angel, Val, and Joe entered into a cave. Running her fingers along the smooth, granite wall, Angel was surprised by the coolness. She was having a hard time wrapping her brain around the stories Rachel and Josh told of Black Rock. She saw a beauty where others saw darkness. There was a horrific smell that almost made her eyes water, though. That was something she could live without. It almost smelled of death and burnt flesh. "These are steep tunnels," she remarked while they descended into the extensive pathways. She marked the wall with chalk every few feet to mark their journey, so they knew how to get out when the time came. They would also know if they were going in circles.

"There's light down there," Val pointed out the faint light deep within the recesses of the mountain.

"Then that's where we'll go," Jon said decisively.

Heading down, they were suddenly met with a colony of ghost bats flying above and around them. Angel let out a scream as the guys yelled, ducking the bats, and flailing their arms.

"Run!" Joe shouted.

"No! We'll lose our way. Stay together," Angel yelled, ducking closer to the ground until they were prostrate, with their hands over their necks waiting for the colony to pass over them.

Looking up, Jon found himself mesmerized by the bats. The thin membrane that covered them, almost made them look translucent. Covering his head, he felt their sharp teeth scratch his hands more than once. The diverse animals of the world that God created frequently captivated his attention. How God made them all different and unique never ceased to amaze and astound him.

Once the bats cleared, Angel stood, brushing herself off from the dust. "That was *not* fun."

"I don't think *anything* about this is fun," Val pointed out as the others got off the ground.

"Let's keep going," Jon pushed. "We need to get to the girls. The others will be waiting. We need to be a *lot* quieter than we're being or we'll get caught."

"Of course. If we didn't have bats flying around our heads, it would make things a lot easier," Angel said under her breath as she pushed on.

The deeper they went into the bowels of the caverns, the faster Angel's heart raced. She was grateful Jerrod suggested the chalk to keep track of their path, or she knew she wouldn't remember how to get back out. As a secondary tracking system, Val set down a sprig of rosemary every five feet. She did *not* want to be lost in the caverns.

When the light from a fire in the middle of an opening danced off the cavern walls, the group tucked behind a couple boulders, shielding them from sight of those around. As Angel peeked around the boulder, she could see several demons sitting around the fire, while two others wondered around, keeping an eye out. Seeing the two little girls sitting in a cage in the dark part of the cavern, her heart broke. They looked petrified as they huddled in the corner, dirty, and disheveled.

Hearing one of the demons cackle in laughter, she turned her attention back to the hideous creatures that were about seven feet tall, had blackish-red scales covering their bodies, and black wings. Their yellow and black eyes darted in every direction, watching for movement, while the talons on their hands looked as sharp as razor blades. 'Terrifying' was a kind word for it.

"*What* is *that*?" Val asked in shock.

"Those are demons," Jon whispered. "You'll get used to it."

Val shuddered. "I don't think I'll *ever* get used to *that*."

"Please tell me y'all put something in my water this morning and that I'm hallucinating?" Joe asked. "They're really creepy. Knowing they're real, makes horror movies look like child's play."

"I didn't drug you. I've been too busy trying to take care of my desperately not wanting to be here." Val sighed, shaking his head. "Unfortunately, I think this is all too real."

"You are neither hallucinating, nor is this a horror movie," Angel whispered. "It's real. Do you guys think Rachel's team is ready yet?"

"We'll find out momentarily," Jon said, checking his watch. "Jacob should be setting the first one off in less than a minute."

Thirty seconds later they heard an explosion that rocked the walls around them, bringing down part of the ceiling of the cave.

"I would say they're ready," Val shouted over the falling debris and screeching of the demons on the other side of the cavern from them.

"Nothing personal, but I would *love* to be anywhere but here," Joe exclaimed. "Can we get the girls and get out now?"

They ducked, covering their heads as another explosion rocked the caverns again.

"Wow! He's good," Jon said, keeping an eye on the number of demons left in the cavern. When it was down to four, he said, "Time to go. There's one each."

"Not yet," Angel held them off.

Another explosion went off a little closer this time, sending two more running. That left only two guarding the children.

"Now!" Angel yelled, as the four of them ran around the rock into the center of the cavern. Angel and Val took on one demon, while Jon and Joe took off after the other one.

"Get the girls!" Val shouted to Joe before he took another swing at the demon.

"Forget this!" Angel yelled. Whipping out a knife, she ran for the demon from behind, running up its back. Wrapping her arm around his shoulders, she used her knife to slit his throat, while Val kicked him in his stomach, sending Angel and the demon back into a rock. Taking her breath away, she went to the ground with the demon on top of her. A gurgle was the only thing that escaped its mouth, while the yellowish-green blood spurted out, coating its skin.

Watching the creatures face distort before it flamed and then turned to ash, sinking into the cavern floor, Val helped Angel off the ground. "So, you've seen this before?"

"Yes. Help Joe get the girls, I'm going to help Jon get rid of his before any more come running."

"Probably a good idea."

"Hi. I'm Joe," Joe explained, as he picked the lock on the cage door. "Are you Allie and Callie?" he asked the two little girls. Their big brown eyes looked into his, fear evident in every muscle of their little bodies. Their dark brown hair was a tangled mess. When they nodded, he explained, "Your mom and Terrik are waiting to see you. She said to tell you the code word is 'apple pie'."

Nodding, Allie crawled out of the corner of the cage, where they were cowering together at the horrific scene before them.

Joe glanced back to see Angel jump on the back of the one Jon was fighting to slit his throat. This one struggled more before Angel was able to get a good grip enough to run the cold steal across its neck. When she did, she shoved off the creature, while it bent forward, dropping on its hands and knees. It hissed at Angel and Jon, and then dropped to the ground for a brief moment until it burst into flames and then turned to ash.

Val ran over to Joe. "We need to get them out of here," Val ordered, "Preferably before their friends come back."

"Got it," Joe said, unlatching the lock. "Come on, ladies. We need to get you to your mommy. Come on now, we won't hurt you. Apple pie, remember?"

Allie got up, pulling her sister with her. Val grabbed one, while Joe grabbed the other, just as another explosion went off in a different direction than the others.

While the group ran into the pathways, Angel led the way, keeping an eye on her chalk markings. "This way," she said, leading them out of the maze of pathways.

Hearing another explosion in the distance, Angel ordered, "Let's get them out of here!"

"Your wish is my command," Joe shouted, as another explosion went off toward the back portion of the range.

Running down the tunnel, Angel kept a close eye on the chalk markings she made on the way in. Hearing the little girls scream, and the guys yell, Angel looked up in time to stop.

In the middle of the passageway stood a demon. "*Where* do you think you are taking them? Those preciousssss little onesssss are oursssss," he said, crossing his arms in front of him.

"Shoot him," Val said quietly into Angel's ear, as he held one of the girls.

Hearing only her own heartbeat in her ears, Angel slowly went for the knife on her side.

"We don't have time for this!" Jon snapped, pulling his gun from the holster on his side. Hitting center mass with each bullet, he emptied his magazine. "Get us out of here!" Jon yelled as the creature dropped to the ground in a fiery pile before changing to ash. "Preferably before others come!"

Once they stepped out into the bright sunlight, they were almost blinded. Gunfire went off near their head before it was returned from where Rachel and Jesse were in the distance.

"That way!" Angel shouted, leading the crew to where the helicopter was to be waiting.

*       *       *

Setting up his last C4, Jacob stood, satisfied. "Well, my job is done," he said, picking up his backpack.

"What job is that?" he heard behind him and froze.

Eyes wide, Jacob spun, and found himself face-to-face with a demon. "Umm…well," he gulped, "you're an ugly one, aren't ya?"

"What are you doing here?" the demon demanded.

Slowly reaching in his bag, Jacob kept talking, hoping to distract the demon from what he was really doing. "Well, this looked like a nice place for a stroll. And, while I *did* see the keep out signs," he said, feeling around until his hand landed on the can of hair spray. Slowly pulling it out, he continued, "I just can't help myself. I'm one of those guys who, when you're told 'no,' does it just to find out what will happen if they do." Reaching into his left pocket, he grasped the lighter with his other hand. "What do they call you, by the way? I'll bet it's 'Tiny.' You know, because you're kind of big."

"We are everywhere. We are many. And we *will* destroy you."

"Well, again, I beg to differ. Pretty sure we'll get out of here just fine."

Uncrossing his arms, the demon went to lunge at Jacob. Aiming the hairspray can at the demon, Jacob lit the lighter as he pushed the button on the hairspray, creating a flamethrower.

The demon lit up! Watching in horror as the demon teetered side-to-side before dropping to the ground in a ball of fire, Jacob was stunned when it immediately turned to ash, putting the fire out. "Well, that's new."

Hearing a hiss behind him, Jacob turned to find that the fuse was lit for one of the bottles in his backpack. Throwing it to the side before it caught, he shouted, "Time to go!"

While running to meet up with the others, he quickly lit the ropes he was using as a fuse for the bottles of Vodka that were sitting beside the C4 already in place, while making his way to where the helicopter was supposed to be.

*   *   *

"Whose bright idea was this?" Rachel snapped, while she and Jesse dove behind a rock just in time to escape getting shot. As a barrage of gunfire ricocheted off the rocks around the pair, debris rained down. Praying for the safety of the rest of their team members Rachel knew were getting away, she brushed off the debris, took a deep breath, and looked around the rock to find her target before firing her weapon in the direction of their pursuers, praying those attacking would focus on them and not those escaping. Emptying her magazine, she then ducked back behind the rock to change it out. "I only have three more left. Do you know if they're clear yet?"

"I saw them heading for the helicopter," Jesse assured her. "Pretty sure they're clear by now, but I haven't seen the chopper take off yet."

"Should we make a break for it?"

"I don't know if we can get clear enough to make it out without putting the others in danger," Jesse said, and then emptied his weapon. "I've only got two magazines left."

"Well," Rachel said on a sigh with her thick Australian accent. With her face coated in dirt from the rock and dust-filled terrain surrounding them, she said, "If this is it, I want t' let ya know it was an honor t' serve the Kingdom with you."

Jesse shook his head. "Don't think like that." Seeing a cave a short distance away, he grabbed her hand and pulled her with him. Dodging the flying debris the gunfire created as it ricocheted off the rocks, he was thankful each shot missed its mark. When his eyes adjusted to the dim light inside the cave, his heart filled with hope at the tunnels that jetted in every direction. "Looks like the Lord's not done with us yet. Ever play hide-n-go-seek?"

Ignoring the hope in Jesse's voice, Rachel resigned herself to the idea that this was the end. "If it wasn't Josh, I'm glad it's you here with me."

Cupping her face with his hands, he kissed her. "I love you, Rachel. Focus for me."

"Was that just to distract me?"

"Did it work?"

"Yeah. But if you do it again, I'll have t' kill you."

Jesse chuckled as he continued to pull Rachel down one of the dimly lit, chilly tunnels. Unable to form a plan in his mind, he prayed for God's leading.

"We're gonna die, an' you're laughin' at me?"

"It's because your hair is a disaster. I even saw dirt on your teeth."

"We're being shot at an' you're concerned with my looks?"

Stopping in the tunnel, he spun toward her. "You may have given up, but I'm not done yet."

"I haven't given up."

"Then snap out of it! We *are* getting out of here!"

"Are ya sure?"

"If not, we're going to give it our best shot. The others got away. Now it's our turn."

*   *   *

Landing the helicopter in an area out of sight of the lookout point for Black Rock, Terrik left it in idle mode so when they saw the crew coming, he could quickly engage the blades, and get the girls out. "Now we wait," he announced.

"I can't believe all of this is happening." Amber shook her head. "As of a month ago, my biggest problem was Mathers…whatever he was."

"Yeah. Have to say I have *never* seen one of those creatures before! I never even knew they existed."

Studying him for a moment, Amber asked, "Can I ask you a personal question?"

"Pretty sure we've passed that point in our relationship. I'd kind of like to think we're moving forward."

"We are," she said hesitantly.

Hearing her tone, he asked, "What's wrong?"

"I'm just going to ask you bluntly. Are you a Christian?"

"Am I a what?"

"A Christian? You've been around this stuff for long enough. You've seen the good side of Christianity, and the dark side of Satan."

Nodding, he admitted, "I have. It still gives me the creeps. I've seen what some people do to others. But whatever Mathers was, I have never seen that before."

"What do you think about Heaven and Hell?"

"I don't know. Are they real?"

Momentarily stunned, Amber asked, "Are you saying you don't know that Heaven and Hell are real? Even after you've seen what all you have seen since the girls disappeared?"

"Have to admit that it scares me that it may be real."

"Oh! It is! Do you know who Jesus is?"

"Not really."

"Oh boy. This could be a long conversation."

Seeing the first few bombs go off in the distance, Terrik said, "Head's up. Things are starting. We need to stay alert."

"We do, but your salvation, to me, is extremely important."

"I have time. We'll take care of that once we get the girls to safety."

"What if we talk about it until then?"

"Can't. Watching for the team is more important right now."

Sighing, Amber shook her head. "I disagree. Your salvation is the most important thing in the entire world. I almost made the mistake of waiting too long. As soon as I did, He sent me the A.N.G.E.L.s to help. And, even though things are scary right now, I've seen how things were already lined-up, I just needed to take the step and trust Him to take care of it. However this turns out, I know God is in control. He will take care of all of us. Romans 10:9 tells us, *'Because if you confess with your mouth that Jesus is Lord and believe in your heart that God raised Him from the dead, you will be saved.'* It's the easiest, most simple, yet most crucial decision of your life. I'm sure you've heard John 3:16, most people have, but I'm going to go on to verse 17 as well. They say, *'For God so loved the world that He gave His only begotten Son, that whoever believes in Him should not perish, but have everlasting life. For God did not send His Son into the world to condemn the world, but that the world through Him might be saved.'* This isn't rocket science here. What if we don't get out of this alive?"

"Look, I'll talk to you about it after this is all over. Right now, I want to concentrate on getting Allie and Callie out."

"Their hearts would be for you in this moment too. I know them. They prayed for me every night when they did their prayers. God forbid something happens to them before we can get to them, but if it does, then I know beyond a shadow of a doubt that I will see them whenever God takes me home. I almost waited too long. I had the answers for so long, but I waited. I don't want you to wait until it's too late. That's why we need to talk about your salvation. Once you die, you can't change your mind. You *have* to accept Jesus as your personal Savior from all your sins before it's too late. In Romans 6:23, it tells us, *'For the wages of sin is death, but the gift of God is eternal life in Jesus Christ our Lord.'* You are born into sin, you have to *choose* Jesus."

"What happens if I don't?"

"You will never know," a demon hissed, and they both jumped. Four demons had snuck up behind the helicopter while they were talking, and now both Amber and Terrik had a gun pushed against the base of their skull.

"Can't we negotiate here?" Terrik asked nervously. "We're just tourists."

One of them came to the front of the helicopter, and crossed his arms. "And we're a couple of kangaroos. We know exactly why you are here. And we –" He was cut off by another explosion. Turning back to the helicopter, he ordered, "Kill them. We need to get to the others!"

"Lord, please take care of my girls," Amber whispered. The last thing she remembered was the searing heat that momentarily penetrated the back of her skull before she was surrounded with a peace, and heard Revelation 21:4, *"He will wipe away every tear from their eyes, and there will be no more death or sorrow or crying or pain. All these things are gone forever."*

# Chapter 13
# A Broken Heart

As Angel and her crew made it to the helicopter, they were horrified at what they ran up to. Joe and Val covered the girl's heads so they wouldn't see that someone had shot and killed both Amber and Terrik, leaving their bodies in the helicopter.

"What happened?" Jerrod asked, when he and Josh ran up to the group.

"We need to get out of here," Jacob said with hushed tone.

"Why?" Val asked as an explosion went off, and Jerrod checked for a pulse on Amber and Terrik.

"That. And there should be four more. I set off mazel tov cocktails by using a rope as a wick, setting them near the C4, creating fireballs. As a matter of fact..." he started, but was cut off when two more went off. "One more," he announced. "That's all I got."

"Is there anything you can mix for one more to blow that?" Jerrod asked, nodding toward the helicopter.

"Why would I?"

"Because if you don't, there'll be a deeper investigation, and it'll look bad for all of us since we have the girls. They're just bodies. They're not in there."

"I see," Jacob said, still not sure if he should do it. When Jerrod crossed his arms, Jacob sighed. He took his backpack off and pulled out the hydrogen peroxide and nail polish remover. "I really didn't want to use it if I didn't have to, but –"

"We need to blow it," Jerrod said sternly.

Jacob sighed again, shaking his head. "Fine. Everyone take cover."

Combining the hydrogen peroxide and nail polish remover in a bottle, he slipped the rope in for a fuse. Setting it near where he knew it would ignite the fuel in the tank, he lit the fuse. After setting off his homemade concoction, using a shorter fuse than the others, everyone in the group made a run for the vehicles. Just as they reached them, the fourth bomb went off within a split second of the helicopter blowing in a huge fireball.

"Let's bail," Angel said. "This place is about to be crawling with EMS people shortly due to all the explosions."

"What about Rachel and Jesse?" Jacob asked, panic evident. "We need to wait for them."

"No. We'll meet them at the ranch," Angel said decisively. "We'll leave the jeep for them. We have to get these little girls to safety. They're our priority. They've been through enough."

"They'd better make it out of there," Josh growled, getting into the van, "or you're not going to have a happy crew on your hands!"

"Just get us out of here!" Joe shouted. "Sooner rather than later! I've had my fill of crazy for the moment. This situation is what is known as a tornado on the back of a hurricane."

"That's a new one," Jon said over his shoulder, peeling out of the parking lot.

Joe shrugged. "That's what this feels like."

"Shouldn't some of us go back once we get the girls to safety?" Jacob asked. "What happened to 'never leave a man behind'?"

"Those two are both well-trained," Jon explained. "I have confidence they'll get out and make it back to the ranch."

"Glad *you* do," Josh snapped. "I don't agree with this in the least."

"It's *my* twin. I know how he was trained."

"And it's *my* sister. She knows Queensland like the back of her hand, but she's also dealing with unnaturals…which is new."

"We're going to be running into a lot of new experiences. This'll be a test."

"I'd rather not test her with her life. What if we get everyone to the station and then come back? I think that's a fair compromise. And, only those who want to."

"No," Angel said firmly. "We'll stay at the station and wait for them."

"We'll see," Josh huffed, sitting back in his seat with his arms crossed, as he worked on a plan to rescue Jesse and Rachel in his head. He knew if he went back to the station without Rachel, he would have to answer for it to his parents and he was *not* looking forward to explaining this one.

*   *   *

As Rachel and Jesse ran deeper into the belly of the caverns, a bomb suddenly went off, sending them both flying backward into the air, landing with a thud.

While the debris settled, not feeling Rachel immediately near him, Jesse called out over the ringing in his ears, "Rachel? Are you okay?" Coughing, he had to catch his breath before trying again, "Rachel? Where are you?"

Not getting an answer, panic flooded his system. Feeling like he was suffocating with all the dirt in the air, he coughed. Crawling in the darkness with his hands feeling in front of him, he finally felt the warmth of her skin. "Rachel?" he asked. Feeling his way up her arm to the head of her motionless body, he pulled his flashlight off his belt with his other hand. "Oh, Rachel," he sighed, running his fingers through her hair. That's when he felt the warmth of the blood from under her head.

"Rach?" he asked, his body shaking. "Rachel? Please? You can't give up on me."

*    *    *

Pulling up to the front of the main house of the station, they were met by Nico and Kit Sullivan. After giving Josh a hug, she went to hug the others. Noticing who all was there, Kit asked, "Where are Jesse and Rachel?"

When a silence fell over the group, Nico cleared his throat and said, "Let's get the little ones in and settled, and then talk. As the group went in, Nico grabbed his son's arm to stop him, while Kit followed the others inside. "Not so fast."

Jacob hung out near the door to keep an ear out on both sections of people. He didn't feel comfortable at all in leaving Rachel and Jesse. His hope was that Josh would do something.

"What?" Josh groaned, dropping his head.

"Whose idea was it t' leave Rachel an' Jesse behind?" Nico questioned.

"Angel an' Jon."

Rachel's twin, Leah, rode up on her horse, excited. "Was that Rachel?" she asked, sliding off her horse. Giving her brother a hug, she asked, "Where is she? I have wonderful news!" Getting a good look at Josh's face, Leah's face dropped before anger replaced the smile that was there only moments before. "Where is she?" she demanded.

"She's still at Black Rock with Jesse," Josh admitted.

"She's *where*?" Nico shouted. "You know better than to go there! What were you thinkin'?"

"I'm thinking we need to go back and get them," Jacob said, walking out onto the deck.

Seeing Jacob duck out, Angel followed him onto the porch. "Noooo, we're staying here. We're not losing anyone else." She quietly added, "We've already lost Amber and

176

Terrik. I'm still not sure how I'm going to explain this to the twins, or how we're going to handle the situation."

Anger flashed across Nico's eyes. "You *are not* leavin' them there!"

"Jacob, go inside," Angel ordered, not taking her eyes off Nico.

"No," Jacob stood his ground. "I didn't want to leave them in the first place."

"Go inside, *now*," Angel growled. "If I give you an order, I expect you to follow it. And for the record, that's an order."

"Obviously you don't know me very well."

"I mean it. Do it now!"

"No," Jacob said, moving to the other side of Josh. "If they go, I'm going with them."

Angel dropped her head, shaking it. With her hands on her hips, she took a deep breath, hoping to control her emotions. Her body hadn't stopped shaking since that morning, but she knew she had to get control of the situation. Looking up at them, she hoped they would understand her heart. "This is not as easy as it sounds. Leading such a large, diverse group of people into this type of situation is the most difficult thing I have ever had to do. I didn't ask for this. I didn't want…" She swallowed as the tears slowly crawled down her cheeks. "I didn't want anyone to die. I only wanted to help people. We lost an ally in Terrik, along with the mother to those two babies in there," she said, pointing toward the house. "I don't know what I'm going to do with them. Who is going to raise them? *Definitely not* their father."

"Worry about that *after* you find Jesse an' Rachel," Nico said. "Stay focused on getting who you can t' safety."

"How are we going to do that?"

"Are you not trained?"

"Yes, but I don't know the area."

"Do you not trust the Lord t' help you? You're one of his A.N.G.E.L.s. What makes you think He's just going t' let them die in there in a demon lair?"

"Can we? I don't know if my heart can take losing my brother. It's already breaking for those two little girls in there."

"Yes!" Josh shouted. "You need to have faith! We are God's A.N.G.E.L.s! He *will* help us. He won't leave them."

"And neither will we," Jacob finished.

*     *     *

Deep in the recesses of the caverns of Black Rock, Jesse sat on the ground with the unconscious Rachel. With her head on his lap, he sighed. "You know, growing up with this group was an experience," he said, talking in a low voice, while keeping an ear out. "Being trained, going on missions…we always had back-up, though. We had Derek, Dad, Mom, and the Colonel." Tears formed in his eyes, as he continued, "I'm going to miss him so much! I know I never told him how much I appreciated him. And now I'll never have that chance. Why did I waste that? He was a good man. A hard man, but a good man." Looking down at Rachel, he ran his fingers through her hair. "Please wake up? I don't think I could handle losing someone else so soon. I know we will eventually, but it's too soon to lose anyone else just yet."

*     *     *

"What's the plan?" Jacob asked while Nico drove the van. Josh, Jacob, Nico, Angel, and Jerrod were in the van, leaving Joe, Jon, Val, and Kit with the children at the station to protect the others.

"We know where they were firing from," Angel said, forming a plan. "If it were me, I would have found a cave to duck into until it was clear to get out."

"I would do the same," Jerrod agreed. "Question is, was that anywhere near where one of Jacob's cocktails went off?"

"Yes," Jacob said quietly. "That was one of the reasons I wanted to make sure they were okay. I would feel responsible if anything happened to them."

"You are *not* responsible," Nico interrupted the conversation. "You set those off to keep the evil inside, right?"

"Yes."

"You had no idea where they were going to be, right?"

"No, sir."

"Then you did what you were supposed t' do. You're not responsible if anything happens t' them. Besides, we're going t' get them out."

"No, Dad," Josh corrected, "*We*'re going t' get them out. *You* are going t' stay in the van. If anything happens t' you, Mum would never forgive me. You have your gun in case someone tries t' shoot you, right?"

"Yes, I do, but – "

"No," Josh said firmly. "We need t' do this on our own. We're big boys an' girls."

"I don't know you," Jerrod said to Nico, "but I *do* know you raised two fine warriors for Christ. Trust the training. Trust the Lord."

"I appreciate that, an' I do," Nico agreed. "I just feel somewhat helpless in looking after my own children."

"*Train up a child in the way he should go, and when he is old, he will not depart from it*," Jerrod reminded Nico of Proverbs 22:6. "Trust the Lord."

"Right oh," Nico agreed. "I'll stay in the van. You'd better bring them back...and alive...or your mother will kill us both!" he warned Josh.

Josh nodded. "Understood."

"If you can't bring them home alive," Nico added quietly, "Just bring them home."

# Chapter 14
# Faith As Small As A Mustard Seed

With his flashlight on the ground beside him, Jesse sighed. Looking to the Lord, he prayed, "Father, we know where two or more are gathered, that You will be there. We know You're with us. Please allow us to get out of here alive? Please allow the others to have escaped without harm? Please allow them to have found the little girls, and they are now united with their mother? Lord, that young lady has been through a lot in her life. I ask You to give her strength. I ask You to wake Rachel. In Jesus' name I pray, Amen." Sighing, he rested his head back on the granite wall of the cave. "I miss my family. If this is where You want my path to end, though, here with Rachel, I'm okay with that. The only thing I pray is that the kids got out." Shaking his head, he looked down at her. "I thought we could get out of this. I'm sorry for giving you hope."

When she didn't respond, Jesse sighed. "Time. I know it'll take time for you to wake up." As he sat there, his mind wondered back to his childhood. "You would think I would be used to these type of situations. Growing up in a foreign country, being blond with green eyes, I stood out. And the fact that there were two of us, it made us stand out even more. Our dad trained us from the point that we could hold a knife, gun, and bow and arrow. We went on missions starting around sixteen years old. My first one was scary. Wanna hear it?" he asked. When she didn't respond, he said, "Of course you do….

*     *     *

…Sixteen-year-old Jesse was on his first mission. He body filled out over the last year, and with the skills he picked up over the years, his dad finally thought he was ready. "Okay,

181

while we're in there, you stay beside me like glue. Do you understand?"

"Yes, sir," Jesse responded.

Their mission was to get a family out who were marked by the locals to be taken out for standing up for the local pastor. The pastor and his family were evacuated the night before, but he insisted on getting this family out as well, so the A.N.G.E.L.s stayed to pull them the next night, preferring to do it under the cover of darkness.

Juan, Mauricio, and Mauricio's son Pedro, along with Mark and Jesse, had a plan, but the question was if they could implement it in time.

"It's that one," Juan whispered pointing out the home.

"How many?" Mauricio asked.

"Parents, and four small children."

"We'll take the back. You want all three in the front?" Mark asked.

"I'm going to keep watch, and potentially lay cover fire if necessary," Juan explained. "Pedro and Mauricio go to the front, but give Mark and Jesse time to get to the back."

Nodding in agreement, Mark and Jesse disappeared into the backyard. "We'll sit right here, because it gives us a clear view of the entire backyard. That way Mauricio and Pedro won't end up with a surprise."

"Dad?" Jesse said, feeling the hair on the back of his neck stand on end.

Hearing the tone, Mark nervously asked, "Do I want to know?"

"They're here."

Gulping, Mark scanned the back yard. Into his radio, he said, "Head's up. Jesse said they're here."

"Copy," came from both groups.

Hearing Mauricio knock on the front door, Mark and Jesse crept slowly toward the back door. Just as they were under a window, the light flipped on. They could hear the mother yelling at the child to throw some clothing into a bag and to grab one stuffed animal.

"Dad?" Jesse whispered.

"Not now," Mark said, keeping an ear out toward the window, while looking out at the lawn.

"Dad, they're at the front," Jesse said with urgency in his voice.

"Then, let's get them out through the back," Mark ordered. As shots were heard at the front of the house, Mark kicked in the back door to find a stunned wife staring at him in horror. "They're at the front, you have to come out this way."

"No, I –" she was cut off when the front door was kicked in, and there was a sudden shower of gunfire.

Jesse dove for the little girl beside the mom, while Mark dove toward the mom.

"Dad! We need to get them out!"

"No!" the mom yelled. "Ferdinand is upstairs with the little ones."

Turning to Jesse, Mark ordered, "Get these two out! I'll go upstairs with Mauricio and Pedro to help get the others out. Go!" Mark shouted before returning fire to give Jesse cover.

Running outside with the mom holding one hand, and the daughter holding the other, they ran face-to-face with a demon.

The mom stopped in her tracks. "¡Oh Dios mío!"

Jesse let her hand go so he could pull his gun out. Firing four shots at point-black range, the creature let out a hellish screech that deafened the trio. Holstering his weapon, while the creature dropped to the ground in flames, Jesse pulled the mom and daughter to the front, to Juan's previously known position.

"Seriously?" Jesse said, stunned when Juan wasn't there. Looking back toward the house, his heart skipped a beat at the sight of fire jetting out of one of the upstairs windows. "No. Please, Lord! No," he whispered, shaking his head.

To his horror, a body flew out the window, landing on the ground with a thud, not moving. The wife turned into Jesse's shoulder, as she clasped her daughter closer to her.

Just when Jesse was about to give up, Mark, Juan, and Pedro ran out the front door, each with a child. "Go!" Mark shouted to Jesse. "Get to the van! Go!"

Without another word, Jesse practically dragged the mother and daughter to the van, with the mother continuously tugging to go to her dead husband. Once he got them to the van, he jumped in the front seat and started the van. Out of the corner of his eye, Jesse saw three demons coming his way. As the other guys got in, they barely got the door closed before Jesse slammed his foot on the gas.

Even after twenty minutes, the mother was still yelling and wailing, while the kids were crying and screaming. It was beginning to give him a headache, but he completely understood. That family not only lost their head of household, but their father. The wife lost her lover, her anchor, and her best friend. Life for them would never be the same. Along the same lines, all four children and the mom were saved that night, along with all the A.N.G.E.L.s, and for that, he was grateful.

*     *     *

"So, yeah, my track record with this type of thing is sort of good, sort of not so good," Jesse said. When Rachel didn't move, he sighed. "Come to think of it, there weren't many where something big *didn't* happen."

In his mind, God gave him a verse, '*So do not fear, for I am with you; do not be dismayed, for I am your God. I will strengthen you and help you; I will uphold you with my righteous right hand.*'

"Isaiah 41:10. That's one of my favorite verses. Thank you," he said to God.

'*Peace is what I leave with you; it is My own peace that I give you. I do not give it as the world does. Do not be worried and upset; do not be afraid.*'

"Another good one…John 14:27. What about Psalm 27:1? '*The Lord is my light and my salvation – whom shall I fear? The Lord is the stronghold of my life – of whom shall I be afraid?*' I do not fear if this is it. You have given me many adventures. You have honored me beyond measure in allowing me to grow up the way I did. I cannot thank You enough for my parents, brother, and sister. I know without them, my life would be vastly different. I know without the A.N.G.E.L.s, my mom wouldn't be alive today. Thank you for allowing me to meet such wonderful people through the years. Thank You for protecting me and my family, and our friends. If it's Your will that we get out of here, then I will be grateful, and as always, will not waste what You have blessed me with. If this is it, then I know I will be with you today in paradise, knowing I have served You to the best of my ability."

Hearing the dismay in his voice, Rachel struggled to open her eyes. At first his voice sounded far away, but the more he talked, the closer he sounded. "Jesse?" she asked, weakly.

"Rach!" he softly exclaimed. He was excited, but didn't want the demons to hear them if they were in the area. He could normally tell how close they were, but with all of the explosions and his concern for Rachel, all he knew was the obvious…they were around. "Was that you?"

"I think so," she groaned. "Where are we?"

"We're still in the caves. We need to be quiet, though. I don't feel them immediately near, but they are still around in here."

"Ugh!" she sighed, closing her eyes for a moment. Looking back up at him, with his tiny flashlight as the only light in the tunnel, she asked, "Do you know how to get out of here?"

"Not really."

With Jesse's help, Rachel sat up, resting her head on her knees while she took deep breaths. "Wow. I'm dizzy."

"Just take slow, deep breaths until your head is clear. You hit it pretty hard. You actually have blood in your hair."

"How much?"

"Quite a bit, I'm afraid. What's that in your hand?" he asked, noticing a small baggie in Rachel's hand for the first time.

Holding up the bag with the small seed in it, she explained, "Amber gave it to me this morning before we left. It's a mustard seed. She said to have faith that we'd get the little ones out. She gave it to me because she knew I was nervous being the first team in."

"I see. And, does it help?"

She nodded. "Actually, yes. Before we covered their get-away, I grabbed it, praying for the courage to do what needed to be done. The Bible said if we have faith, even as small as a mustard seed, that we can move mountains."

"Well, we are *in* a mountain. Maybe that faith can get us *out* of the mountain."

"Maybe," Rachel agreed. Looking down the tunnel, she squinted. "Jesse?" she whispered. "Am I hallucinating or is there a light down there?"

Seeing the light, he quickly shut his flashlight off.

"Do we go down there?" she asked.

"We should check it out."

"What if it's *them*?"

"Well, we have two choices. We can either sit here and see if they notice us, or we can go investigate and see what's there. What do you want to do?"

"I *want* t' go home."

"I know. I do too. However, we need to figure out right now if we want to sit or go where the light is."

"I have a feelin'," Rachel said, pushing herself off the ground, "we're supposed t' go toward the light."

"Are you okay to walk?" he asked, resting his hand on the small of her back, bracing her in case she stumbled.

"Yes. With our faith being bigger than a mustard seed, let's move this mountain an' get out of here."

*     *     *

Pulling into the parking lot with a plan in place, Nico slammed the van in park. "Right oh. You ready?"

"Ready or not, here we go," Angel said, as everyone but Nico climbed out of the van. "Two teams. Everyone has radios, right?"

"Yep," Jerrod said, holding his up. He and Jacob were one team, while Angel and Josh were the other. "Let's go get them. Do you have your toys, little buddy?" he asked Jacob.

"I'm *not* a little buddy," Jacob snapped, glaring at him out of the corner of his eye, "but yes, I have my toys."

Jerrod smirked. "As long as you blow things like you're supposed to, and can shoot your way out, I'll call you whatever you want."

"Then you can call me the Master Blaster," he said with a grin.

"You can very easily earn that nickname. C'mon, let's get Jesse and Rachel out of there."

*     *     *

Clutching the baggie containing the mustard seed in one hand, while holding Jesse's hand with her other one, Rachel and Jesse made their way down the tunnel toward the light.

"I think it's moving," Jesse said after a few minutes.

Rachel furrowed her brow. "How can the light move?"

"Do we keep following it?"

"Your knives handy?"

"Yep. Yours?"

"Always," Rachel said, tapping the knife set on her hip with the baggie hand.

Cautiously, they continued down the tunnel, listening for some sort of sound that may signify danger.

"In Psalm 43:3, it says, '*Send me your light and your faithful care, let them lead me; let them bring me to your holy mountain, to the place where you dwell.*' While it's normally not a literal light, I'll take it," Rachel said with a smirk.

"Good one. Want to do a verse challenge?"

"How does that work?"

"Well, we come up with a subject, and find a verse to match it. It'll help pass the time," he offered.

"Okay, well, I got one. What about you?"

"Well, there's the obvious, Psalm 119:105, '*Your word is a lamp unto my feet, and a light unto my path.*'"

"Too easy. I thought you were up for a challenge."

Jesse smiled, as his cheeks flushed. "Well, I wanted to get the obvious one out of the way."

"Then give me another t' be fair."

"All right," he agreed, debating in his head for another verse on light. "What about, Matthew 4:16?"

"Good one."

"That's, *'the people living in darkness have seen a great light; on those living in the land of the shadow of death a light has dawned.'* Will that work?"

"That'll work," Rachel agreed. "Now for me. Hmmm."

"Don't try too hard. I don't want you to hurt your head anymore."

Sticking her tongue out for a moment, she then responded with, "John 18:12 says, *'When Jesus spoke again to the people, He said, 'I am the light of the world. Whoever follows me will never walk in darkness, but will have the light of life'.* How's that?"

"Good. Oh! I got one! *'The city does not need the sun or the moon to shine on it, for the glory of God gives it light, and the Lamp is its lamp.'* That would be Revelation 21:23."

"Nice! Good onya!" Rachel smiled. "Okay, new subject."

"Shh!" Jesse hissed, as he pulled on her hand to stop her from moving. Feeling the hair on the back of his neck standing on end, he knew what was in the tunnels ahead of them.

"What?"

Putting his finger in front of his mouth, he then pointed down the tunnel, where there was a scratching noise.

As the adrenaline flooded her body, Rachel clutched the baggie with the mustard seed in her hand, praying with every bone in her body for protection.

Pulling his gun from the holster, his body on edge, Jesse wrapped the arm with the gun in it around Rachel's body, while he covered her mouth with the other. He knew what was coming. He didn't have to see it. From a young age, he could feel when the other side was near.

Dragging its nails along the wall, the demon looked in every direction. Jesse knew his gun was already ready to go. He patiently waited for it to cross his path.

"Well, hello precioussss," the demon said, leaning on the wall of the alcove the pair were hidden in. "Cassiusss will be happy to ssssee you. I'll get a grand reward for you two."

"No. You won't," Jesse said, and then emptied his gun into the demon.

Looking down at its chest, the demon then looked up at Jesse before dropping to the ground in a ball of fire, and then immediately dissolved into a pile of ash.

"Time to go," Jesse said, dragging Rachel behind him by the hand.

"Don't have t' tell me twice!" Rachel said, glancing back at the pile of ash before running full speed with Jesse.

Suddenly stopping in his tracks, Jesse saw another light in the distance, dancing off the walls.

Rachel gulped. "More company."

*　　*　　*

While Angel and Josh went one way, Jerrod and Jacob went the other. "They'd better be okay," Josh said, while they slowly made their way toward where they knew Rachel and Jesse were last seen.

"We'll have to trust God for that one," Angel said in a low voice.

"Would you be so flippant if it were *your* life?"

"What are you asking?" Angel stopped and stared at him, angry. Pointing toward the mountain, she yelled, "That's my brother in there!"

"Keep it up an' we might as well paint a target on us!" Josh hissed. "Shut it!"

Narrowing her eyes, balling her fist at her sides, she growled, "Do *not* even *attempt* to shut me up when you've challenged my integrity!"

Standing toe to toe with Angel, Josh confronted her. "Ever since we met, you have attempted t' assert your place as leader of this group. You get all argy-bargy when someone possibly challenges you as leader, an' heaven forbid we point out your flaws in leadership."

"Don't know what that means, but using my intuition it doesn't seem nice."

"You get your britches in a bunch if someone challenges you. Why is that? Who said *you* were t' lead this team?"

"I did," they heard behind them, and spun toward the archangel, standing less than a foot away from them. "She was given leadership by me. Rachel has as well."

"We're here t' get her," Josh explained.

"I am aware. They are being helped as we speak. However, this situation needs to be resolved in order for you to move forward as a team. Joshua, please explain your concerns."

"She gets in a tizzy if someone even challenges her leadership. She also feels it's her place t' boss us around. An' t' top things off, she left Rachel *an'* Jesse behind. Jacob's right. You *never* leave a man behind."

"I am aware," the archangel said with a nod. "She is working on this with Jesus."

"In the meantime, we're cleanin' up her messes," Josh countered.

"What *messes*?" Angel demanded.

"The one we're in right now is a perfect example. There are police crawling all over the place, an' we're tryin' t' rescue two people *you* made us leave. How are we goin' t' do this?"

"*You* are not," the archangel asserted. "Return to the van and speak with your father. He will help you sort this out."

"Yes, sir," they mumbled as they walked back to the van.

"What are you two doing in here?" Nico asked when the pair got back in.

"The archangel sent us back in here t' sort out our anger issues with each other," Josh explained.

"Are you bloody serious? There are lives on the line, an' you two are bickering?" Nico snapped. "Get your bloody bums out there an' go save your brother an' sister!" When they didn't move, Nico growled, "NOW!"

"The archangel told us to stay in here until we sorted it out," Angel argued.

"Probably because he's madder than a cut snake that you two are snippin' at each other when there are still two lives on the line. What's your problem?"

"She's a horrible leader – very selfish," Josh said.

"And he won't ease up," Angel shot back.

Nico sighed, shaking his head. "We don't have time for this. Rachel an' Jesse don't have time for this. What do you reckon will happen when they find out what *you two* were doin' when you're supposed t' be savin' them?"

"Her calls are self-centered, not carin' what people think. She thinks she's his nibbs, not lookin' for anyone's input. She doesn't take into account our skills either."

"What skills do *you* have?" Angel snapped.

"I can speak just about any language known t' man. Go ahead an' test me," he challenged. When Angel didn't say anything, Josh continued, "See. She doesn't care. She's arrogant in her calls of leadership, an' she's *forever* narcissistic in her attitude. We don't need the enemy t' take us out with her in charge. She'll send us all t' our deaths!"

Angel scoffed. "Tell me what you really think."

"You don't want t' know what I *really* think."

"Fine!" Nico snapped. "You two sit there until Kit can sort this out back on the station. Just pray that Jacob an' Jerrod are havin' better luck than you two, or we'll lose 'em for good. Seriously? I can't *believe* what I'm hearin'!"

"But –" Josh went to object, but Nico cut him off.

"Shut it!"

*     *     *

"Faith as small as a mustard seed," Rachel whispered, clutching the baggie in her hand. "Faith as small as a mustard seed."

"It's okay," Jesse said, still holding her hand while he prayed in his head for safety for the pair. "God's got us."

As the light moved closer, Jesse and Rachel plastered themselves into a tiny alcove in the wall of the tunnel. Deciding she didn't want to see the end coming, Rachel tightly shut her eyes, clasping her clenched hand with the baggie to her face, praying with all her might against it being the end.

"There you two are," Jerrod said, shining the flashlight on the pair.

"You two look horrible!" Jacob exclaimed, wide-eyed.

"Oh! Thank you, Lord!" Jesse said in relief.

Opening her eyes, Rachel was never so grateful to see two people. She threw her arms around them both with tears in her eyes. "Thank you for coming back for us!"

"You *never* leave a man behind," Jacob explained, firming in his mind to not do so again no matter what Angel said. "Let's get you two out of here."

"We don't know our way out," Jesse explained. "The tunnels behind us are sealed."

"That's why we marked it. C'mon," Jerrod said, leading the way. "Rachel, your dad is in the van waiting for you."

"Dinkum?" Rachel asked, stunned.

Cocking his head to the side, Jerrod said, "I don't know what that means."

"It means, 'are you serious'?"
"Yes. He's waiting for you. Let's go."
"Lead the way."

*　　*　　*

Arriving at the van, under the cover of the brush, the group hoped to avoid the police and medical personnel who were crawling all over the area. While they knew the personnel were doing their best to determine what happened on that day, they didn't want to have to explain what they were doing there.

"Praise the Lord!" Josh jumped out of the van, grabbing Rachel when they got close enough. "I'm so sorry we left you."

"Get in!" Nico snapped. "We have t' get out of here before they figure out that we're not just onlookers. Good heavens, Rachel! Your Mum is goin' t' kill you. You look like a dog's breakkie."

Ignoring her dad, Rachel just sat in the middle seat with her head back, closing her eyes. She was relieved just to see the outside of the caves again.

On the way home, Jerrod looked at Rachel's head. Content to know that she would be okay until they could get home where he could stitch it up, he rested, knowing God had taken care of His A.N.G.E.L.s.

# Chapter 15
# Flesh And Blood

The entire ride home to Kit and Nico's station, the van was completely silent. Anger, fear, relief, and general thoughts of what happened swirled all around them, but no one said another word.

"Rachel!" Kit yelled when they pulled up.

Pete ran out of the house on her heels. As soon as Kit hugged Rachel, Pete grabbed Rachel's hand, setting her down on a chair to look at her head. "What happened?" He asked, pulling through her hair to find the cause of all the blood.

"There was an explosion that brought the roof down," Rachel explained.

"I'm sorry," Jacob said, feeling horrible that it was his fault. "I didn't mean to lock you guys in there, or worse yet, bring the roof down on you."

"Come here." Rachel put her hand out to him. When he knelt in front of her, she took his hand into hers and explained, "You did your job…an' you did it well. You did what you were supposed t' do. We didn't get clear before it went off. Had we been, they would have all been sealed in, with the exception of how y'all got in. Speakin' of which, how *did* you get in?"

"There was an opening on the top, just big enough for one person," Jacob explained. "I sealed all the side entrances. Unfortunately, if we can get in, they can still get out."

"So did we. And that's what's important. You have t' remember, we're not fighting against flesh an' blood. General rules don't apply. As long as you guys completed the mission, an' got the girls out an' t' their mum, then the mission was successful."

Jacob cringed. "The girls got out, but Amber and Terrik didn't."

"What do ya mean?"

"That big, black charred piece of equipment in the open field was their helicopter."

"What happened?" Rachel demanded, her heart racing.

Ignoring the others, Pete started stitching a small cut on her head. Knowing her hair would cover the stiches, he was grateful that was the only real wound she had. He knew Jerrod could have easily taken care of it, but he watched her grow up. He wanted to take care of her one more time. Feeling like he too was losing one of his children, he knew the Lord had them in the palm of His hand, and for that, Pete was grateful.

In a low voice so the twins wouldn't hear, Jacob explained, "By the time we got to the helicopter, Amber and Terrik were shot and killed. Their bodies were still in the chopper. In order to give us all a chance to get out with the girls, and so there wouldn't be too many questions in regards to them, Jerrod had me blow the chopper. Now, as you briefly saw, the police and EMS are scrambling to figure out what happened."

"I see," Rachel said, looking down, upset. "So, we got the girls, but lost our charge?"

Lifting her chin, Jesse made sure she looked at him before he said, "Her time was done. The twins are safe. We'll sort this out. Know that God has a plan."

With her bottom lip trembling, she said, "I know it's all in His plan, but now those babies have t' grow without parents." Tears crawled down her cheeks as the emotions from the day caught up to her. "We did what we could, but that wasn't enough. Haven't those two little ones been through enough? Why would God do this?"

"This wasn't God's doing," Jesse said. "Free will did this. Free will from the other side hoped to take out those of us they could. God knew it would happen, so he had a back-up plan."

"There's no one t' raise them, though," Rachel said, dropping her head in her hands. "We *are not* giving them to Eric!"

"No we're not," Jon said, coming out on the porch with a piece of peanut butter toast, drinking a soda. "And, there *is* someone to raise them."

"What do you mean?" Rachel looked up at him with her tear-streaked face.

"My mom and dad are going to raise them."

"Really?"

"Yeah. I remembered something interesting while you were gone."

"What's that?" Jesse asked, straightening up. "We could use some good news."

"Well, when we were writing the names down, there were two names on the next generation list that both have the last name of 'English' by them from Spanish Springs."

"Really?" Angel asked, crossing her arms. "I never connected that."

"Yep, and I don't see any of us having any babies any time soon, especially mom and dad. So, we put two-and-two together and figured out that Allie and Callie are going to be A.N.G.E.L.s. Then, when we told Mom and Dad what happened, they agreed to raise them. Now," he started, turning toward Jerrod, "Considering that *you* are the only one the twins really know, would you be willing to stay with Mom and Dad until the twins are comfortable?"

"Of course!" Jerrod agreed. "I've known them since before they were born. I won't abandon them now. There's a lot going on in their little lives."

"They're actually sleeping right now," Jon said, finishing up his toast. He then drained the rest of his soda before he explained, "Kit fed them until they couldn't eat anymore, and then she put them down. She also gave them some of Pete's tea to help them sleep."

"Good idea," Josh said. "That stuff'll knock 'em out 'til mornin' at least, if not a couple a' days. Poor things probably don't know what t' think."

"I reckon there are a few other young people who also need t' go into a food coma," Nico pointed out. "Why don't y'all get some food an' then get some sleep? I doubt anyone would trace y'all back t' us. But if they do, we'll head them off."

"Thank you," Jesse said. "We appreciate it."

"Annnnnd, you're done," Pete said, covering the stitches with Rachel's hair. "Go get some sleep, an' when you wake *gently* wash your hair an' then come find me."

"Will do." Rachel gratefully gave him a hug. "Thank you."

"Go get some tucker, an' then get some rest," he said before returning to the barn.

"Sounds like a great plan," Jesse agreed, heading into the house with everyone but Jerrod and Nico.

Once they were inside, Jerrod and Nico each took a seat on the two rocking chairs on the porch. "What's going through your mind?" Nico asked. "I can see the wheels turnin' from here."

"There's a lot," Jerrod admitted. Taking a few moments before he continued, he formed the thoughts in his mind. "Did they tell you how they found me?"

"Nope."

Sighing, Jerrod looked out across the station. "I guess being in this beautiful place, you wouldn't see the evil in the world."

Nico burst out in laughter. "Ohhhhh, mate. You have *no idea*! I used t' be an FBI agent. I've seen a lot over my lifetime. That's not even includin' what happened here on the station. There's been some interestin' situations around here."

"What do you mean by that?"

"Well, Ephesians 6:12 reminds us that, '*We wrestle not against flesh and blood, but against principalities, against powers, against the rulers of the darkness of this world, against spiritual wickedness in high places.*' There is so much more goin' on around you than what you see."

"Yeah. I caught that when we saw what we did in those mountains." Jerrod shuddered. "Those creatures were something I've never seen before. They were worse than what I even saw in the field in Iraq…and that was horrific."

"I'll bet. I'll tell you what. I may not be able t' help you in the way ya need, because what you saw was different than what I saw an' experienced. However, I happen t' know of two people who *can* help you. You're on your way back t' Nevada t' see Mark an' Casey. Mark an' Derek were both former spec ops. They, I'm sure, have the answers you're lookin' for."

"You think?"

"I know. Look, I can help you with those two dingbats inside with their issues when they wake, but I'm pretty sure you need Mark an' Derek for what's goin' on inside a' you."

"What two dingbats?"

"Josh an' Angel. Those two need a different kind a' intervention than you do."

"Yeah. I don't want to touch that one with a ten-foot pole."

"Then work on gettin' yourself t' Nevada, an' I'll handle the other mess."

"Nico, we got comp'ny," Nico heard one of the ranch hands over his radio.

Watching the police vehicle bound up the drive, Nico groaned. "I got it," he said into his radio.

"You knew they were going to come. That van has a license plate they can trace," Jerrod pointed out.

"I know. I was hopin' it wouldn't happen, though."

As the vehicle pulled up, two police officers got out and walked up to the van.

Nico got up and shook their hands. "G'day! How's it goin'?"

"This van was seen at Black Rock near Cooktown twice t'day," the first officer pointed out.

"Okay. An' why is that important?" Nico asked, playing dumb.

"Because there were explosions up there, includin' a helicopter that killed two people."

"Really? Is *that* what happened? We were wonderin' what all the fuss was about up there."

"Yes. Mind explainin' what you were doin' up there?"

"Well, we took a family trip there t'day, an' when we got home, we realized we forgot somethin', so we went back for it. No worries. Sorry if it was an inconvenience for y'all t' come out here."

"So, you're tellin' me you didn't notice the explosions?"

"Of course I did. Blind Freddy coulda seen 'em! But they weren't from me or my family."

"I see. Do you know where they were from?"

"Not from me or my family," Nico reiterated, which was true. Jacob set them off, and technically he wasn't family.

"Did you happen t' see anything?"

"Not note worthy."

"Right oh. Thank you for your time," the officer said, and they left.

When they pulled away, Jerrod asked, "Do you think that'll take care of things?"

"Who rented the vehicles?"

"They were in Josh's name, since he's Aussie born and old enough."

"Then they can't get traced back t' Terrik or Amber?"

"No."

"What about the rooms?"

"Those are in Rachel's name."

"Good."

"Terrik and Amber both bought their own tickets too."

"Okay then, y'all should be good. How are you gettin' home?"

"Derek is supposed to send the IDs for the girls, and then we'll order the tickets and fly home."

"No rush. In the meantime, enjoy Serenity Wells an' all it has t' offer."

"Sounds like a plan."

*   *   *

The next morning the group went down to breakfast, while Kit got the two little girls up and ready. When they came downstairs, Kit introduced the girls to Caleb and Willow's children, who the twins stuck to like glue for the rest of the day. She was happy to see the girls laughing and having a good time, but she knew that would be short-lived. She understood that eventually, they would want to know where their mom was, and she prayed Mark and Casey would be able to successfully navigate that conversation with the Lord's help.

Groggy-eyed and looking beat-up, the rest of the group trudged down to the table shortly after Kit and the girls got downstairs.

"Well, aren't y'all a bag a crushed biscuits," Adoni, one of the ranch hands, remarked. "What happened t' ya?"

"Had a bit of a run-in in town," Josh said quickly.

"Looks like your blood-n-blister got the worst a' it," another ranch hand Barwon, remarked, concern evident. "Weren't ya watchin' 'er?"

"I *was* watchin' 'er," Josh snapped. "We got separated."

"May wanna keep a better eye on 'er," Barwon pointed out. "Yer friend too," he said, gesturing toward Jesse as he took a bite of his eggs. "Seems 'e needs it too."

If it wasn't for Barwon's size, and the respect the Aboriginal had for his family, Josh would have jumped him. However, he knew that wouldn't make his Dad happy at all. Since it wasn't his station, he would let him get away with it. "We got separated, an' these two got the brunt of it," Josh said, feeling the anger churning inside.

"Calm your brumbies, mate," Kendall, another ranch hand, said. "Both a' ya. There's enough tension around here. Y'all are scarin' the little ones," he pointed out, nodding toward Allie and Callie. The girls were sitting on either side of Rachel and Angel. When Kendall mentioned them, they moved closer to the one they sat beside. Allie was next to Angel, and Callie sat beside Rachel.

"Are y'all done yet?" Kit snapped. "This is the table. Everything is left at the door and not brought in here. That's the rules, and y'all know it."

"Well," Barwon continued, "Pretty sure this has somethin' t' do with Hawk an' his crew. I thought they were supposed t' be lookin' out for them."

"God is," Josh corrected.

"Then He'd better keep a closer eye on you."

"They're alive, aren't they?" Nico pointed out.

"Yeah, but they –"

"Then that's all that matters," Nico cut Barwon off, effectively ending the conversation. "Now, eat. We have a busy day."

Just then a car pulled up to the front of the house. "Ohhhh, what now?" Kit groaned, dropping her head in her hands.

"I got it," Nico said, getting up. Jon and Josh followed him out the door. "Can I help you?" Nico asked the young man who got out of the car.

"Just a delivery, sir," the young man stammered at the size of the trio who came out onto the porch. "I was told t' get it 'ere yesterday, but the rain that hit yesterday afternoon slowed me a bit. I'm really sorry."

"No worries," Nico said, signing for the package. "Have a good one."

As the small group entered the house, Nico opened the package to find new identities for the two little ones with their new last name as 'English,' along with plane tickets. "Looks like y'all are leavin' this afternoon," Nico said, scanning the tickets. "They have y'all separated into two groups."

"Pretty sure that was for safety reasons," Josh said, sorting them as Nico handed them to him.

The two groups were: Rachel, Jesse, Jacob, Jerrod, and Callie; and then Angel, Josh, Jon, Val, Joe, and Allie. Handing them out, he also gave the young one's tickets to Rachel and Angel. "First group leaves at noon," Josh said, sitting down, "an' the second at four."

"Why is it they keep separatin' you two?" Barwon pressed. "I would feel better if y'all were t'gether."

"Because if they don't, Rachel won't stand on her own an' be the leader she's supposed t' be," Danny Hawk, the head of the Australian A.N.G.E.L. group said, as he and Charlie walked in from the kitchen.

Kit jumped. "Where'd you come from?"

"Kind of thought we'd see you sooner." Nico took a bite of his toast. "Where ya been?"

"Cleanin' up the mess at Black Rock," Hawk explained. "Seems it got a bit ugly over there."

"Well, grab a seat an' eat," Nico gestured toward the table that was full of the breakfast of steak, eggs, hash browns, and fresh bread.

Both Charlie and Hawk sat down. "Are these the little ones?" Charlie asked.

"Yes," Rachel said, resting her hand on Callie's shoulder.

"You are lovely little ones. Your Mum must be proud."

"Where *is* Mommy?" Callie asked, looking around. Those were the first words she spoke since they were rescued.

"She's with Terrik," Rachel explained. "We'll tell you all about it when we get t' the States."

"Are you sure?" Allie questioned.

"Apple pie, remember?" Joe said with a wink. "She wouldn't have told us the code word if it wasn't from her."

"Okay," Allie said, digging back into her breakfast. Noting Allie's lead, Callie started eating again, keeping an eye on everyone at the table.

After breakfast, Nico sent the ranch hands to their assignments for the day, and the kids out to the backyard with Willow and Caleb to watch them, leaving Hawk, Charlie, Nico, Kit, and the young A.N.G.E.L. team at the table.

"That will only be a temporary fix," Nico said as the door closed behind everyone leaving.

"What will?" Hawk asked.

"That Amber is with Terrik story."

"But, it will get them to Nevada where Mark, Casey, Derek, and the Colonel can settle things," Charlie said. Noting the sudden silence, he asked, "What?"

"The Colonel passed about two weeks ago. Why didn't you know?" Jon questioned. "Actually, there were many A.N.G.E.L.s there, except y'all. Where were you? Why did you miss it?"

"We were on a mission," Hawk explained. "I haven't had time t' tell the team yet."

"I see."

"I don't think you do," Hawk continued. "We were sent t' South America t' get Cristiana, Pablo, an' Pedro out of trouble."

"Where's the rest of their team?"

Nervously clearing his throat before he spoke, Hawk explained, "They're spread out doing missions. Unfortunately, none of them could get t' the trio in time. *We* almost didn't."

"Are they okay?" Angel asked, feeling like she would vomit if something happened to them.

"They're recoverin'," Hawk said hesitantly.

"Meaning?" Angel pressed.

"Meaning God's not done with them yet. You are all young teams. You are not immortal by any stretch of the imagination. The sooner you learn that, the better off you'll be. This is dangerous work."

"We know," Rachel said, touching the back of her head.

"I don't think you do," Hawk pushed. "We're not fightin' flesh an' blood here. The enemy takes many forms. You never know where he'll be or what he has in mind. He's had *years* t' study you *an'* your weaknesses. He knows you better than you know yourself. He's a cunning individual. There's a reason for that verse in 1 Peter 5:8, which says, '*Be sober, be vigilant; because your adversary the devil, as a roaring lion, walketh about, seeking whom he may devour.*' You are a very integral part of the Kingdom, an' he knows it. He'll try t' take you out at every turn. I was aware when the Colonel went home. It felt like a swift kick in my gut when he went. I know, though, that he more than earned his rest an' place in Heaven with the Lord. He's gettin' ready for us t' meet him up there when our time is done." Seeing the look on the face of the group, especially Jon, Jesse, and Angel, he continued, "You are all strong. You had the benefit of his counsel an' trainin' for over twenty years. There were many lives saved durin' his tenure as head of the American A.N.G.E.L.s. His loss was felt among all of us. His life touched us all, an' we'll never forget him, but there is more work t' be done, an' you have all stepped up t' do it. Those more experienced will step in where they can, but this is now *your* cross t' carry. It's *your* divine legacy. You *must* fulfill your callin'. You *need* t' pass it down t' the next generation so the work can continue. This is as big as it gets. The balance of power in the world is at stake. In order t' do so, you'll have t' stay focused an' remember who you're dealin' with." Before they had a chance to respond, he said, "I know. I know. You all know everythin'. But, you *don't*! You *are not* immortal. I don't know how else t' spell this out for you. You almost lost two of your own yesterday. Do you understand the seriousness of what you are doin' out there?"

"Yes," Angel huffed, crossing her arms. "We are aware."

"Then remember, you *do not* leave a man behind!" Hawk growled, glaring at her. "Never! I can't believe you did that. You are responsible for these team members lives. Do you get that? What possessed you t' leave them?"

"You've left some behind. What happened with Shawn O'Brien and Victoria Stanton?" Angel shot. "You left *them* behind."

"Angel!" Jon and Jesse objected, seeing the fury on Hawk's face at the mention of his lost team members.

"They did what they set out to do. We don't always come back. We know the risks when we go. Our mission is bigger than any one person."

"You *left* them behind, though," Angel challenged. "What's the difference between what you did, and what I did?"

"We had to get Mark and Casey to safety. By the time we went back for them it was too late. I learned my lesson the hard way. Look, they were A.N.G.E.L.s for *years* before they were called home. You don't think I didn't feel it when they left this Earth as well?"

"Why is it different when we do it than when *you* do it?"

"Angel! Seriously!" Jon stood, leaning on the table in front of Angel. "Shut it! Have respect! He's been at this *way* longer than you have! Your leadership skills are in serious need of an overhaul! I can*not* believe who you are challenging right now! You need to take lessons from these men, not act like the know-it-all you have been! If you're not careful, you'll lose your leadership position."

"What do you mean?" Angel asked, taken aback.

"You need to take some lessons from Rachel. As a matter of fact, I want to switch teams."

"Meaning?"

"I want Rachel in charge."

"Wait! What?" Rachel shook her head, confused. "When did we divide up in teams? An' who placed Angel an' I in charge of those teams?"

"God did, an' you have been since the beginnin'," Hawk said calmly, as he watched the team go at each other.

"Are you bloody serious? I don't remember volunteering for that!" Rachel snapped.

"Watch your mouth!" Nico shot.

"But – "

"Look, you are both strong leaders in your own right," Hawk said, doing his best to keep a lid on the tempers flying around the room. "Let's try it this way. Who wants to be on Rachel's unit?" When everyone raised their hands except Angel, Rachel shook her head. "Why not?" Hawk asked.

"I don't want this! I *want* t' be part of a unit, a team, but a leader of the entire thing? No. No way," she insisted. "I don't want it."

"You always have a choice," Hawk explained, "But you're a natural leader…as is Angel."

Joe raised his hand. "I vote 'no confidence' in Angel."

"Wow," Angel huffed. "Anyone else?"

"Tell you what," Hawk jumped in, "Before we hang Angel, what if Nico an' I work with her?"

"Can't." Jon shook his head. "She gets on a plane here at noon."

"We have until then. That'll give us five hours. Think we can do somethin' in five hours, mate?" Hawk asked Nico.

"I reckon that'll work. We'll take Jerrod with us. That way what we don't finish, I'm sure he can work with the others in the States t' complete," Nico offered.

"Fair enough," Jerrod agreed. "I can do that."

"Don't I get a say in this?" Angel asked, stunned.

"Depends." Hawk shrugged. "Do you want t' lead or not?"

"I do, but –"

"Then let's do a leadership 101 crash course. C'mon, we don't have much time," Hawk said, pulling Angel outside with him, Jerrod, and Nico.

Once they were outside, Kit calmly said, "Now for the rest of you. I believe we need t' have an open and honest conversation."

"I didn't ask for any of this," Rachel groaned, dropping her head in her hands. "And it's makin' my head hurt worse."

"You didn't *have* to ask for it," Val explained. "You were *born* to do this."

"What if I don't want it?"

"You always have a choice," Kit explained. "But even when you're not a leader, you seem to inherit the position."

"Meanin'?"

"As Val said, you're a natural. Look," Kit said, taking her daughter's hand, "I would think all of them raising their hands for you would have proved that to you."

"It did, but it hurt Angel."

"We've all tried to give her hints," Jon explained. "No, scratch that. We've been pretty blunt about it her poor decisions."

"I understand that. I've put my own input into her choices as well, but I still don't want t' see her hurt."

"Your heart is what makes you a strong leader," Kit explained. "You take their skills, their lives, and their hearts into consideration when making *your* decisions."

"Look," Joe jumped into the conversation, "You put us where we're strong."

"You also make sure everyone makes it out," Jacob added.

"And," Jesse continued, "you got to know each of us, where our strengths and weaknesses are, and who we work with better than others before you paired us up. She just took charge and started a dictatorship. Technically we're older, so we could pull rank, and did so a couple of times."

"But, you won't anymore," Kit corrected. "That's not your position."

"But if we don't, who will? She could have gotten us in a heap of trouble over these last few weeks," Jon pointed out. "Her attitude was disturbing at best…dangerous in a high intensity situation at worst."

"I understand that, but the authority wasn't given to you."

"If we didn't, people could have gotten hurt…or worse. I'm not going to stand by as my team members get hurt if I can help it."

"I do believe that's what Nico, Jerrod, and Hawk are working on."

"Right."

"Then, what's past is past."

"That *past* cost Amber and Terrik their lives," Jon corrected. "As well as Allie and Callie their mother."

"You can't blame that on Angel," Kit pointed out.

"Maybe…maybe not. *Should* Amber and Terrik have been on their own without a weapon? *Should* there have been someone guarding them while they waited?" Jon asked. "If we did, would they have made it out alive?"

"Those are questions only God can answer," Kit said, using the calmest tone she could muster. "You are not God. You guys cannot be second-guessing your missions. Now," she put her hand up to silence the objections, "you *do* need to talk about the mission, but only in order to find out what you can do better next time."

"Better leadership for one," Jacob said under his breath.

"What do you mean by that?" Kit asked.

"She *made* us leave," Jacob said, still upset. "We didn't want to. We *wanted* go back and get Jesse and Rachel, but she made us go. She originally said we couldn't go back, until Nico overrode her."

"Do you think maybe she did that because she wanted to get the little ones to safety, knowing they were already traumatized?"

"If so, then why wouldn't she let some of us stay?"

"Because she was trying to get as many to safety as she could."

"And it could have cost the lives of Jesse and your daughter. Her theory was that they could get out on their own. I know. I asked." Jacob said, stewing.

"She has confidence in their abilities," Kit explained.

"Glad *she* did," Jesse scoffed. "We were in major trouble. I *highly* doubt we would have gotten out without Jerrod and Jacob's help. They found the way in *and* out. Who knows if we would have *ever* found that *one* entrance? Nope. I'm not happy with her right now."

"Is that because you like Rachel and you would have been angry if anything happened to her?" Kit probed.

"What?" He looked at her, wide-eyed. "Rachel's a great girl, but –"

"I am?" Rachel looked at him in surprise.

"Look, that's not our priority right now. There are lives on the line. There's no time for romance anywhere in this," Jesse pointed out.

"When it comes to matters of the heart, passions and feelings tend to escalate unless aired out," Kit explained.

"Fine," Jesse huffed, crossing his arms. "I like Rachel. *But* that *won't* distract me from what I'm supposed to be doing."

"Really?" Rachel asked, stunned. "You like me?"

"Oh! Seriously!" Joe threw his hands in the air. "We have to deal with this *now*?"

"Like you don't like her too," Kit challenged.

"Stop," Rachel insisted, hands in the air. "Just stop. We're not doin' this, Mum."

"Why not?"

"Because this is my team."

"You're owning them now?"

Narrowing her eyes at her mother, Rachel snapped, "That's not fair."

"Fair or not, you are now claiming ownership of them," Kit said, satisfied.

Rachel rolled her eyes as she crossed her arms. "I *hate* it when you do that."

"But," Kit said with a satisfied smile, "am I right?"

"Fine! I'll lead. But I don't want the *entire* team. That's a *ton* of responsibility that I don't want."

"And I *believe* that's what the guys are working on," Kit said again.

Rachel sighed. "Fine. Look, my head hurts. We're on the four o'clock flight. I'm going t' grab a kip," she said, getting up from the table. "An' no one else talk about any type of relationship with me when I'm gone," she warned.

Kit saluted. "Yes, ma'am. We'll talk about attitudes while you're resting. Go on."

"Fine," Rachel sighed, leaving for upstairs.

"Okay," Kit started when Rachel was out of earshot, "now for the rest of you nice gentlemen, I *do* believe we have some things t' clear up."

"Look, I know we have a lot t' cover," Josh started, "but I feel that I owe Angel and apology. I jumped all over her when I shouldn't have."

"No. You were right," Angel said, walking in with the guys from the kitchen. "The guys had me listen in the kitchen so I could understand where you were all coming from, uncensored. Having said that, Jacob's right too. I should have sent a few to the ranch with the girls, while the rest of us went after Jesse and Rachel."

"Look, I have a feeling we're going t' continue t' rub each other the wrong way," Josh said. Before she could respond, he explained, "You're kind of like my spiritual sandpaper…but I wouldn't have it any other way. As iron sharpens iron, we'll keep each other in check."

"Agreed," Angel said, putting her hand out to shake his.

When he reached for it, he pulled her in for a hug. "Sorry, in this house we hug."

"Just something I'll have to get used to," Angel said, relishing in the fact that Josh hugged her. She knew she had to keep her feelings separated, so she would take the closeness when she could.

"Okay, now that that's settled, let's iron out more of the wrinkles I've been hearing about," Kit said.

"Ma'am, may I go upstairs and talk to Rachel?" Jesse asked.

"You may. I only ask that the door is left open," Kit agreed.

Running up the stairs before she changed her mind, Jesse had to guess at which room she was in. He quietly opened one of the three closed doors, to find Rachel asleep on the bed, fully clothed, on top of the covers. Lightly knocking, Jesse said, "Rachel? Are you still awake?"

"Yeah. C'mon in," she said, sitting up. Flipping the lamp on next to the bed, she leaned against her pillow with her legs crossed in front of her. "What can I do for you?"

"How's your head?"

Scoffing, Rachel explained, "That depends on the temperature of those around the station right now. As far as I last knew of their temperaments, yeah, my head hurts pretty bad."

"I'm sorry."

"Thank you, but I'm sure you didn't come up here just t' check on my head."

"I didn't," Jesse said cautiously.

"Then?"

"I don't want to sound conceited by any means, but I feel like there is a strong attraction between us."

Rachel only nodded in response.

"Can you give me a little more than a nod?"

"Well, I will admit that I like you, but I don't know you well enough yet to make an accurate assessment on you."

Pulling his legs up, he wrapped his arms around them, as he sat on the end of the bed. "I guess I wanted to address the feelings before we go any further into things."

"Probably a good idea."

Jesse nervously chuckled. "Can you give me a little bit *more*?"

"Right oh." Rachel leaned forward, resting her elbows on her knees. "I *do* like you. I actually am *very* attracted t' you, to be honest, *but* I'm not sure if it's a good idea t' start somethin' in the middle of just startin' our teams. We're also heading into heavy stuff."

"Exactly. I mean, is there *ever* really going to be a good time to potentially start a relationship in the work we do?"

"That's a good question."

"Do you have a good answer?"

"Let's go take a walk," Rachel said, getting out of bed. Sliding into her boots, they headed downstairs and out the door, avoiding eye contact with the group still at the dining room table deep in their own conversations.

Jesse chuckled at the looks they got from the table. "Okay, now that we've *really* set the rumor mill flying…"

"No doubt," Rachel agreed.

As they went out into the bright morning sunlight, Jesse remarked, "Wow. This is peaceful."

"It is," Rachel said, stopping to lean on the fence of the corral, where two horses were eating their breakfast. "Being raised here, I'm sure, was considerably different than what you faced in Mexico."

"Definitely. You're talking apples and oranges. We were in a pretty big city in Mexico. There was private school during the day, training outside of town in a field at night and on weekends. As soon as we were old enough, we started missions with the group."

"This was my first. I guess it didn't go very well, huh?"

"Actually, it went very well. We got the twins out."

"Amber an' Terrik didn't make it out, though," she said, discouraged.

"Things happen. On my first mission, we lost the husband. I kicked myself over and over. It hurt deep. My mom was actually the one who sat me down one day and read to me Ecclesiastes 3:1-8. It's a long passage, but it eased the pain in my heart. I took the next month to memorize the entire section, so on those days, days like today, I would recite it and know that I did my best...and my best was good enough."

"Okay. Go for it," Rachel said, looking out over the station. From where they were, they could see quite a bit of it.

"'*To every thing, there is a season, and a time to every purpose under heaven: a time to be born, and a time to die; a time to plant, and a time to pluck up that which is planted; a time to kill, and a time to heal; a time to break down, and a time to build up; a time to weep, and a time to laugh; a time to mourn, and a time to dance; a time to cast away stones, and a time to gather stones together; a time to embrace, and a time to refrain from embracing; a time to get, and a time to lose; a time to keep, and a time to cast away; a time to rend, and a time to sew; a time to keep silence, and a time to speak.*'"

"'*A time to love,*" they heard Kit say, as she walked up to them, and leaned on the fence beside Rachel, "*and a time to hate; a time of war, and a time of peace.*' There is a lot going on," she explained. "I would imagine at this point, the conversation between the two of you is in regards to the '*time to love*' portion of those verses?"

"Some days you can be a little *too* observant," Rachel said under her breath.

"Are you kidding? Anyone with a pair of eyes could see as soon as you two laid eyes on each other that you were attracted to each other."

"I don't know if now is a good time, though."

"Is there ever a good time for love?"

"I'm trying to be practical here."

"I know. You are quite a bit like me in that area…unfortunately," Kit admitted. "I pushed your dad away for way too long before I relented. Once I did, my heart was free to love his, and what God joined together, no man will ever tear apart."

"That's sweet, but we've not been together all that long," Rachel pointed out.

"Relationships are a tough thing to navigate."

"So is being an A.N.G.E.L.," Rachel countered.

"All I'm saying is maybe, just *maybe*, you can learn from my mistake of waiting to the point that you're almost killed before you decide to give love a shot," Kit suggested. "I almost waited a little too long. God saw fit to keep us together, though, and alive. For that, I'm grateful."

"Me too. I wouldn't be here if you didn't."

"Do I need to go? I mean – "

"No," Kit cut Jesse off. "You are as much a part of this conversation as she is. I'm just pointing out that God gave you those feelings for a reason. Maybe you should take some time to explore them before you potentially lose each other."

"I'll take that into advisement," Rachel said hesitantly.

"Okay. My job is done." Kit stood. "I need to go find the guys to see if I can help regarding Angel and *her* issues."

"Now *that* is a conversation I *would not* want to be near," Jesse said as Kit walked away. "She can be a brat when she wants to. She always feels that she's right, too. Unfortunately, she hasn't been told 'no' too often growing up, so she's learning the hard way."

Watching until her mother was out of earshot, Rachel then groaned, dropping her head onto her arms. "I hate it when she's right."

"What do you mean?"

"We may not have a lot of time," Rachel said, looking up at him. "But what I want to do is pray about it. I'm kind of scared. I've never gotten into any type of romantic relationship before, because I knew I would be an A.N.G.E.L. – that kind of puts a damper on that area."

"Know the feeling. However, since we're already both A.N.G.E.L.s, do we continue to fight it, or do we go forward?"

"We pray, an' let God tell us," Rachel said, decisively.

*   *   *

Later that day, Leah found Rachel and pulled her aside to talk with her. "I've been meanin' t' talk t' ya sooner, but you were a bit busy," Leah said, hopping onto the fence of the sheep paddock, while Rachel leaned on it with her crossed arms.

"What about?"

"Well, you remember me talkin' t' you about Finn Walker?"

"The one from your Veterinarian classes?"

"Yep. That's the one."

"Why?"

"Well, he talked t' Mum an' Dad about a month ago, an' I was waitin' t' tell you face-to-face, an' then Josh face-to-face before we announce it t' everyone."

Standing, with a grin on her face, Rachel asked, "Leah? Are ya tellin' me what I *think* you're tellin' me?"

Holding her left hand up for Rachel to see the shining diamond ring on her finger, Leah said, "That I'm engaged. Yes!"

Squealing in delight, Leah hopped down, and Rachel hugged her like she didn't want to let her go.

"I want you t' be the maid of honor," Leah said, with a thrill of excitement.

Rachel stopped smiling. Biting her lip to stop from potentially crying, Rachel shook her head.

"What? Why?"

"I don't know when I'll be back. I almost didn't make it back t'day. While God's got me in the palm of His hand, I'm not guaranteed a tomorrow. I don't get days off, or vacation time in doin' what we do either."

With her bottom lip trembling, Leah stammered, "But…I thought…are ya sayin' that you can't be in my wedding? My own twin sister won't be there?"

"I don't know for sure. I don't want you t' count on me, only t' have me potentially bail on you last minute."

"You *have* t' be able t' come!"

"I honestly don't know."

"I'm sure God'll understand," Leah said, desperate.

"When is your wedding date set for?"

"We were goin' t' make it whenever you two would be able t' make it. We were hopin' for Christmas time."

"Please don't plan around us. I don't think this is goin' t' be a matter of every six months coming home."

"You don't know what it's like for us," Leah started. "Havin' the two a' you around all our lives, it's been difficult for both Caleb an' I, let alone Mum an' Dad, t' not even know if the two a' you are alive. Don't get me wrong. We do love an' trust God, but not even knowin' if your own twin is still on this planet is extremely stressful!"

"I'm sure. But, we've known about this for a long time. We knew we were meant for a higher callin' since we were little ones. We can't control our assignments any more than we could control who got the call."

"I get that."

"Then what's your problem? I *need* you t' understand! I need you t' support an' encourage, not get upset when I can't make it back when ya need me to."

Upset, Leah explained, "We've talked since we were little girls about our weddings. We talked about having children around the same time. We had dreams that included each other."

"And, *you* will fulfill those dreams *for* me. I don't even know if love is a possibility in this line of work. Mum talked t' me about it earlier, but I don't even know," Rachel said, shaking her head. "Our lives are not our own in this job."

"I understand that, but you're tellin' me that you can't even come t' my wedding?"

"Leah, please understand."

"I think I need t' take a ride," Leah decided. "I need t' clear my head."

"My answer will still be the same when you come back," Rachel warned. "It'll be up t' God."

"Then that's Who I'll talk to," she said firmly, stomping her way to the stables.

"Well," Rachel sighed, "that went well." Looking to the Heavens, Rachel prayed, "Your will, not mine, Lord. Your will not mine."

# Chapter 16
# The Ends Of The Earth

With the final group landing in Reno, Nevada, they loaded into the vans with Derek driving, and headed for the English home. Once there, they unloaded and met up with the rest of the team.

While Casey fed those who just arrived, Jerrod asked Mark and Derek to talk. Heading out to the back porch, the men sat around the table.

"What's going on?" Mark asked. "I understand you guys had a bit of trouble over there. I also know we still have to talk to the little ones."

"We do, but that's not what I wanted to talk to you two about," Jerrod admitted. "The girls can wait a few."

"What's wrong?" Derek asked, sitting back in his seat with his arms crossed.

"Well, I tried to talk to Nico about it, but he said you two would probably understand better."

"About?"

"Well, two things actually. The first is when I was in the field, I heard about the A.N.G.E.L.s. A lot of guys would tell stories of you guys, but I dismissed it as a myth."

Mark chuckled. "Little did you know that you'd be working with us directly."

"Exactly! I mean, these are the older guys, mind you. Some of the stories were told by sons of guys you helped. However, it was dismissed by most as stories, because the A.N.G.E.L.s hadn't been seen in over twenty years. And, now I know why. You guys are legends in your own right."

"Make no mistake. It's not us. It was all the Lord. We can only do what He wills. Anything else will cause us to fall. All of the credit goes to Him and Him only."

"I understand." Jerrod nodded. "That brings me to my second thing. Did anyone tell you how they found me?"

"No. What happened?" Mark asked, concerned.

"They, um…" Jerrod sighed, looking toward the heavens for help. "I, uh," he cleared his throat. "I was ready to check out."

"Meaning?" Mark pressed.

"The nightmares," Jerrod explained, nervously fiddling with his phone. "They won't stop. They slowed while we were out, but they just won't stop."

"Nightmares from combat?" Derek asked.

Nodding, Jerrod continued, "I would see people, not really knowing if I knew them from overseas, work, or if they were really there or my imagination. Does this make sense?"

"Unfortunately, yours is not a story we haven't heard before," Mark said, leaning forward. "You *are not* alone."

"How do I make them stop?" Jerrod asked, desperate. "When will they quit? I see faces in my nightmares of people I couldn't save. They're of men and women that I couldn't do anything to help. I just had to watch them die, knowing I couldn't do anything to save them."

"You're not God. It's not your job to *save* anyone. That's God's job. Yours is to do your best. And, I'm sure you *did* do your best."

"Of course!" Jerrod looked at him, stunned that he would think otherwise.

"Then your best was good enough. You can only do what you can do."

"You don't understand. They haunt me! I can't get away from them. Don't *even* get me started on storms or fireworks.

When we were at Black Rock, to the others I may have looked like I was in complete control, but it was all instinct. With the explosions, the loss of life, and leaving Jesse and Rachel behind…" He shook his head. "There are days that I feel I'll never get away from it."

"But, you tried to get away from it that night," Derek said in understanding, sitting forward, resting his hands in front of him. Feeling the Spirit pressing him to push forward, Derek asked, "You were trying to end it all, weren't you?"

Hesitating, Jerrod debated for several moments before he admitted, "Yes."

"What happened? Why didn't it work?"

"The gun misfired," Jerrod said, slowly letting out a breath of air, as his body was on edge. "The gun misfired twice, and then your group kicked in my door."

"And, you think that's a coincidence?" Mark asked.

"No," Jerrod said firmly. "I don't believe in coincidences."

"Do you believe in God?"

"I believe in a higher power," Jerrod admitted. "And after what I saw at Black Rock, I'm pretty sure things are a lot more black and white than I gave it credit for. I now know there are real demons in this world. I know there are real angels here as well. Knowing those two facts, I can't help but think God is real too."

"So, you don't know Jesus?" Mark asked.

"I know of what is written in the Bible of Him."

"Then you know the Bible?"

"Some of it."

"Then you know some of God's Words?"

"Yes."

"Are you familiar with Psalm 37:17-19?" Derek asked. When he shook his head, Derek quoted, "*The righteous cry out, and the Lord hears, and delivers them out of all their troubles. The Lord is near to those who have a broken heart, and saves such as have a contrite spirit. Many are the afflictions of the righteous, but the Lord delivers him out of them all.'* He loves you and wants to help you. He doesn't want you to take your own life. Do you not know how important you are to Him?"

"I don't feel important," Jerrod admitted. "I feel like I let a lot of people down. I lost lives over there."

"You didn't lose any lives. They were taken from them. You did your best to help them survive what was done to them," Derek countered. "Just like you would do anything to help those Marines and soldiers, God would go to the ends of the earth to help one of His children. You don't know what you're missing, man."

"Jeremiah 29:11 says, *'For I know the plans I have for you,'* declares the Lord, *'plans to prosper you and not to harm you, plans to give you hope an a future,'*" Mark continued. "He has a plan for you. Your purpose in life didn't end once you left the service."

"It sure felt like it did. It's frustrating at times. People don't understand what it's like. To see faces of people you know are dead? To have to feel like you need to watch everyone and everything around you, wondering if anyone would potentially want to take you out? Having to sit where you can see all exits. Making sure you can see all vehicles around you, along with the potential areas where there could be IEDs? It makes you feel like you've lost your mind at times. I know you understand this stuff." Jerrod growled. "This *can't* be new information for you."

"It's not. While you lived on edge, ducking the other side overseas, we did it everywhere we went, even here in the United States. There was no safe place for us," Derek explained. "Why do you think we live out here in the middle of nowhere?"

"So you can see anyone coming."

"Exactly. But, we can't be on edge 24/7 or we'll lose our sanity. Sleep at times is a struggle," Derek admitted, "but I know where my faith is – it's in God. While it *is* there, there are days where I still can't shake feelings or nightmares. But, and this is key, that doesn't discount my faith by any measure. My brain still remembers those events. My body still feels it. When thunderstorms come, or fireworks go off, do you not think we're on edge?"

"I'm sure. I am too."

"Does that mean our faith in God is any less at those times?"

"No."

"Are you a Christian?" Mark asked.

"I think so."

"'I think so', and 'I know so' are two different things. That may be something you want to get sorted really quick, especially in this line of work."

"I think you're right. What I saw in Black Rock gave me heart failure. We also almost lost Jesse and Rachel."

"Really?" Mark asked, taken aback.

"Yes. There were these creatures in that mountain. They were…" Jerrod shuddered. "They were covered in black scales. They had yellow eyes, and these talons on the ends of their fingers that could probably cut your heart out in one swipe. They were worse than any movie I've *ever* seen!"

"I'm sure. We call them unnaturals," Derek explained.

"In John 10:10, it tells us, '*The thief comes only to steal, and kill, and destroy. I came that they may have life, and have it abundantly.*' Do you really think God wants you to take your own life?" Mark asked. "He put you here for such a time as this. He put you here to help this crew. He put you here to help us with the twins."

Jerrod took a deep breath, and then slowly let it out. "I'm sure. How did He know they would need me?"

"Because he's omniscient," Derek said, matter-of-factly. "He knows everything."

"Do you think He knows what I'm struggling with?"

"Of course."

"Do you think He'll still be able to use someone who's broken?"

"Who said you're broken?" Mark asked, taken aback.

"My brain is not where it should be. The flashbacks are strong."

"They'll still come, but we can help you work through them. You may never fully get rid of them, but talking about them may help you clear some stuff up in your mind. You see, there is still unfinished work somewhere in the recesses of your mind. That's the battle when you're asleep. It's trying to correct it. It may never be corrected, but know you are *never* alone. You never have to be alone ever again."

Looking into their eyes, Jerrod hoped they would understand. "The struggle is beyond real. I see people who I *know* are dead. I have these images that haunt me. Thankfully the nightmares haven't scared anyone…yet. But who knows if one of these nights I'm in the middle of a waking nightmare, and I scare those around me?"

"Meaning?"

"I usually wake up sweating and yelling. Sometimes I'm not even in my right mind. When I wake up, I'm standing in the middle of the room, yet I don't remember getting out of bed. I wake in a fog, feeling like I'm still in the middle of Iraq. It fades away like a mist, until I realize I'm at home and am safe. What will happen if one of these waking nightmares happens in the middle of a mission?"

"We'll make the team aware of it. They'll work with you."

"You don't think it'll scare them?"

Derek chuckled. "If they're not scared of Jacob and what he can do with simple household items, then I'm pretty sure they can handle your nightmares and dreams."

Jerrod had to smile at that one. "He's an interesting one, but I love that kid. He's got a great heart, but a unique mind. Still not sure how we found him, but I'm glad we did."

"That would be a God thing," Mark clarified. "He puts people in our lives when we need them. Look, your purpose used to be to serve the military. We need to find a new purpose for you. What about serving in the Lord's Army? What about taking what you learned in *our* military, and using it to help others in the *Lord's* Army? Some of these missions will be big, like the one you just completed. Some will be as simple as delivering food to a family in need. Now," Mark put his hand up to stop Jerrod's objection, "you'll still have your nightmares. You'll still have those visions, but we can work through some of it as it comes up."

"You're willing to do that?"

"I'm going to be honest with you."

"You haven't?"

"I have, but we're about to go deeper."

"Okay. Go ahead."

"There are things we have both seen," Mark said, gesturing toward Derek, "there are things we have experienced, that I know you would fully understand. However, in this position as an A.N.G.E.L., you can help people that you may not have the chance to otherwise. You can use those skills taught to you by the service to help people who need you. You can also use them to continue to train those around you."

"I agree."

"So you'll stay?" Derek asked, hopeful

"Yes. I'll stay. If nothing else, you guys will have your hands full with those two little ones." He chuckled. "Once they come out of shock, you're in trouble."

Derek looked him in the eyes. "I'm sure, but for now, we need to sort another issue out."

"Which is?"

"Your questionable eternal security."

"Yes. Please…and thank you."

*   *   *

Pulling different colors of spray paint from the garage shelf, Jesse made his way out to the rock. This would be one portion of the job he would have a love/hate relationship with. It was his honor to be the one to paint the names. However, when he had to paint on the rock, he knew it would be because of a loss to their team.

Heart breaking, Jesse put Amber and Terrik's name low enough for the girls to see, but high enough that they wouldn't get lost on the boulder. Once finished, he took a step back. "There," he said, satisfied.

For the Colonel's, he painted it with block letters, filling them in with camouflage paints, intertwining a set of dog tags within the letters of his name. For Amber and Terrik's names, he painted them with red, white, and blue lettering. He also painted a stethoscope looping through the middle of Amber's name to signify her medical background.

"Good job, mate," Josh said, coming up behind Jesse, resting his hand on Jesse's shoulder.

"Thanks. I don't know if I like this job or not."

"As long as ya don't have t' paint your own name, you should be good."

"Good point. I would rather not have to paint anyone else's name on this rock any time soon."

"From your mouth, t' the Lord's ears. Let's pray this won't be a habit."

"Definitely, brother. Definitely."

*   *   *

Later that night, Jerrod, Mark, and Casey sat Allie and Callie down, along with the other A.N.G.E.L.s. "This looks big," Allie, the more vocal of the two, said, looking around at the group.

"Remember when I told you that your mummy was with Terrik?" Rachel asked, taking each girl by the hand. After each girl nodded, Rachel went on, "Each of us have lost someone in our lives we were close to. At this point, I still have my mum an' dad, so do Angel, Jon, an' Jesse." When Allie furrowed her brow, Rachel pushed forward. "Your mum is in heaven, with God. She's sittin' up there watchin' the two a' you, makin' sure you are looked after. In the meantime, Jerrod will stay here for a bit, until he's needed in the field. Know God will look after you an' your Mum as well."

"Are you saying we won't ever see her again?" Allie asked, tears brimming her eyes.

"In the Bible it tells us, *'Precious in the sight of the Lord is the death of His saints.'* Know that God's heart hurts for you t'day, as does ours. I'll make you a deal," Rachel said, after quoting Psalm 116:15.

"What?" Allie asked, wiping the tears from her eyes.

"You pray for us, an' look after us, an' we'll do the same. We'll look after each other as a family should."

"Tell you what," Angel said, sitting beside Allie, "Since your parents aren't here, what if Jon, Jesse, and I share our mom and dad with you?"

"But," Allie's bottom lip quivered. She took a deep breath and shuddered. "We want Mommy."

"What if we take it from here?" Casey offered. "I think this needs a 'mom touch' to get this one sorted. You guys are trying, but I almost think you're making things worse. Let Mark and I take this," she said, effectively sending others away.

Once the room was cleared, Mark sat down, cross-legged on the floor, with Casey and the girls. "I would like to welcome you to our home. Here, you will be loved, cherished, and we will do our best to raise you for the Lord's Kingdom."

"But, what about Mommy and Terrik?" Callie asked. "When will we see them? I want to see her."

"I want to hug her," Allie added.

Letting out a slow breath of air, Casey said, "This may take a bit. You know who Jesus is, right?"

"Yes," both girls responded.

"Good. At least that gives us a place to start."

*     *     *

With such a heavy conversation going on inside the home, as others scattered about the property, Rachel headed outside into the desert and found a good-sized rock to sit on. Once landed, she pulled the baggie out of her pocket and held it up to see the seed still in tact within the bag.

"Ya know, you may want to keep a closer eye around you," Val said, climbing onto the rock with Rachel. "You didn't even see me coming. Do you mind?"

"No, go ahead. I just came out here t' get away from the heaviness a' the house. There are some heavy feelings in there. I'm just glad the anger finally cleared."

"I know what you mean," Val said, looking out at the vastness before them, as the sun began its decent behind the rocks, reflecting onto the clouds as it slowly set, setting off deep shades of reds and oranges. "I know we're going to head into heavy situations, but we need to clear all the feelings before we move on."

"I know. I'm just wondering what *is* before us. Things will only get heavier the deeper we get into this."

"In 2 Corinthians 10:3-4, it reminds us, *'For we walk in the flesh, we do not war according to the flesh. For the weapons of our warfare are not carnal, but mighty in God for pulling down strongholds.'* Our battles are not the normal battles people think of when they talk of war. While ours is a battle of the mind, it's also the spiritual battles that people only see in their nightmares. Our enemy knows us better than we know ourselves. We need to be ready."

"Oh, trust me, I know," Rachel agreed. Holding up the baggie, she asked, "Do you know what this is?"

Examining it, he said, "Actually, yeah, it's a mustard seed."

"And you know that verse?"

"Yep. *'Truly I tell you, if you have faith as small as a mustard seed, you can say to this mountain, 'move from here to there,' and it will move. Nothing will be impossible for you.'*"

"Amber gave it t' me before the mission. She knew I was nervous."

"Really? I never knew you were nervous. You always seem so confident."

"Nooooo, I was terrified out of my mind. There were two little girl's lives on the line. Little did I know, it was Amber and Terrik we should have been keeping an eye on."

"So, you think that was *your* fault?"

"No. I know I was doin' what I was supposed t' be doin'. But, knowin' it in my head, an' understandin' that in my heart, are two different things. I was ready t' give up, but Jesse wouldn't let me. He said if faith only this big could move a mountain," she said, holding it up, "then it surely would get us *out* of a mountain. And, he was right. I didn't have faith, but he did."

"We all have those mini crises. What's important is where our faith is in the process, and how we react to it. We are ordered to fight the good fight. In 1 Timothy 6:12, he tells us to, *'Fight the good fight of the faith. Take hold of the eternal life to which you were called when you made your good confession in the presence of many witnesses.'* Things may not work out how we want them to, but we know they'll work out to better the Kingdom. We have to have faith in that, or we'll lose ourselves, and all our work will be in vain. We have to know in the midst of chaos, that God is ultimately in control."

"I get that, but why did Amber an' Terrik have t' die?"

"I don't know the answer to that, but I do know the One who does, and I take comfort in knowing that He knows why, and that they're with Him right now in Heaven."

"But – "

"Stop questioning Him. There are some things we'll never know the answer to here on earth, but we may get answers when we get to heaven. However, pretty sure once we get up there, we're not going to have any more questions. Pretty sure we'll be too busy worshipping the Lord God Almighty, and won't care what else went on in this life. This is only a brief moment in time compared to thousands of years in eternity.

Look, we do the best we can while we're here. We do what we feel He wants us to do, help those who we can, and pull those out of danger that we can get to. We have to leave the rest up to God."

"I guess it never occurred t' me that we would lose our original charge."

"It's not our decision, nor is it in our power."

"But it's in God's," she said, turning toward him. "Why didn't God save them?"

"Ours is not always to know."

"Why not?"

Hearing a voice behind them, they jumped. "Because we have to trust that the Lord God Almighty knows the plan," the archangel said.

Seeing the archangel behind them, they got off the rock and faced him. With Val's eyes wide, he asked, "Are you seeing that?"

"Yes." She shrugged. "That's the archangel. Have you not seen him before?"

"No. Are you kidding? I mean, seriously! I have now actually seen both sides. This is wild!"

Glancing down at the seed, Rachel sighed. " I know you said t' trust the Lord God Almighty, an' I do. I just don't understand why they had t' die," Rachel admitted. Looking up at the archangel, she asked, "I know Amber was a Christian, but Terrik wasn't a Christian prior t' the mission. Did he become one before he was killed?"

"I am afraid he waited too late. Amber spoke with him regarding Jesus and salvation, but he chose to wait until after the mission."

"Wait a minute," Val jumped in. "Are you saying that Terrik was working with us, and he wasn't a Christian? And," he turned to Rachel, "how do *you* know?"

"I know, because I can see if someone is a Christian or isn't. I can see if they are an A.N.G.E.L. by how bright they are, or if they're on the other side," Rachel explained. "What I *don't* understand is why he didn't accept Jesus when Amber talked t' him. Knowin' everything he saw, how could he not? Also, the biggest problem I'm havin' is why God didn't protect them? Why didn't He alert us that they were even in trouble? I don't know if I can do this."

"You are not always the one *to* understand," the archangel explained. "Yours is to obey."

"I *do* honor an' trust Him," Rachel clarified. "I just don't know why Amber an' Terrik had t' die. Why didn't Terrik accept Jesus? And, I *really* don't understand why those two little girls back there are now parentless."

"These are struggles of the human heart," the archangel started. "They are also understandable. Terrik had the free will to accept the sacrificial love, forgiveness, and salvation of Jesus at any point and time. Most people would ask questions when he saw the demon at Amber's apartment, but he did not. Amber also spoke with him before they were taken, but he chose to wait until after the mission. People unfortunately make this mistake more often than I would like. Jesus wants everyone to choose Him. He wants to help them. He loves them. He waits, hoping they will make the right choice. People are not immortal. They never know when their time is gone." The archangel's heart broke as he explained, "They do not understand how much this hurts the Father. They do not understand what Jesus did for them. This is the most important decision people have to make in their lives, but some feel as if they could make it at any time. Some feel as if they can wait until the last minute. Then there are others who know what they are seeing, hearing, and feeling, and act immediately upon it. The gift is theirs to claim, but some do not claim it in time. The angels rejoice when one of His children make the choice to follow Jesus and accept His gift of salvation. We are all called to serve Him, wherever you are. In His word, Jesus reminds you that, *'For whoever wants to save their life will lose it, but whoever loses their life for Me and for the gospel will save it.'* As an A.N.G.E.L., you have chosen to give your lives for the gospel. You will have struggles. You will have heartbreak. Your lives are not your own, and you know this, but have still chosen to give it to the Lord."

"Mark 8:35 is a good reminder. I give you that," Rachel said. "I don't mean t' question you or the Lord in takin' them, but I'm strugglin'. Where's the logic in takin' 'em an' leavin' the twins by themselves."

"First of all, they are not alone. They are not only a child of God in the family of God, but they are also part of the A.N.G.E.L. family, and part of the English family now. We take care of our own."

"Why didn't God take care of Amber then?" Rachel snapped, and then realized what she said and quickly covered her mouth.

"Rachel, your heart betrays you. Your heart is tender. That is the way God made you. That is what makes you a good leader. It hurts because you operate with your heart."

"Don't know if this will help," Val jumped into the conversation, "but when I was in high school, I lost a close friend. Adelaide reminded me that Isaiah 57:1 and 2 tells us that, *'Good people pass away; the godly often die before their time. But no one seems to care or wonder why. No one seems to understand that God is protecting them from the evil to come. For those who follow godly paths will rest in peace when they die.'* We don't know what God may be saving Amber from. We don't know what was coming for her. Who knows? Whoever shot them could have taken them hostage and tortured them, but God allowed them to be killed instead. Now," Val held his hand up to stop Rachel, "I know your concern, as is mine, that Terrik didn't accept Jesus as his Savior, but we can't control that. We all want everyone to be a Christian. For one, it would make our job immensely easier. For another, we wouldn't hurt so much when someone passes that we know isn't a Christian. Your heart hurts, because you couldn't save them. Your heart also hurts, because you now have a hole in it. We were with Amber for quite a while. We all got to know her and her spirit. She struggled with accepting Jesus, but once she did, she was all in. She even encouraged you on that day by giving you the mustard seed. Keep that to remind yourself that even with a little bit of faith we can do great things, but with large amounts, we can change the world."

"Thank you," Rachel said, tightening her hand around the baggie.

"Rachel, did you *always* know why your parents made the choices they did while you were raised on the station?" the archangel asked.

"No."

"Did you always understand those choices?"

"No."

"Then why didn't you question them?"

"Because they're my parents. I figured they knew better than me."

"Why do you not trust the Lord God Almighty as much and more?

Rachel nodded, as she processed the conversation. "I get it. I don't always need t' know everything," she said. "Sometimes I just have t' trust."

"Jeremiah 17:7 and 8 says, '*But blessed is the one who trusts in the Lord, whose confidence is in Him. They will be like a tree planted by the water that sends out its roots by the stream,* "' Val quoted, " '*It does not fear when heat comes; its leaves are always green. It has no worries in a year of drought and never fails to bear fruit.*' Rachel, your strength is in the Lord. With roots that deep, nothing will take you down. You were given the gift of leadership, because those roots *are* deep, and God trusts you to lead this team through safely. People look up to you because of your strength. We know where your strength is, and where your heart is. We know you care and that you will listen with your heart and give guidance with your heart."

"The bigger plan is actually more vast than your mind can remotely comprehend," the archangel explained. "There are people's lives you cross into each and every day. Sometimes it is a blessing, such as the case with Jerrod. Sometimes it is a lesson, such as the case with Kent Shepherd, the contractor. Either way, there will always be questions of 'why' and 'why not.' Yours is not always to get that answer. I will guide you in the plans I know exist. However, it is your responsibility to follow what you know to the best of your ability. You know The Master. You have been given people who have gifts granted to them by the Spirit to help you. Do not question when one is taken. Celebrate that they had life and lived it well. Your job is to fight the good fight, helping others, until it is your time to go home."

"I understand," Rachel agreed.

"You are to lead a portion, and Angel is to lead a portion. Both will be successful if you keep your focus on the Lord. You are wise. You are a born leader. God made you that way. He created you for such a time as this. Now, go back to your teams and bond with them as a complete unit. Angel is learning. Have patience with her. Teach her. Show her."

"I will."

"That is all I ask," the archangel said before he disappeared into the skies.

"Well, pretty sure that answers most of your questions," Val pointed out.

"Definitely. Now, let's get back t' the others. We have some groups t' lead an' people t' find."

Shaking his head as they slowly made their way back to the house, Val asked, "Do you ever get used to that?"

"Nope. I'm just glad that God has so much confidence in me that He actually shows me what and who we are fightin'…and who is fightin' with us."

"Who knew they were really real?"

"I did, and now so do you. Our responsibility, though, is t' listen an' follow Him, no matter what we see."

"With the gifts He's given us, and things He's already shown us, I'm pretty sure there are big things coming."

"Right. I'm just glad God's on our side. We have the stronger power, an' in the end, we win."

"Thank the Lord!"

*    *    *

Returning to the house, Callie pulled Rachel aside to talk with her. "Do you want company?" Val asked.

"No," Callie said, shaking her head, as she pulled Rachel out to the back porch, where Allie and Angel were waiting for them.

Crouching in front of Callie, Rachel took both of her hands and asked, "What's going on?"

"We need to talk to you," Callie explained, setting Rachel down next to Angel.

"What is it?" Angel asked.

Pulling a picture she and Allie drew out of her pocket, Callie handed it to her. Rachel gasped when she saw the picture of all of the A.N.G.E.L.s. In the upper corner of the picture, there was a drawing of Amber and Terrik with angel wings, with pure yellow behind them.

"Mommy and Terrik are home," Allie explained. "You guys are our family now."

"That's right," Rachel said, kneeling in front of them. As she tucked a portion of hair behind each of their ears, she said, "And as a sister, we will look out for you as best we can."

Callie gave her a hug. "I know."

"You are lovely young ladies, and I know my mom and dad will take great care of you," Angel added.

"You'll take care of us too?" Allie asked.

"Definitely!" Angel said, giving her a hug. "You're part of our family now."

"You were brought into this home, into our lives at this moment, for a reason," Rachel explained, as tears brimmed her eyes. Pulling away, she pointed to the picture and continued, "Our lives, however long they are, are given t' us by God. When our job is done, we will join your Mum in Heaven. We'll celebrate in a place where there are no more tears. There will be no more cryin', no more pain. Until then, we will be your family."

"I know," Allie agreed.

"And know that we will do our best to love and protect you," Angel added. "Until we are called home."

Callie nodded. Wrapping her tiny arms around Rachel, she begged, "Don't leave me. Please?"

Rachel's heart broke. "Oh, love, know I will come back after every mission until it's my time to go t' the Lord."

"Please don't let it be your time anytime soon," Callie said, tears in her eyes.

"That'll be up t' God, honey. An' if He does, know you have a lot of family surroundin' you. You will *never* be alone as long as you are here. That is my promise t' you."

*   *   *

Sitting down at the dinner table that night, after prayer, while everyone dove in, Mark cleared his throat. "Seems there are some things we need to get moving."

"Such as?" Derek asked.

"Well, while I know Angel, Jon, Jesse, Josh, and Rachel are trained, pretty sure the others would like some training under their belts."

"That would be appreciated," Joe agreed.

"Definitely," Val agreed as well.

"That would be nice," Jacob said. "I ran into an interesting creature at Black Rock. I'm just glad I had the fire power to deal with him."

"We're going to teach you to use more than just fire power," Derek said confidently.

"And, I have a surprise for *you*," Casey said to Val.

"Really? What would that be?" Val asked, intrigued.

"We're going into town tomorrow to go shopping," she announced. "Now, while some of you will be getting weapons, *you* and I will be going shopping for herbs, plants, spices, and seeds," she said to Val.

"Really?" Val asked, a thrill of excitement running through him. "I get a garden?"

"Oh yeah! I'll even let you pick where you want it. The others will also be getting what they'll need for protecting the garden as well so it won't get eaten. We'll get you all set up so when you come home, you can replenish."

"That would be great!" Val grinned. "Thank you!"

"We're also going to get some computer and surveillance equipment," Mark announced. "When you guys gather the rest of your team, I want them to have somewhere to start. We'll, of course, have to add to it when they get here, giving them whatever they need and are used to using for their jobs. We'll set up the basement for them."

"You mean like a cyber cave?" Jacob asked.

"Exactly. This is a base of operations, a safe haven if you will," Mark explained. "We need to make sure everything is ready as much as possible."

"In the meantime, we'll work on training, techniques, and learning how to see what cannot be readily seen," Derek started.

"To feel what cannot be readily felt," Casey continued.

"And to know the enemies movements before even they do," Mark finished. "When you're finished, you *will* be ready. We only need you to trust us."

"We do," Joe said.

"While you do now, we're going to be asking you to do some unique things. Know it's to protect you and keep you safe. Once we're finished with you, we're confident you will be able to handle whatever the enemy has planned for you."

*   *   *

In the dead of night, the demons, led by Cassius, crawled out of their hole in the Black Rock. They crept out of the area, under the shadows of the night, deep into the Outback.

Once landed, Cassius knew he had to get his remaining troops warmth. While the Outback was hot during the day, it was bitter cold at night.

His second in command, Dorius, was killed during the explosions. His first order of business would be to appoint a new second hand man. Snapping his fingers, he lit the pile of wood, instantly starting a fire. Several of his followers started dancing, celebrating still being alive after the attack.

He let them enjoy the moment. Watching his followers, he planned in his mind just what he would do to those who destroyed his home and some of his followers. That's when it hit him. "The archangel," he said aloud.

"What, sire?" the young recruit Korax, asked, who was sitting beside him.

"This was the doing of the archangel."

"You mean the A.N.G.E.L.s are back?"

"They never left. That young group wasssss the new team. They will be a delight to take down. If we do, it will destroy the archangel." Then he added under his breath, "He has been a thorn in my flesh since the beginning of time!"

Fearing the temper of his master, Korax chose to only nod in response.

Studying the flames as they danced along the wood, Cassius knew what he had to do. Standing, he cleared his throat. As his followers settled, Cassius walked around the fire, over and over, speaking with a newfound fervor, "With Dorius gone, I am promoting Korax into his position." Cheers were heard throughout the group for the newly promoted Korax. "Yesterday we lost many of our numbers. Those A.N.G.E.L.s invaded our home. They blew up our sanctuary. They thought they killed us, but we have and will recover. Our numbers are strong. We *will* recover from this. We will recruit and become strong once again. And then we *will* take vengeance on those who thought they could bring us down!"

Cheers were heard from around the group. Pushing forward with new found momentum, Cassius went on, "I swear to you, as your leader, we will not stop until every last one of those A.N.G.E.L.s are brought down to their knees. We will not rest until each of those little beasts are wiped from this earth!"

# Chapter 17
# Fight The Good Fight

The group lined up on the firing line, with the targets out by three yards. Mark did a small safety course on guns before he said, "Now, there will be times, as Jesse and Rachel found out, where your accuracy will be crucial. The amount of ammo you have is not limitless, so you need to make each shot count."

"Yes, sir," the group responded.

"This is just an evaluation to see who needs training in what areas. Okay, put on your safety glasses and ear protection. Go one at a time so we can keep track of who is hitting what target."

"Thanks for the vote of confidence," Jacob said, tongue in cheek.

While each member fired, Mark, Derek, and Jerrod kept track of where each shot landed. Moving the targets back to seven yards, Mark then went and compared notes with Jerrod and Derek. "All right," he said, "Go another round." After they went another round, they compared notes again.

"Can I?" Jon asked his dad while the three men talked.

Mark chuckled. "Go ahead."

"All right!" Jon said, and emptied his magazine by making a smiley face on the target.

"That's awesome!" Jacob laughed.

After moving the targets one more time to fifteen yards, Mark said, "Okay, one more time. Same order." After they each went and compared notes, Mark stood in front of the group. "Okay, you all did pretty good. Joe and Val need from seven yards on, and add Jacob for the fifteen-yard. You're a good shot Jacob, we just want to sharpen that a bit more."

"Thank you, sir," Jacob said, appreciatively.

"I don't really care for guns," Val admitted.

"But, one day that may save your life," Derek pointed out.

"I used to feel the same way," Casey explained. "I used to be a paramedic before joining this crew. I would help save lives, not take them. One day, however, that gun saved my life. It may do the same for you some day."

"All right," Val agreed. "Show me what needs to be done."

*     *     *

The next assessment was on knives. With targets about eight feet away, four at a time, they would throw three knives.

"Please be careful with these," Derek said. "They aren't butter knives."

"Yes, sir," they responded.

They again did two rounds. Rachel, Jesse, Val and Jacob hit their targets with extreme accuracy. "Okay," Derek said, taking the knives from the targets. As he talked, Jerrod and Mark moved them back to twelve feet. "Okay, let's go another round. Same order." After they were finished, as Derek pulled the final set from the boards containing silhouette targets, he said, "Everyone but Rachel, Jesse, and Jacob, will need further training in knives."

"I tend to like to use my knives in closer proximity, if you know what I mean," Angel explained, as her face flushed in embarrassment at her name not being called.

"The idea, is to not let them get so close," Derek pointed out, causing her face to go even redder than it already was.

Angel nodded. "Right."

"Okay, next?" Derek asked Mark.

"They're not going to like this one," Mark said hesitantly.

"What's next?" Val asked nervously. "I know we had a crash course for those two weeks. Are you saying we're going to be training even harder?"

"Oh yeah. You need to be ready. The training you got was a temporary fix. You guys need to be able to handle yourselves if you get separated. We can't send you out to the field in good conscience with what we see here. Not saying you're bad," he quickly added. "We just want to have the confidence of knowing when you are sent out that you'll come back."

"Scary stuff, huh?" Joe sighed, rubbing the back of his neck.

"Scary stuff," Mark confirmed.

"Okay then, what's next?"

"Hand-to-hand."

"Really?" Val squeaked. "I guess I can't continue to stay a pacifist in this, can I?"

"You *can*," Derek said cautiously. "But you may not like the end result."

Val sighed. "Fine."

"We'll keep an eye out for you," Jacob assured him. "You hang back with me, and we can just blow stuff up."

"All right, Master Blaster, what happens if they catch you off-guard like at Black Rock, only you don't have anything to light them on fire?" Jerrod asked.

"I do this," Jacob said, and threw the knife, landing center-mass on the silhouette.

"Fair enough. But, what happens if you don't hear them? If I remember the story, two *girls* took you down when they first found you, and almost took you out."

"That was two on one!" Jacob said in his defense, regarding when Rachel and Angel first found him in the desert.

"Think you can take me by yourself?" Rachel challenged.

With his cheeks burning red, Jacob said, "No. I can't fight a girl."

"They can possess girls," Derek pointed out. "You may have to do just that."

"Are you afraid?" Rachel asked. "We're about the same strength, so I don't think it's a strength issue."

"No. It's that you're a girl."

"Wanna take me first?" Jon asked.

"Uhhhhh no. I'll pass."

"Tell you what," Mark said, thinking through his options. "We're going to play a game."

"I like games. What are we talkin' about here?" Joe asked.

"Casey?" Mark asked. "Remember the Challenger - Aggressor game from the Outback?"

"Yep. I'll go get it," Casey said, and disappeared into the house.

"What's she going to go get?" Joe asked.

"While we normally play this at night, we're going to go a round with everyone one time during the day. After that, they'll all be at night from that point forward."

"How do we play?" Val asked, intrigued.

"Here," Casey said, handing him a thick neck scarf for a blindfold.

"Oh no," Rachel groaned, dropping her head, shaking it, while resting her hands on her hips. "I *hate* this game."

Mark chuckled again. "That's right. You were trained by Hawk, Charlie, Ethan, and company. Weren't you?"

Rachel nodded. "Yes. And I know where this is going."

"Josh, were you as well?"

"Yes," Josh groaned, rolling his eyes.

"Then you guys will start at night. There's no reason to give you a dry run."

"Gee. Thanks," Josh said under his breath.

"What is this?" Jacob whispered to Rachel.

"Something you're not goin' t' like," Rachel whispered back. "Just do your best."

"Gee. Thanks."

"Jacob, you're first," Mark said.

"Seriously?" Jacob said with a frown. "Why can't Val or Joe go first? Joe said he liked games."

"You *may want* t' go first," Rachel pointed out. "After you see it, you'll buck it even worse."

"Fine," Jacob sighed, shaking his head. Walking over to Mark, he stood there with his arms crossed. "All right. I volunteered for this job. Train me, oh wise one. What do you want me to do?"

"Having a willing spirit is crucial, and I appreciate that," Mark said, resting his hand on Jacob's shoulder. "Take off your shoes and socks, and put them on the deck."

Jacob raised an eyebrow. "You *are* aware we're in the middle of the desert, right?"

"Try doing this in the middle of the searin' hot sands of the Outback?" Rachel pointed out.

"Fair enough," Jacob said before he ran his shoes and socks to the deck.

"Val and Joe, you two head up to the deck. You guys are next," Mark said. Once they were on the deck, Mark blindfolded Jacob. As he spun him in circles, the group fanned out in a circle, surrounding him. Mark then nodded toward Rachel. She was going to be the aggressor.

Rachel slipped her shoes and socks off and stepped into the circle. Mark then stopped Jacob and let him get his bearings, with his blindfold still on. "Okay," Mark said, with his hands on Jacob's shoulders to steady him, "In a few minutes, I'm going to let you go. You will keep the blindfold on the entire time, until I tell you to take it off. I have already picked the person you will be fighting."

"With a blindfold on? How is *that* fair?" Jacob growled.

"We have to learn to see what cannot be readily seen," Derek reminded him. "You have to be able to also feel what the enemy is going to do, even if you can't see him. Remember Ephesians 6:12, *'For our struggle is not against flesh and blood, but against the rulers, against the authorities, against the powers of this dark world and against the spiritual forces of evil in the heavenly realms.'* Does that sound like someone who will play fair?"

"No," Jacob admitted.

"You can't always rely on your knives and explosives. You never know where they'll show up," Casey pointed out. "Or *who* they'll show up as."

"We're going to be giving you verses of encouragement along the way, so you learn to rely on His words. They will trigger in your mind when you face adversity out there in the field. Trust us. We've been doing this for a while," Mark said.

"I know. I just don't like that I can't see anything. How am I supposed to fight what I can't see?" Jacob asked.

"The quieter you become, the more you'll hear," Josh explained.

"Easy for *you* to say!" Jacob snapped.

"Are you ready?" Mark asked.

"No."

"Philippians 4:7," Josh said, *"And the peace of God that surpasses all understanding will guard your hearts and minds in Christ Jesus."*

"That's fine. But who'll protect my body?" Jacob asked nervously.

"First Peter 5:7," Rachel said from the other side of the circle from Josh. *"Cast all your anxiety on Him, because He cares for you."* Afterward, she moved to the opposite side of the circle as quietly as she could in her bare feet.

"All right," Jacob said, putting his hands in the air. "I'll be quiet and listen."

"We'll give you about thirty seconds to acclimate and get used to the silence," Mark explained. "Pray in your head to the Lord for clarity of mind, and for Him to open your eyes."

Jacob cocked his head to the side. "Even though they're covered?"

"Yes," Mark chuckled. "Even though your eyes are covered. He can show you what's not there. Let the Spirit guide and direct your mind and body."

"Okay," Jacob said, standing in the middle of the group, still blindfolded. As Rachel slowly moved around the inside of the circle, looking for the best spot to throw the first punch, Jacob took a couple deep, cleansing breaths. He imagined those who formed the circle. He remembered Val and Joe on the porch. He smelt the desert sands, along with the heavy sweat of each of the members from being in the blistering sun all day.

The longer he stood, the crisper his other senses became. Hearing the noises of the creatures of the desert, it was almost deafening at how quiet it was. In this day and age, with media playing 24/7, along with social media, and cell phones, that was not the norm.

That's when he heard it. To his left, he heard a pebble move. Then he heard the foot crunch into the sand. "Lord, help me," Jacob said, feeling his own heart pounding in his ears. Another crunch to his right. He spun toward his right with his hands in front of him. "I don't know who you are, but I can hear you." Then, looking toward Heaven, Jacob asked God, "Please let me see what I cannot see?"

Mark nodded toward Rachel to take the first swing. She nodded before she ran behind him and kicked him in the lower back.

Letting out a yell, Jacob was propelled forward, and then dropped to his knees with his hand on his lower back. "Ow! Why would you actually hurt me?" he snapped.

"The enemy will not take any mercy on you," Casey said. "Remember Psalm 18:39, *'For you have girded me with strength for battle; You have subdued under me those who rose up against me.'*"

"Listen to Ephesians 6:18," Jon said, *"With all prayer and petition pray at all times in the Spirit, and with this in view, be on alert with all perseverance and petition for all the saints."*

"Sure. Easy for you to say."

"You can do this, Jacob," Jon said. "Listen with your body."

"What do you mean by that?" Jacob snapped.

"Pray."

As he was about to talk, Rachel kicked up, hitting Jacob in the jaw. Yelling, he rolled on the ground in pain, blood dripping from his mouth. Rachel looked to Mark, who held his hand for her to wait.

"Jacob," Mark said, crouching next to him.

"I *really* don't like this game," Jacob growled. "And when I find out who it is, I'm going to kill them!"

"Jacob, listen to my voice," Mark said.

"I *seriously hate* this game!"

"Jacob, I need you to concentrate on my voice. Block everything out, including the pain." As Jacob sat up, resting his arms on his knees breathing heavily, he nodded for Mark to go ahead. In a calm and soothing voice, Mark continued, "In Hebrews 12:1 & 2 we are reminded, *'Therefore, since we have so great a cloud of witnesses surrounding us, let us also lay aside every encumbrance and the sin which so easily entangles us, and let us run with endurance the race that is set before us, fixing our eyes on Jesus, the author and perfecter of faith, who for the joy set before Him endured the cross, despising the shame, and has sat down at the right hand of the throne of God.'"*

"And that helps me *how*?"

"Jacob, you are not alone in this. As a child of God, you will *never* be alone. You not only have all the Saints of the past cheering you on, but more importantly, Jesus is with you wherever you go. He will *never* leave you or forsake you. That's a promise."

"Right. But how does that help me here?"

"They're cheering you on. They *want* you to succeed. *We* want you to succeed. You can do this. I wouldn't have picked you first if I didn't think you could handle this."

"All right. Would you like to give me any hints on how to beat this?"

"I'm going to give you a few minutes. It will feel like an eternity, but it's not. In those minutes, I want you to pray. I want you to ask for the Lord to show you who is fighting you, and where they are before they come for you again. Can you do that? You have to have faith, *knowing* the Lord will help you."

"Yes, sir," Jacob said resolutely.

"You got this," Mark said, and retook his place in the circle. "Okay, Jacob, listen carefully to the words of Romans 5:3 & 4. *'And not only that, but we also glory in our tribulations, knowing that tribulation produces perseverance.'* You have perseverance charging all through you, Jacob. You are a survivor. This is just a test. You *will* persevere *and* prevail! The verse goes on, *'knowing that tribulation brings about perseverance; and perseverance, character; and character, hope.'* You can do this. You are not alone. The others are praying for you," he said, and those in the circle immediately joined hands and bowed their heads in prayer.

"Now we need *you* to believe in Jesus, the Spirit, and God, that They will help you in this test. It will prove your character. It will also give you hope for your future."

Jacob only nodded in response as he prayed for clarity of mind, sensitivity in hearing and feeling, and sight, even though he was blindfolded. That's when he saw it. "Rachel!" Jacob said in shock. "Is *Rachel* my aggressor?"

With a smile, Mark simply said, "There ya go. Keep it up. Rach, give him a couple minutes before you begin again. He's learning."

She only nodded in response, as she cautiously moved around the circle. Whatever direction she moved, he would spin toward her with his hands in front of him. Pride swelled in her, as she knew he unlocked a power he didn't even know existed. As much as she hated this game, she knew the benefits were invaluable.

After a couple of minutes, Mark nodded toward Rachel to go ahead. She knew she couldn't go behind him, because he would continuously turn in every direction she moved. "Sorry, Jacob," she whispered. Seeing him brace for impact, she kicked his shoulder with her heel. When he went back, she waited a moment for him to get back up. As he wavered in his step, holding his shoulder, she kicked his stomach. Sending him back a couple of steps, she knew she took his breath away. "Find me, Jacob," she whispered. "You can do this."

With Rachel sweeping with all her might behind his knees, he went to the ground, legs in the air. When she went to kick him in the head, he grabbed her foot at the ankle. Standing, she hopped to keep her balance. Triumph written all over him as he held her ankle tightly, it was short-lived.

Knowing he had a good hold on her left foot, she jumped, swinging her right foot into his lower back where she originally hit him. He let out another yell as he let go of her foot and dropped to the ground.

"Blast it!" Jacob grumbled. "That's it!" He jumped toward where he knew Rachel to be. Just missing her, he hit the ground, hard. "Umph!" Spitting the dirt and blood out of his mouth, he stood, facing where he knew Rachel was. Standing tall, he waited for her to make her move. "You are mine now!" He sneered.

Facing Jacob, she knew he was getting sharper with each minute. She had to take him down in order for the challenge to be over. Those have always been the rules. One person had to give. She knew Jacob well enough to know he wouldn't give up easily. She could hear the groans from the deck of Val and Joe, knowing they would be next. Then, turning back to Jacob, she took a slow breath of air and let it out just as slowly, focusing on where to take him down in the kindest way possible.

"Any day now, Rachel," Jacob taunted. "Unless you're scared that *I'll* take *you* down."

"You asked for it," Rachel said, not giving him mercy. Dropping to the ground, she swept his ankles out from under him. When he was on the ground, she got behind him, and put him in a sleeper hold, but didn't use pressure yet. "Say you give," Rachel ordered, "and I'll stop."

"Never! You'll have to knock me out first!" he shouted.

When he tried to kick his legs up, Rachel ducked to the side, and then tightened her grip around his neck, beginning to knock him out. "Give, Jacob."

"No!" he shouted as he squirmed to get free.

"Jacob, I don't want t' knock you out, but I will," Rachel threatened.

"Let me go, Rach!" Jacob said, his face turning bright red. "Give!"

"No!"

Rachel tightened her grip. "You're going t' sleep."

"I…don't…give," Jacob said before his arms dropped to his sides, unconscious.

"Done," Mark announced.

As Mark and Derek picked Jacob up and carried him up to the deck to lay him down on the bench, Mark said to Val, "You're next."

Sighing, Val said, "Can I just give now?"

"No," Derek laughed. "Trust me, everyone will get theirs at some point through the next several weeks."

Val's face went pale. "*Weeks?*"

"Yes. You might as well get it over with. Just keep in mind the lessons that Jacob missed, and try not to get yourself knocked unconscious."

"Yes, sir," Val mumbled, as he headed down to the circle without his shoes and socks.

Mark covered Val's eyes with the scarf, as he nodded toward Angel. Deciding to take it easy on the guys for their first time, he decided the girls would be the easier ones to take them on.

After he spun Val, and Angel got her shoes and socks off, Mark stopped Val. Down near his ear, he asked, "Did you hear everything I told Jacob?"

Val only nodded, already praying in his head for sight from the Spirit, as he could only see black due to the scarf.

As Mark took his spot in the circle, Casey said, "Val, keep Joshua 1:9 close to you through this. *'Have I not commanded you? Be strong and courageous. Do not be frightened, and do not be dismayed, for the Lord your God is with you wherever you go.'* You can do this!"

"Yes, ma'am," Val said, taking deep breaths. To his surprise, Val could slowly see the circle of people in his mind come into focus, even though his eyes were still covered. He could see Angel moving silently around the circle. Thanking the Lord for the gift of spiritual sight, he knew what he had to do.

"Have they started yet?" Jacob asked, groggy, sitting up next to Joe.

"Not yet," Joe said. "Dude, you got the tar beat outta you. You okay?"

"Yeah. I'll get her next time."

"Shush you two!" Val snapped.

"Sorry, man," Jacob said. "You got this, though."

"Thank you. Now, shush!" Seeing Angel to his left, he continued to stare straight ahead. When Angel went to jump at him in a kick, Val took a step back just in time, and Angel flew across the circle, hitting the ground with a thud.

"What?" Angel looked at him, stunned. When she looked toward Mark, he shrugged, and gestured for her to try again. Getting off the ground, she brushed herself off, angry. *How dare he get the better of her! Rachel took hers down, Angel had to do the same to Val or she would look bad, especially considering that Val was the more passive of the two.* Silently, she circled Val, looking for the best option.

"Second Timothy 4:7," Jesse said. "I'm going to replace the 'I' in this verse with 'you,' so you can hide this in your heart. *'You have fought the good fight, you have finished the race, you have kept the faith.'* You are strong already, Val. Keep focused! Finish this race. You got this."

"God will lead me," Val said confidently. Following Angel's every move in his mind, he knew exactly where she was at each moment thanks to the Spirit.

Spinning, she went to kick him behind the leg, when he spun and grabbed her ankle. Jamming his elbow into the back of her knee, she let out a howl of pain before crumbling to the ground.

"Angel?" Jesse asked.

"He's mine!" She sneered, getting off the ground. Limping, she punched toward his head. When he went to grab her hand, she slammed her foot into his back. When he went down, she grabbed him by the neck. "Give!" She growled.

"I give," Val said, putting his hands in the air. "I don't want to end up unconscious."

"I'll let you get away with it this time," Mark said, slipping the blindfold off as he crouched beside him. "Mainly because I think Rachel needs to take a look at Angel's knee."

"I'm fine!" Angel grumbled.

"Just let me take a look. I'm an RN, remember?" Rachel pointed out.

"No!" Angel snapped.

"Angel!" Casey looked at her wide-eyed. "What's wrong with you? You know full well how this works."

"I do, but…" Angel's voice trailed, as she turned away, still holding tightly to her leg. She wanted to cry. She wanted to yell and scream. She wanted the pain to stop. However, she was mortified that Rachel took hers out, and she had to trick hers in order to win. And the fact that he gave so easily made her even angrier.

"At least let me put ice on it," Rachel coaxed.

"Don't touch me!"

"Angelina!" Mark warned.

"Fine," she said, letting Jon and Jesse help her up to the deck, while Rachel went to grab a bag of ice. "I can't believe I get the one who has spiritual sight!"

"Relax," Jon coaxed. "You'll get your turn to try it again on another day. Pretty sure you're done for today."

"Just leave me alone," she said, snatching the bag of ice from Rachel.

"You're welcome," Rachel said sarcastically before going back down to the group.

Jesse followed Rachel down to the circle. When he got down there, he stood beside Casey. "Mom?"

"What?" Casey asked.

"Little Miss Priss is up there pitching a fit and being rude."

"Jesse!"

"Seriously! She needs to stop. If she's leading a team, she has to get this competition stuff out of her. She is being rude because Rachel took her man down, but she couldn't."

"Mark, why don't you take this one?"

"Oh, trust me," Mark stood, "she doesn't *want* to deal with me right now. I heard every word."

"Got it," Casey said. Once she got up to the deck, she sent Joe down for his turn, along with Jacob down to watch on a rock while he recovered. "All right. You want to tell me what's going on?"

"I *did* this training," Angel started. "On the first time, *he* goes and can see already. Of course it's on me, and not on Rachel, the golden one."

"Stop! Rachel's not in competition with you. There are two units, but you must work as one."

"I get that."

"Then why do you keep trying to one-up her?"

"Because she's better than me at just about everything…prettier too."

"James 3:16 says, *'For where jealousy and selfish ambition exist, there will be disorder and every vile practice.'"*

Angel rolled her eyes. "I know what the Bible says."

"Obviously not, because Proverbs 14:30 reminds us that, *'A tranquil heart gives life to the flesh, but envy makes the bones rot.'* You are rotting on the inside. Anyone can see that. You are a beautiful young lady too, but you look ugly to those who can see into your heart. You know, like Josh."

"What?" Angel gulped, as the color drained from her face. "How did you know I liked him?"

Casey sighed, shaking her head. "*Everyone* can see it, including Josh. Unfortunately for you, I can tell he's a man who looks deeper than the surface. And, if that's the case, right now you don't have a prayer."

"What does *that* mean?"

"You are ugly on the inside right now."

Angel scoffed. "I can't believe you're saying this!"

"You *can* and normally *do* have a beautiful heart, but you're choosing to show your ugly side right now. In doing so, you won't have to worry about Satan, Cassius, or whoever else comes at you guys to take you out. You'll take your own team out all by yourself from the inside."

"Mom!"

"Mark 7:21-23," Casey continued, despite Angel covering her ears, "'*From within, out of the heart of men, proceed the evil thoughts, fornications, thefts, murders, adulteries, deeds of coveting and wickedness, as well as deceit, sensuality, envy, slander, pride and foolishness. 'All evil things proceed from within and defile the man.'* Or in this case, woman," Casey finished.

"I am *not* taking my team down from the inside," Angel defended herself.

"Yes. You are. They have to trust you, but from your actions today I highly doubt they'll trust you right off. They'll be keeping an eye on you. I know the archangel and God are as well."

Angel dropped her head. "He already talked to me once," she admitted.

"Psalm 73:26 says, *'My flesh and my heart may fail, but God is the strength of my heart and my portion forever.'* You need to rely on God and not on yourself. You *are not* in charge of anything He hasn't given you. You are His servant, but you're acting like you're the one in control. You have been given a gift, obviously so has Val. He can see things with the help of the Spirit. We haven't quite run into that one yet. I think that's pretty cool. While Rachel can tell what side they're on, he can see what God shows him. I would think that would be a good thing."

"Why did this gift have to hurt, though?" She asked, rubbing her leg

Casey smirked. "Because, my dear, you are a very stubborn young lady. Pretty sure you got that one from me." Nudging Angel, she reminded her, "We all have to start somewhere. This will be a test for you on many levels. The lesson, in particular, is the fact that there's a young lady who's stronger and faster than you."

"Not to mention a better leader," Angel added. "*And* better looking."

"Not true! Beauty is in the heart. Right now, though, that *is* true, because you're heart is a little on the dark side."

"I know."

"Growing up, because your eyes are green and you're fair-skinned, the guys had their eyes on you as soon as they saw you. You were different. You stood out."

"This is true. But why is it when I actually find one I like, why can't I get his attention?"

"You mean Josh?"

"Yes." Angel sighed. "He won't even look at me."

"That's because your heart is dark. Your brother already told me that your heart attitude was suffocating him. He said your jealousy was irritating, and your anger was overpowering."

"He *would*."

"You know he can feel the emotions of those around him. When you were angry, there was a reason he didn't say a verse. He was supposed to, but he was trying to block your anger and frustration. You could see him fighting it with everything he had."

"Good for him."

"Seriously, Angel!" Jon snapped from the circle, where Jesse was fighting Joe. "You about done?"

"Yes," Angel said, narrowing her eyes at Jon.

"Mark? Honey?" Casey called to him. "I do believe I need back up, and Angel needs to be away from Jon for a bit. He needs a break."

"Got it," Mark called back. Before he left the group, he said, "Keep going." Once up to the porch, He grabbed Angel by her elbow, taking her to the basement, where she would be able to punch her feelings away on the punching bag. Unfortunately, her leg hurt, so she half-limped, half-ran to keep up with her Dad. "Can you please slow down?"

"Nope. You need to get that anger out of you before you go anywhere."

"I will. Just slow down for now. Please?"

"You're not being fair to anyone out there. I am extremely disappointed by your behavior. If this is how you have been acting the entire time, I'm surprised your brothers didn't leave you somewhere. You're going to sort this out, and you *will* do it tonight."

"Yes, she will," the archangel said from the basement, as they came down the stairs.

Looking at him, in wide-eyed surprise, Angel said, "You're here?"

Crossing his arms, the archangel sternly, but lovingly said, "Yes, my dear. You and I have to have a *serious* discussion."

*   *   *

After dinner that night, the group, minus Angel who was still in the basement with the archangel, headed outside to do more work with the challenger/aggressor game. With each round they did, the individual members got stronger. Pretty soon, those new to the game connected with the Spirit, which made the matches longer and a lot more painful as the challenger fought back.

Later that night, after the games, they were on the back porch eating ice cream cones, relieved to be done for the day.

"Remind me to never make you mad," Jacob said to Rachel.

Laughing, she asked, "Why?"

"Because you can kick my behind into next Tuesday with your eyes closed. As a matter of fact, you proved that twice tonight," he said, rubbing his chin. She punched him when she was blindfolded, and Jacob was the one sneaking up on her. "Even blindfolded, you took me out."

"You'll get there," she encouraged.

"Hey, Rach, can we go talk?" Josh asked.

"Sure," she said, and followed him off the porch into the house. Once they were in his room, he closed the door. "This looks serious," Rachel remarked, with a smirk.

"It is," he said, and her smile faded. "I need help. Let me correct that to I need *your* help, Rach."

"Really?" She sat back, leaning on her hands with her legs stretched out in front of her.

"I *really* like Angel, but I don't think I can handle her attitude anymore. I don't know what t' do. I can speak just about any language known t' man, thanks to God. I can wrestle the best of them. Some men are even afraid of me. I can even hold my own in a match of logic and whit with Pete, and the aggressor challenge against Jon. While I have all that understandin', strength, an' logic in me, what I *can't* figure out is why Angel's being such a brat right now."

"Because she likes you."

"I don't understand. If she does, then why doesn't she let her heart shine through? Why is she hidin' it with all of that ugly?"

"She's strugglin'," Rachel explained. "She's been downstairs with the archangel all day. I'm sure she'll be up soon enough, but she has t' work it all out before he lets her leave. If her team will have any amount of confidence in her, she'll have t' get rid of that pride, anger, an' jealousy."

"Too true," Josh said, deep in thought. After a moment, he asked, "Do you think she's capable of gettin' rid of all of it?"

"I do. With God, all things are possible. You know that."

"I do. I've just never run across this before."

"We have. You just never saw it in someone who you liked as well."

"What do *you* think of her?"

"I think she's lookin' in the right place t' find answers," Rachel said cautiously. "And when she's done wrestlin', she'll come out better in the end if she stays focused on God. I would caution you t' watch an' make sure it sticks. She went after Val with a vengeance. Her problem was that he could see her an' wouldn't take her beating."

"Her problem was also that you choked your challenger out."

"I gave him an option." She shrugged. "Jacob just chose t' keep going until he passed out. If I didn't, he could have seriously hurt himself."

"I'm sure. He's a tough little guy."

"Careful using those words around him. He's startin' t' get a complex."

"I know. I do like him, though."

"I know. Um," Rachel tucked a portion of her hair behind her ear as she sat up. Wrapping her arms around her legs, she asked, "What, um, what do ya think of Jesse?"

A smile slowly formed on his face as he exclaimed, "You like him, don't you?"

"Yep."

"I approve wholeheartedly! He's a great man of God. Mum an' Dad would approve as well."

"Well, we decided to pray about it, *but…*" her voice trailed.

"But *what*?"

"Well, he kissed me in the caves."

"Really? You were both covered in dirt!"

"So."

"If he kissed you then, then he's *definitely* a keeper!" Josh burst out in laughter as Rachel hit him with a pillow. "He still kissed you when you were stinky an' everything."

Hitting him with the pillow again, she explained, "He did it t' distract me."

"Yeah. Uh-huh!"

"Brat!" Rachel yelled, jumping on him, as the pair dropped to the floor, wrestling. "Give!" Rachel yelled, with her legs locked around his neck.

"I would *never*!" Josh shouted back.

The door flew open, and everyone rushed in at the yelling. "What's going on?" Mark demanded.

"Just wrestlin'," Rachel said innocently, as she released Josh.

"Can she seriously take you down?" Jesse asked, impressed.

"No," Josh said, getting up off the floor. "She does her best, but she can't take me out."

Jumping on the bed, Rachel then jumped on his back, taking him back to the bed in a sleeper hold.

"Let…go…Rach!" Josh squeaked.

"Say that I win!" she shouted, tightening her grip.

"No," he said, turning them side-to-side until he rolled onto his feet and flipped her onto the other bed over his head. When she went to get up, he grabbed her in a headlock. "You give?"

"Actually, yes. I know you," she said, and he released her. "Good idea."

"Are you two done?" Mark asked, with a smirk.

"Sure. For now," Rachel relented. "We spar all the time."

"Well, save it for the games."

"Yes, sir."

"Hey, all," Angel said, walking into the room. When people moved out of the way, she made her way to the center.

Seeing her eyes red from crying, Rachel asked, "Are you okay?"

"Not really," she admitted. "The archangel and I have been wrestling all day. I know I screwed up big time. You guys even gave me a second chance, and I blew it. Do you think you guys could forgive me for being a jerk?"

"Maybe," Rachel said. "Is this goin' t' stick, or is it temporary again?"

"I deserved that."

"It's genuine," Jon said. "I can feel it. She's extremely remorseful."

"Okay then. I accept your apology," Rachel agreed.

"Me too," Jon said. "Just stay focused on the good, huh?"

"I will," Angel agreed.

"Then, we're willing to give you another shot," Jon said, giving her a hug "Just don't blow it again."

"I won't."

*     *     *

After several weeks of training, setting up the basement, and planting the garden, Mark sat everyone down in the study for a meeting. While Casey put Allie and Callie to bed for the night, he started, "All right, pretty sure you are all now up to the tasks that God has intended for you. However, we have a bit of an issue."

"What's that?" Jacob asked.

"You only have half of your teams."

"Really? Who are we missin'?" Josh asked. "Pretty sure we have quite a diverse group here as it is."

Pulling the list from the safe in the wall, Mark unrolled it. Scribbling on two pieces of paper, he split the list in two before handing one to Rachel and one to Angel.

Rachel scanned the paper, and asked, "Who's going with me?"

"And, who's with me?" Angel asked.

"That, young ladies, are up to them," Mark explained. Glancing at the group of guys, he asked, "How do you guys want to do this?"

"I think we should be separated," Jon volunteered. "I'll go with Angel if Jesse wants to go with Rach?"

"I agree," Jess said, appreciatively, as he took his spot beside Rachel, while Jon moved next to Angel.

"Nothing personal, but I like working with Rachel," Jacob said, moving next to Jesse.

"I'll go with Angel," Val said, moving next to Jon.

"Josh?" Mark asked.

Debating in his head for a few tense moments, Josh moved next to Angel. "I know Rachel's covered."

"What's that mean?" Jon asked.

"I've seen her in action," Josh explained. "I know she's got this. And what she doesn't, I know *your* brother will protect her. Therefore, I'm protecting *his* sister."

"Gotcha. Fair enough," Jon said, giving him a fist bump.

"If you don't mind, I'd like to go with Rachel," Joe said. "I think there should be a person on each side who has dreams or visions."

Angel nodded. "I agree."

"Jerrod?"

"Well, I think if they're just going to gather teammates, that I may sit out for a couple of these. If there's a big one, let me know and I'll meet you wherever you need. I'd like to be considered on Rachel's team, mainly to keep the Master Blaster in line," he said with a smirk as he nudged Jacob.

"That'll work," Mark agreed.

"In the meantime, I'll work with you guys regarding the little ones. I think they need a familiar face around for a bit longer."

"Good thinking," Mark agreed. "You guys understand that half of the support teams are going to one group, and the other half to the other group. So, Rachel, if you notice on your list, you're going to Ireland, Egypt, and Jordan, while Angel's group is going to England, Russia, China, and Japan. With Josh being the linguist, I feel that's the best way to separate the assignments. Angel's group is picking up two more field agents for her team in Russia and one in England. Once you pick them up, that'll even the two teams a bit more. Now," he held his hand up to stop the conversations that erupted, "none of the new teammates know of any of your past. This is a clean slate. You were all called for a reason. You were called to fight the good fight for the Kingdom. This is not a position that will land you with fame and fortune. You'll never be on television, nor will you be a startling success in the eyes of the world. You will not lead a normal life in this job. You will operate in the shadows. But, you will receive blessings beyond measure for what you do. There's a new army rising up all over this world – The Lord's Army. You are all a part of this. Your job is to bring those into this to help others. The Spirit has given you an assignment. You are to free those who are bound in spiritual chains. You will help provide what is needed for those who are His. You will fight some literal battles, as well as spiritual ones. You will literally take on the gates of Hell. I will caution you in this, and I pray you heed my warning. Do *not* underestimate the other side. Don't think for a moment that Black Rock was a victory. You may have woken a sleeping giant when you attacked the den. They will be waiting around every corner. They will do their best to stop whatever it is that the Lord God Almighty wants you to do. This will be a race for lives, while trying to stay alive yourselves. The rewards will be great, but the cost will be tremendous. Amber and Terrik have already paid a portion of the price. There will be many people you will meet along the way. Sometimes you will get there in time to help. Sometimes you will not. Know whatever you choose on this day, there will be no turning back. If you choose to be sent, you are potentially volunteering for your death. You *will* be marked. Satan would like nothing better than to take you out. He has had a lot of time to study you. He knows you better than you know yourself. Having said all of that, I feel each of you are here for a purpose. I feel you were each brought here for such a time as this. The Kingdom needs you. They need your training and expertise. You have been called. What is your answer?"

"I'm game," Jerrod said. "I was brought here for such a time as this. I've already learned that."

"Me too," Jacob said. "Pretty sure this is my calling."

"We've already volunteered," Jon said, referring to himself, Jesse, Angel, Josh, and Rachel.

"Here I am. Send me," Val volunteered.

"I've said from the start I've wanted a family," Joe said, "I'm not giving up now."

"Then, here are your tickets," he said handing Angel and Rachel their team's tickets, "The Lord reminds us in Luke 10:2 that, '*The harvest is plentiful, but the workers are few. Ask the Lord of the harvest, therefore, to send out workers into His harvest field.*' You are part of those workers. You leave in the morning. Get a good night's sleep. You're going to need it."

# Epilogue
# Army Rising

As the A.N.G.E.L.s gather their forces, so is the other side. Though they were dealt a blow at Black Rock, the unnaturals are more determined than ever to exterminate the A.N.G.E.L.s, who have been a thorn in their flesh since the ascension of Christ.

Are the A.N.G.E.L.s ready for the battle, or is the next generation in over their heads? Have all of the issues within their unit been fixed, or will they implode? Find out in *Army Rising*, the next adventure of the *Divine Legacy Series*.

**Luke 10:2** *'The harvest is plentiful, but the workers are few. Ask the Lord of the harvest, therefore, to send out workers into His harvest field.'*

**Ephesians 6:12** *'For our struggle is not against flesh and blood, but against the rulers, against the authorities, against the powers of this dark world and against the spiritual forces of evil in the heavenly realms.'*

*The books in the Divine Legacy Series –*

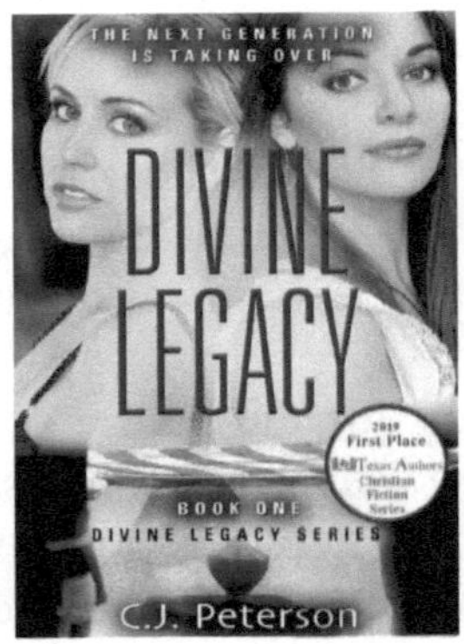

**Connect with CJ – _CJPetersonWrites.com_**

**Meet the previous generation of A.N.G.E.L.s -**

## Grace Restored Series

Book 1

Book 2

Book 3

Book 4

Book 5

Katie MacKenna experienced one storm after another in her life. When Leukemia stole her mother from her and her father, Katie was only seven-years-old, and her father didn't know how to cope after such a catastrophic loss. His response was to shut down and become abusive. The overwhelming devastation which surrounded Katie throughout her journey in life forced her to shut down just to survive as well.

Trust is a difficult thing for many people, but for Katie it's virtually impossible. Every life has Seasons of Change. Will those seasons open Katie to new opportunities or will they forever isolate her in survival mode? Will she be able to overcome the storms that have surrounded her to answer a call for help?

**Meet the previous generation of A.N.G.E.L.s -**

# *The Holy Flame Trilogy.*

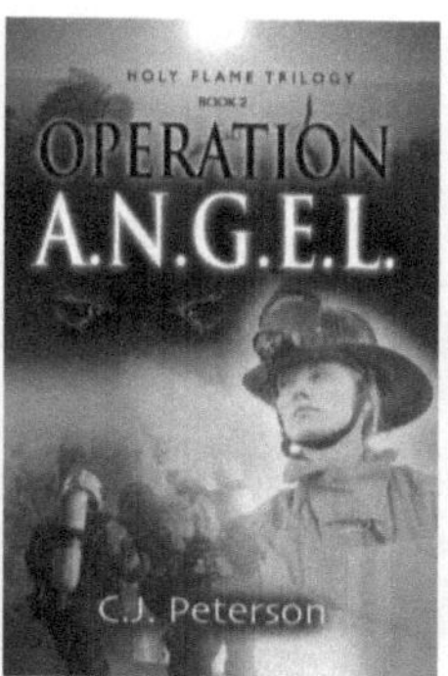

Book 1          Book 2          Book 3

# Summary

Courageous. Brave. Fearless. Valiant. These synonyms are often used to describe firefighters/paramedics, police officers, and military personnel. They face danger and lay their lives on the line when they leave for work. What are their struggles? Could that hinder their job proficiency? Who is taking care of those who are taking care of the citizens of this country?

Casey Carter is a 'newbie' to the firefighting family of Engine Company 15. Not only does she have to prove herself as a probationary firefighter, but she also has to battle misconceptions of females within her newly chosen profession. As situations begin to arise, can she count on the firefighter brotherhood to have her back? Will she be able to pass the tests placed before her, or are there aspects that she was not even aware existed?

Often in life there are two realms in play. There is the physical realm - what is right before you; the other is the spiritual realm - what is unseen. Each can directly affect you, whether you believe they exist or not. Can Casey keep them in balance when she is not exactly sure what she is fighting? Can a group of men help her see what cannot be readily seen, hear what cannot be readily heard, and be able to overcome what she never knew existed? Will they be able to show Casey her true Call To Duty?